MURDER

BY THE

RIVER USK

Welsh detectives investigate a puzzling cold case

PIPPA McCATHIE

THE
BOOK
FOLKS

Paperback published by The Book Folks

London, 2020

ISBN 978-1-913516-50-5

www.thebookfolks.com

To James, Toby and Sam

Prologue

May 2010

Inspector Fabia Havard looked up from the report she was reading. Her lips tightened when she saw who was standing in the door of her office. Sergeant Gerry Fairweather was not one of her favourite colleagues.

"Yes Gerry, what is it?"

"So sorry to disturb you, ma'am." His tone made it clear that he wasn't in the least bit sorry. "There's a missing person report just come in. Young university student called Caleb Morgan, Caerleon campus; his housemates are concerned about him, they say he's not been around for a couple of days."

"Did they say whether or not that's unusual for him?"

"I suppose they think so, otherwise they wouldn't have reported it, would they?" he said.

Fabia gritted her teeth. Best not to react. "Has anyone checked with his family?" she asked calmly.

"Yes. They've not seen him either. The parents are very worried, particularly the mother. She says it's completely out of character for him to bugger off without warning." Fairweather had come further into the room and slouched down into a chair opposite her desk, not waiting to be asked.

"Did you take the call?" she asked.

"No, that new chap did – the posh one."

She knew exactly who he meant but she wasn't going to admit it. "The posh one?" she asked, eyebrows raised.

"Sergeant Lambert."

She'd been right. "Well, send him in then."

Fairweather muttered something about not being an errand boy, but Fabia ignored it as he pushed his chair back and left the room. She sighed. He was such a pain, always bordering on insolent, but rarely so bad that she could pick him up on it without seeming over-sensitive. He was just the type to complain that she wasn't up to the job because she was a woman. Sometimes she wished he would really overstep the mark, then she'd have something concrete to deal with.

There was a knock on her door and when she called, "Come in," a tall, slim man in his late twenties came into the room. His dark hair, a little longer than the norm, clear blue eyes and fine features made him stand out amongst his colleagues. Fabia thought he looked more like an academic than a police officer. But she'd been told by his previous boss – he'd come to Newport from the Dyfed-Powys force – that he was sharp as a tack and very talented. A university graduate who'd been fast-tracked but had definitely earned his promotion. It wouldn't surprise her if Gerry Fairweather felt as much scorn for Sergeant Lambert as he did for her. She'd have to keep an eye on that, she thought wearily.

"You wanted me, ma'am."

"Yes, sit down, Sergeant. Gerry Fairweather says you took the call about this lad who's gone missing."

"I did." He took a notebook from his pocket and flipped it open. "His name's Caleb Morgan, he's studying history at Caerleon, sharing a house with three friends, two female, one male. One of them, Gaenor Baptiste, reported

2

him missing. She says they're all very worried, that they've checked with his parents" – he glanced down at his notes again – "Leonard and Marion Morgan, they live on that rather neglected council estate in Cwmbran. They say they haven't seen him for a couple of weeks. His mother is particularly worried as she says he keeps regular contact with her, phones her at least once a week, or she phones him, and she was considering getting on to us herself, but her husband told her not to."

"Anyone else in the family?"

"Just his twin sister. The mother said his twin, Nerys, is also very upset as she says she thinks something bad has happened to him. When I asked why, Mrs Morgan said it was just 'a feeling'. She said the twins are often aware if one of them is in some kind of trouble, as she put it."

"Apparently twins can have a sixth sense about each other," Fabia said. She glanced up and caught a look of scepticism on Matt Lambert's face. "You don't think so?"

"I've heard it can be so," he said diplomatically.

"But you don't buy it?"

"No, not really."

She smiled at him. "Ah. You're one of those that goes for facts and evidence against feelings and instinct."

He shrugged, then grinned. "You could say that."

It occurred to Fabia that dealing with this new chap was very different to dealing with the likes of Fairweather. Quite apart from anything else, he was a damn sight easier on the eye than his heavy-jowled, overweight colleague. His slightly hooded eyes and elegant bearing were extremely attractive. She pulled herself up short. For goodness sake, Fabia, she thought, inappropriate or what?

"So, what do you think?" she asked briskly. "Has he just gone off on his own for a bit of peace and quiet, or are we dealing with something more serious here?"

For a moment he was quiet, looking across at her, and she wondered what he was thinking. Then he pulled his hand down across his mouth and said, sounding a little embarrassed, "You're right, I do prefer hard facts to feelings, but there's something about this that worries me. Both his mother and sister seem convinced something untoward has happened and that his disappearance is completely out of character, and his friend" – he glanced down at his notes again – "Gaenor Baptiste also seemed very disturbed by it all. She says they were due to go to a gig at the students' union, a band that Caleb was really keen on – that was last Saturday. He didn't come home, and he didn't turn up at the union, but he hadn't let her know that he couldn't make it."

"Did you say his father tried to put his mother off contacting us?"

"Yes."

"I wonder why."

"She didn't say, just that she would have phoned yesterday but he wouldn't let her do so."

Fabia looked down at the dry-as-dust statistics she'd been trawling through and then back up at Matt Lambert. She'd much rather be active than sitting in her office.

"Okay," she said, coming to a decision, "I think we should go and talk to the family."

"I'll speak to Constable–"

"No," said Fabia. "I mean you and I, I'll come with you. I want to get a feel for these people."

"A feel?"

Fabia glanced at him and saw his face redden slightly. She got the impression he hadn't meant to say that out loud.

"Yes, Sergeant. Unlike you, I have a great respect for intuition and instinct. Watch me, you could learn a thing or two."

"I'm sure I could, ma'am." His tone was completely neutral, but she got the distinct impression that, behind the cool façade, he was amused.

Chapter 1

For several days, sheets of rain had blown across the land, and wind had howled through the countryside and along suburban and city streets. Even in this corner of South Wales the weather was unprecedented. Rivers had overflowed, fields had turned into lakes, trees had fallen and crushed parked cars, and gardens and farmyards had become sodden stretches of mud or begun to resemble lakes.

On the banks of the River Usk, in the ancient town of Caerleon, a team of archaeologists – students, tutors and volunteers – had abandoned their work. They'd made the dig as safe as they could, spread tarpaulins, dragged in sandbags, laid planks across trenches and erected a temporary fence. But none of this had stopped the landslip. It was as if a giant had taken a huge bite out of the riverbank and spat it out for the fast-flowing water to carry away. But at last the storm was over and calm had returned.

It was when the team came back to the dig on a chilly but dry March morning that they discovered the bones, and at first there was great excitement.

"Prof, come and look at this!"

"Wow! Is that what I think it is? Prof! We've made a find here."

"Maybe it's the remains of a Roman legionnaire, cool."

"Oh my God! A Roman skeleton. I cannot believe it!"

Professor Gavin Roberts trudged along the muddy bank to where the three students stood. What he saw looked like a skull and the first few vertebrae of a neck. He crouched down. As he did so, his boots sunk further into the mud and he nearly toppled over. Steadying himself, he took a closer look at their discovery then turned to another member of the team.

"Tony. What do you think of this?"

Tony Vaughan, who worked at the Caerleon Roman Fortress and Baths museum, had been helping with the dig. He strode across and bent down beside Roberts. For a moment there was silence as they studied the remains.

"What do you think?" Roberts asked again.

"Definitely not Roman, much more recent," Vaughan replied, keeping his voice low. He turned to the students. "Get me a pick or the long-handled trowel, would you?"

One of them handed him a trowel. "Will this do?"

"Thank you, that's perfect," he said. The group of students stood watching and silence reigned as he leant forward and carefully moved some of the earth away. It only took a minute to reveal a jagged indentation in the skull.

"And what's that?" Roberts asked, pointing to a disc that was half embedded in the mud close to the remains.

"I don't know, jewellery of some kind." Vaughan straightened, his face grim. "We mustn't disturb this any further." He struggled up and he and Roberts had a short, murmured conversation, then Roberts turned to the students.

"We'd better get this covered, bring that tarpaulin. The tide's low at the moment so we've got a few hours to make it safe," he said, as Tony Vaughan rummaged in his pocket, took out his mobile phone and punched in 999.

* * *

Chief Inspector Matt Lambert stretched and yawned. In his opinion there was nothing more boring than reading through an annual report, but needs must. He checked the page number he was on, flipped to the end, and checked again. Bloody hell! Forty more pages to go. It was far too expensively produced – all this glossy paper and coloured photographs were a ridiculous waste of money. He leaned his forehead on his long fingers and bent once more to his reading, but rescue walked into his office in the shape of his colleague, Sergeant Dilys Bevan.

"Can I interrupt you, sir?" she asked.

"Absolutely, Dilys, you're a lifesaver. This damn thing" – he flicked a finger at the pages of the report – "is sending me to sleep. Anything else would be a great relief."

She grinned. "Ah, but the Chief Super says we all have to read it, it's a three-line whip."

"Chief Superintendent Rees-Jones can–" Their boss wasn't a favourite with either of them, but best not to go on. "Okay, Dilys, what have you got for me?"

"A call's come through from one of the people working on that dig in Caerleon, someone called Tony Vaughan, apparently he's the new director at the Roman baths and fortress complex."

Matt frowned. The name was familiar, and not in a pleasant way. "I know who he is. Apart from his job at the museum, he's also Fabia's next-door neighbour – pushy bloke. He bought the house where that woman with the telescope lived."

"Rhona Griffiths?"

"That's the one. He moved in a few months ago, and he seems to spend rather a lot of time at Fabia's," he said, without looking Dilys in the eye.

"Ah," Dilys said. The one syllable spoke volumes. She knew Matt's partner Fabia Havard well, and was convinced he would have nothing to worry about when it came to the new neighbour. But wasn't it typical of a man to see rivals where there were none, she thought.

"What do you mean, ah?" Matt said, eyeing her suspiciously.

"Nothing, sir. Anyway," Dilys went on hastily, "he's reported finding a body. They've got a dig going on the banks of the Usk and apparently there's been a landslip after all that rain, some bones have been revealed."

"Isn't that to be expected on an archaeological dig?"

"Not in this case, they're quite recent, at least in this Vaughan bloke's opinion."

"How does he know?" Matt asked scornfully.

"He seems to know what he's talking about, sir," Dilys said.

"A drowning, do you think?" Matt asked, his heart sinking.

Something in his tone of voice rang alarm bells with Dilys. She gave him a quick, sympathetic look. "I don't know, sir."

Fabia had told her that Matt's sister, Bethan, had drowned. She'd killed herself, and it had been Matt who'd had to identify the body. It had been when he and Fabia were first working together and she'd had to support him through the trauma which, in Fabia's opinion, he'd never quite recovered from. But this wasn't the time to refer to that, so Dilys said, her voice calm and neutral, "He did mention something about a head injury, he said it looked as if the skull had been fractured."

"He seems to have given it a detailed inspection. I hope he hasn't contaminated the scene."

"Let's hope so, sir."

Matt pushed himself up from his chair. "We'd better get up there. Let's just check the tide tables, Tuesday 21st March," he muttered as he clicked away at his computer for a minute then looked up at Dilys. "Right, best get going immediately. The tide should be turning in half an hour, so we've got a few hours in hand before it's at its highest."

"So best to get a SOCO team up there double quick."

"Obviously," he said sharply, then gave her an apologetic grin. "Sorry, Dilys, these boring stats have put me in a bad mood."

Dilys somehow thought that wasn't the full story, but she had the sense not to say so. "I'll get the team together, and we'll have to let the Dragon know she's got work to do."

"That's no way to talk about our revered police surgeon," he told her. "Yes, I'll give Dr Curtis a ring now, she'll have to get her skates on too. Tell the SOCOs we'll meet them up there."

* * *

Matt and Dilys arrived at the dig about the same time as a group of civilian scenes of crime officers turned up in a van.

Matt steeled himself as he got out of the car. These situations were never pleasant, but the closeness of the river added to his reluctance. He walked over and had a quick word with the woman heading up the SOCOs and thanked them for getting there so quickly, before the team went off to start setting up an enclosure to protect the scene; then he turned to look at a group of young people standing to one side.

"Probably students from the university helping with the dig," Dilys murmured. "And those two chaps over there look as if they're in charge."

Matt turned to see two older men standing slightly apart. One he recognised. It was Fabia's next-door neighbour. They'd met briefly a couple of times over the last few months. He was tall and muscular with short greying hair, dark eyes and an open, friendly face. Fabia had remarked that he was rather fanciable, which had annoyed Matt intensely. Why wasn't he in his office at the museum rather than down here, poking his nose in? Matt wondered. He and Dilys approached them.

"Mr Vaughan, isn't it?" Matt said.

There was a flash of recognition in the man's eyes. "We've met, haven't we? You're a friend of Fabia Havard's, aren't you?"

"I am," Matt said coolly, then briefly shook the man's hand.

"How do you know her?" Vaughan asked.

Matt felt irritated by the question. "Fabia and I used to work together," he said briefly. "I'm Chief Inspector Lambert, this is Detective Sergeant Bevan. Can you tell us what happened here?"

"It's best if Gavin explains." Vaughan indicated his companion. "This is Professor Gavin Roberts from the archaeology department at Cardiff University. He's heading up the dig, I'm just hanging on his coat tails."

Matt shook hands with Roberts.

"Perhaps you can tell us how this body was discovered."

"Today is our first time back at the dig in a week, the weather meant we had to abandon it for a while," the professor explained, pushing his untidy fair hair back from his forehead as he spoke. "We tried to make things safe, sandbags, tarpaulins, etc., but what with the downpour we've had these last few days, the elements got the better of us. It wasn't until we got back this morning that we realised a section of the riverbank had subsided, and two of my students discovered the bones. We could see that the skull was badly damaged, and I could tell that it wasn't from way back, you know, Roman or whatever."

"How could you be sure?"

Roberts frowned then said, "Experience, I suppose, I've worked on many a dig."

"Is that all you found?" Matt asked.

"Yes. We thought we'd better not disturb the bones, but Tony says he thinks whoever it was is wearing a medallion of some sort."

"Yes," Vaughan said. "I think it might be one of those medical alert pendants, one of my daughters wears one because she's allergic to bee stings."

While they'd been talking, the SOCO unit had been erecting a plastic tent over the area. Matt thanked the two men, told them that they'd be taking full statements from them and the students as soon as possible, and he and Dilys went back to their car to put on regulation white overalls and pull on surgical gloves and rubber boots. After doing so they made their way down to the riverbank to have a closer look.

Matt looked out at the churning, muddy brown waters of the Usk. "They're going to have to work fast."

"They are, sir," Dilys said grimly.

* * *

Since the SOCO team had discovered that the victim had been hit – several times, they thought – with some kind of sharp object, back at the station later on they started the usual routine for a murder enquiry. Matt was waiting for confirmation from the pathologist, but he had little doubt that the SOCOs were right.

It wasn't until much later that Matt managed to get a minute or two to phone Fabia. She was in Bangor staying with her friend, Bella Price, who ran an artists' commune in the beautiful North Wales countryside. He'd found it quite difficult to get through to her over the last couple of days as the reception was intermittent, but when he tried this time, she picked up immediately.

"Hallo, love, how're things going down south?" Fabia said, sounding pleased to hear his voice. "Has the rain stopped yet?"

"Yes, just about, but the weather has, sort of, produced a case for us."

"Oh? How come?"

Matt stretched back in his chair, trying to ease his cramped muscles. Too much sitting at his desk and gazing at a computer screen, he told himself, then went on to tell Fabia about the discovery of the body on the banks of the Usk.

"Has it been identified yet?" she asked.

"Give us a chance, Fabia!" he protested. "No, but we should be able to get an identification pretty quickly as he – the body's definitely male – was wearing one of those medical alert pendants. Once it's cleaned up, we should be able to get a name off it. I'm hoping the info will come through this evening or, at the latest, tomorrow morning."

"Poor chap."

"What? The body or me?"

"Matt!"

"Sorry, not appropriate" – Matt grinned – "but I'm bloody exhausted, you'll have to forgive me. By the way, when do you get back home to Pontygwyn? I need some TLC."

"Thursday afternoon."

Matt could hear a muttering in the background.

"Bella sends her love, she's busy making us the most enormous lasagne, it smells lovely."

"And here am I, sitting in my office with the prospect of a boring takeaway to look forward to."

He could hear her laugh, then Dilys appeared at his office door and he said, "Got to go Fabia. Make sure you do come back on Thursday. I've missed you."

"I've been missing you too, love," she told him. "I'll phone when I get home. Good luck with the new case. I hope you get it sorted quickly. I wish I was there to talk it through with you."

"So do I," said Matt, unaware of how much she'd become involved before very long.

Chapter 2

Two days later Matt and Chloe Daniels, newly qualified as a family liaison officer, were on their way to the market town of Pontygwyn, but it was nothing to do with calling on Fabia. The body discovered on the banks of the Usk had been identified as a young man in his early twenties called Caleb Morgan, and they were on their way to inform his family.

It was a journey Matt could have done in his sleep, but instead of turning right towards Fabia's house once they'd crossed the ancient sheep drovers' bridge, they continued up the high street and, after some time negotiating the Thursday morning traffic and shoppers, they turned left up St Madoc's Road past the imposing entrance to St Madoc's school. After about ten minutes the sat nav told them to turn right and, a few minutes later, informed them that they had arrived at their destination.

Number 20 Morton Road was a semi-detached red brick house, probably built in the 1950s, with a neat front lawn, in the middle of which stood a magnificent magnolia just beginning to flower. A dark blue Mini Cooper was parked on a paved area in front of a garage to the side.

"The fact the car's there means they might be at home," Chloe said to Matt as she looked out of their car window.

"Let's hope so. The sooner we get this over, the better."

"This is a bit of a step up, property wise, from a council estate in Cwmbran," Chloe commented. "I wonder when they moved here?"

"I don't know."

"They're pretty expensive, these houses."

"I know," Matt said. "Perhaps it's inherited."

"That's always possible," Chloe agreed.

They found a place to park a few yards down the road and walked to the front door, the top half of which was filled in with old-fashioned stained glass depicting the sun shining down on a gull flying across a wind-whipped sea. Chloe reached up to ring the bell and they heard it echo through the house. Waiting in silence, they both listened out for sounds of activity and, after a few minutes, they heard footsteps before a shadowy figure appeared behind the glass.

The woman who opened the door looked to be in her early thirties. Her brown hair was tied back at the nape of her neck and her clothes were plain and under-stated. A name tag hanging on a lanyard round her neck told them her name was Nerys Morgan and that she was a child protection officer. So, this was the sister.

"Miss Nerys Morgan?"

"Yes?"

"I'm Chief Inspector Lambert, this is my colleague Constable Daniels. Could we have a word?"

Her eyes widened but she showed no obvious sign of concern. "What's it about? Is it my father?" she asked, her voice cool.

Self-possessed, not easily rattled, that's all to the good, Matt thought, but then, if she works in child protection, she's not going to be, is she. "Perhaps we could come in?"

he said, "We'd like to talk to you and your parents if that's possible."

She hesitated for a moment then opened the door. "It's only Mam and me, my father lives in Usk now," she told them as she stepped aside to let them in.

The hall was neat, a row of hooks to one side were hung with various coats and scarves, and beyond this the stairs rose up to the first floor. Along a passageway next to the stairs a kitchen could be glimpsed through an open door and another door to the right, Matt thought, probably led into a living room.

"Come through," she said. "My mother's in the kitchen."

They followed her along the passage to a bright, sunny room at the back of the house. A large window looked out on a neat garden full of shrubs and nodding daffodils, with fruit trees at the end of a generous lawn. A woman was standing on the other side of a scrubbed pine table, her eyes anxious. Matt guessed she was in her mid-sixties, but she looked older. There were dark shadows like bruises under her tired eyes. She had greying fair hair which fell, rather lank and thin, either side of her face, and her hands were gripped together protectively.

"Mam," her daughter said, "these are police officers, they want a word with us." She watched her mother's face anxiously as she spoke.

Matt introduced himself and Chloe, but his introductions were interrupted by Marion Morgan. "Is it about my husband?"

"No, no it's not," Matt said, keeping his voice as gentle as he could.

She subsided into a chair as if she could no longer stay upright. "Please," she said, "sit down."

"Do you want coffee, tea?" Nerys Morgan asked.

"Thank you, no," Matt said. "Please don't trouble yourself."

They settled themselves, mother and daughter on one side of the table, Nerys protectively close to her mother, and Matt and Chloe on the other. There were signs of preparations for a meal, chopped carrots on a board on the work surface, an onion and a jar of pasta sauce next to it, and a tall jar of spaghetti close by.

Matt looked at the two women, the strong face of the daughter, the tired and defeated face of the mother, and wished himself anywhere but in this kitchen.

He glanced at Chloe who took the hint and said, "I'm afraid we have some bad news. Your son, Caleb, who disappeared almost ten years ago—"

Hope sprang up in the mother's eyes as she leant across the table towards Chloe and interrupted. "Oh, please, tell me you've found him!"

"Mam," Nerys said, putting her arm round her mother's shoulders, "the officer said bad news. What have you found?"

"We've found the remains of a body," Matt told her. "I'm truly sorry to say that it's been identified as your son."

There was the sound of a quick indrawn breath from one of the women but neither said a word.

"I'm afraid there's no doubt," Matt went on. "He was identified, initially, by the medical alert pendant he was wearing, and subsequently by a dental check."

"He was diabetic," Nerys said, her voice expressionless.

"Where was he found?" Marion Morgan asked. The words were muffled behind the hand she'd lifted to her mouth.

"His body was uncovered by archaeologists working on a dig on the banks of the Usk river, at Caerleon. I believe he was at university at the Caerleon campus, as it was then, is that right?"

Nerys nodded. "Yes, he was. And he loved walking along the Usk, he said the beauty of the river was calming. He was a real nature lover, was Caleb."

"You always said you knew he was dead," her mother said to her, her tone almost accusing as her eyes filled with tears. She looked across at Matt then Chloe, pleading. "I can't believe it. You could be wrong, mistakes are made."

"I'm so sorry, Mrs Morgan," Chloe said, "but I'm afraid we're sure of our identification."

"I can't believe it, I can't..." Her voice caught in her throat and she bowed her head, shoulders shaking in grief. "Oh God, my boy, my poor, poor boy."

Nerys's arm tightened round her mother's shoulders. "Please tell us," she begged. "What happened? How did he die? Was he drowned?"

This was the worst part, Matt dreaded having to tell them that Caleb had been murdered. Once they knew that, they would slowly begin to realise the awful disruption to their lives that they would face: the intrusive questions, the invasion of their privacy, the press pack hounding them – everything that came with a murder investigation. There was so little he could do to prepare them for it or protect them. Chloe would be there as family liaison officer, and Matt was confident she'd do her best, but there was a limit to what she or anyone could do to help them.

"His death was caused by a blow to the head," he told them. Neither of the women made any comment, but he noticed Nerys's eyes widen. "Due to the nature of the injury the pathologist doesn't think it was caused by a fall," he went on. "She believes it must have been inflicted by another person."

"He was murdered?" his sister asked in a whisper.

"I'm so sorry," Matt said gently, "but that is the conclusion we've come to."

"Oh no, no!" her mother exclaimed, then her eyes narrowed. "It must have been that dreadful man."

Matt glanced at Chloe, then asked. "What man do you mean, Mrs Morgan?"

But before she could answer, Nerys intervened. "No, no, Mam. Don't start on that."

"Do you know who your mother is referring to?" Matt asked.

She looked from him to Chloe, her eyes pleading. "Yes, but can we not talk about that now? It's been such a shock. I don't think my mother is thinking straight."

"That's hardly surprising," Chloe said, "but we will have to find out more at another time." She glanced at Matt and he gave an almost imperceptible nod. "I'm sure you'll understand that the more information you can give us, the more likely it is we'll find out who's responsible."

"Who else would do such a thing to my poor Caleb?" Mrs Morgan asked, her voice harsh. But the question was unanswerable until they knew a good deal more. Chloe reached out to take Caleb's mother's hand and the fingers gripped hard.

"We will do everything we can to find out who is responsible," Chloe assured her. "Can you tell me who you're referring to?"

But Mrs Morgan didn't answer the question. "My Caleb used to be such a gentle boy, such a quiet boy," she said, her voice shaking, "so loving, he never would have harmed anyone. People took advantage of him because of it, he was led astray, he—"

"Mam!" Nerys said, and the note of warning was back in her voice.

Her mother glanced at her then back at Matt. "You must find out who killed my boy," she said, her voice rising in anguish, "you must."

"As my colleague says," Matt told her, "we'll do our best to uncover the truth. But that will entail a lot of questions. I realise it will be painful for you and the rest of your family, but the more you can tell us about that time," he said, looking at Nerys, "the better. We have records of all the interviews done at the time, with his housemates, his friends, with you and his father."

As he spoke, Matt noticed Caleb's sister glance at her mother. It was a strange look, as if she was about to

19

interrupt this exchange then decided against it. It was a look full of uncertainty, but was there more to it than that? Was it fear? Something had occurred to her, but she'd decided against saying what was in her mind. This was not the time to pursue it, or to push to find out who Mrs Morgan was referring to, but soon, within the next day or two, he would have to probe deeper.

"You'll need to speak to my father, I suppose," Nerys Morgan said, her voice flat and expressionless.

"We will. You say he lives in Usk?" Matt made it into a question.

"We're separated," Mrs Morgan said.

"He's got a flat," Nerys told them, "sheltered housing, it is, just out of town on the Monmouth Road. Do you want me to give you the address?"

Although Matt was sure they'd be able to track the address down easily enough, he was glad when Chloe said, "Thank you, that would be helpful."

Chloe jotted the address down and, as she did so, he caught Nerys Morgan giving her a sharp look, as if she knew this was a bit of a charade. When Chloe smiled across at her, the smile wasn't returned. Matt got the impression she was putting a lot of effort into staying calm – hardly surprising, he thought.

Mrs Morgan suddenly burst out, "When can we have him back? When can we bury my lovely boy? I'll need to speak to the pastor."

Chloe glanced at Matt then back at the two women. "We hope we'll be able to release the body for burial very soon, but there has to be an inquest first. It won't take long, it'll be a formality at this stage, and we'll keep you fully informed. I'll be on hand to help in any way I can."

For the first time Caleb's sister showed some emotion. She gave Chloe a direct look, a look full of pain and anger. "But you can't bring him back, can you?" she said, her voice shaking a little as she said it.

Matt tensed, hoping Chloe would deal well with this aspect of such an investigation – the anger that had to find an outlet somewhere.

"No," Chloe said quietly, "I wish I could, but I can't. But I can help you in practical ways. As a family liaison officer, I can support you through the inquest and the investigation, and I'm here to listen. Anything you can tell me will be helpful to us."

Well done, Chloe, Matt thought.

"And I would very much like to know what your brother was like," Chloe went on. "All we have in the files are some photographs, including the one you used for the posters you put up at the time of his disappearance. Have you any other photos? I would like to see them, very much."

"Would you?" Marion Morgan said. The idea seemed to please her. She took a deep, shuddering breath, wiped at her eyes and pushed herself up from her chair. "I'll go and get them," she said, and left the room.

Nerys watched her go then turned to the two of them and said in a low but urgent voice. "Have you any idea who did this to him?"

"I'm afraid not," Matt said gently, "but we'll do our very best to find out, I assure you. Do you know who your mother was referring to?"

"Not really, there was one person she didn't like, but I'm sure it couldn't have been him."

"Who was that?"

But she didn't give them a direct answer, just said, "You'll be talking to all his friends from back then, won't you?"

"We'll definitely be doing that," Matt told her.

"There were two that he was particularly close to, Gaenor Baptiste and Filly, Felicity Jenner, and then there was Iolo Beynam, they were the three that shared the student house with Caleb. Gaenor was great, a really good friend. Caleb and Iolo, well, they were close, that's for sure." She sounded as if she was apologising for the fact.

"Is there something in particular that you can tell us about him?"

"No, no. And there were several other friends around back then."

Matt wondered what else she would have said about Iolo Beynam. He took a stab in the dark. "Was it Iolo Beynam your mother was referring to?"

She didn't look him in the eye, just said, "It could be. Mam wasn't… well… she didn't like Iolo, but I thought he was a dear." There was a touch of defiance in her voice. "I can give you most of their phone numbers," Nerys went on. "I've sort of kept in touch with some of them, on Facebook and stuff. They'll tell you a lot that my parents won't."

"Like what, for instance?" Matt asked.

She glanced at the door as if afraid her mother would walk back in any moment. "My brother was… was gay, but my mother couldn't accept it, she's very religious, see, and she thinks being gay is a sin and that he was corrupted by… by the people around him. We never told my father, although I'm pretty sure he knew; he used to call Caleb such names." Her voice was tight with anger. "If we'd talked about it openly, he would have gone ballistic, too much of a traditionalist, all macho male and iffy jokes down the pub. Anyway, I think Caleb and Iolo–" she stopped as they heard her mother's returning footsteps. "I'll write down those numbers for you," she said, her voice more normal now as she took out her mobile phone.

Marion Morgan walked back into the room clutching two photo albums and a large folder to her chest. She put them on the table, ran a gentle hand over them as if they were priceless family heirlooms. They probably are to her, Matt thought, remembering the box of photographs he had of Bethan.

"Let me show you," Caleb's mother said.

* * *

Half an hour later Matt and Chloe finally left the house in Pontygwyn. Although Marion Morgan had insisted she wanted the police to inform Caleb's father of the discovery of the body, which Matt found rather sad, as she'd seen them out, Nerys said, "Can you let me tell my father about Caleb before you go and see him? I'll visit him this afternoon. I know Mam said for you to do it, but it'd come as less of a shock from me. He's not well. He's in the early stages of dementia and he can be a bit… well… difficult to manage."

Matt assured her that they understood and said they'd hold off going to see Leonard Morgan until Saturday morning. "I assure you we'll be as careful as we can when we speak to him," Matt told her.

"Please try not to worry too much," Chloe added. "And if there's anything you need, or want to talk about, don't hesitate to contact me. Here's my card."

Nerys took the card and gave her a strained smile. "Thank you," she said. "I must get back to Mam now."

She closed the door firmly behind them.

"There seems to be a complete disconnect in that family," Chloe said, as they started off back to the station. "Split down the middle, it is."

"I think you're right."

"Do you think that it's all down to the boy's disappearance?"

"I don't know," Matt said. "Let's face it, that kind of trauma can destroy the closest of families. I remember the atmosphere being pretty dysfunctional when Fabia and I interviewed them all those years ago, and the parents' attitudes to his sexuality obviously didn't help."

"I got the impression that his sister has more to tell us, about Iolo Beynam particularly."

"So did I. You'll need to keep your eyes and ears open on that one."

"Will do, sir."

23

Matt glanced across at her. "How did you find your first case in family liaison?"

"A bit nerve-wracking," she gave him a shy smile. "Did I do okay?"

"You did very well," Matt said, and returned the smile.

Chapter 3

Nerys checked her watch. It was half past two. She'd better get going. She went in search of her mother and found her slumped in an armchair in the sitting room. There was a book open on her lap, her much-thumbed bible, but it was obvious she wasn't reading it as she sat staring into space, her expression bleak. Nerys's heart was wrenched. How small and defeated she looked. She sat down opposite her, stretched out and touched her mother's knee.

"Are you sure you're going to be okay on your own, Mam?"

"I'll be fine, love, I'm going to give Pastor Harris a ring," she said, giving her daughter a weary smile. "Your father needs to know what's happened. That woman from the police – what was it she said she was?"

"A family liaison officer."

"Yes. She said they'd be speaking to him on Saturday, but I want him to hear about Caleb before they see him, it's only fair."

Nerys's lips tightened a little but she didn't comment. She wasn't sure that fairness came into it with her father.

"I'll be as quick as I can. It'll only take me about fifteen minutes, depending on the traffic, and I should be back well in time to get the tea."

She leant forward to kiss her mother's cheek and give her a quick hug, then she left the room and hurried down the hall and out of the front door. She was dreading this encounter, but it had to be done. The sooner she got it over with, the better.

Her father's flat in Usk was about nine miles from the house in Pontygwyn. The year before, he'd been diagnosed with the first stages of dementia and had had to retire from the steelworks where he'd worked since he was a teenager. With the help of his GP she had managed to find just the right place for him in the Brynmor Care Centre. At first, stubborn as ever, her father had taken some persuading to move from the flat where he'd lived since her parents had split up not long after Caleb's disappearance, but when he'd found out there were allotments nearby that he could work on, he'd agreed readily enough. He'd always been a keen gardener and his mental state seemed to have made no difference to his abilities. Since the move he'd spent the majority of his time on the allotments, and this is where Nerys found him on her arrival in Usk.

She stood watching for a moment before he saw her, psyching herself up for what she knew was going to be a difficult encounter. Leonard Morgan was busy digging a trench, probably for potatoes, Nerys thought. His powerful body was gaunt now, and he moved more slowly than he used to. This man was a long way from the father who used to lash out when angry, which he frequently was, particularly with Caleb. Her twin's gentleness and refusal to play rugby and join in the pursuits that Leonard maintained should be a given for a man, particularly a Welsh man, had always enraged him. As she stood there, the thought that she'd been trying so hard to deny insinuated itself into her mind. She tried to push it aside, shut it away until she got this over with. This wasn't the time. She couldn't afford to be distracted. Taking a deep breath, she walked forward.

"Hallo, Father." She'd never used the diminutive 'Da' with him.

He looked up, unsmiling. At first, she wondered if he recognised her, but a moment later he said, "Ah, Nerys." He dug his spade into the ground and leant on its handle, frowning at her. "What do you want?"

Nerys thrust her hands into the pockets of her coat to hide her clenched fists. It was always best not to show fear or nervousness in front of him. That had been one of Caleb's problems, he was always so transparent.

She stepped towards him. "I'm afraid I've got some bad news," she said.

He didn't respond immediately, and the silence stretched out, then he snapped, "Is it your mother?"

"No, Mam's okay. It's about Caleb."

"Who?"

Oh God, she thought, how could he forget? "Caleb, your son, remember? My twin." Her voice cracked on the word and she swallowed hard.

"Of course, I remember!" he snapped, then his glance slid away from her, no longer looking her in the eye. "He ran off, bloody coward, escaped."

Why did he put it like that? But to ask would be pointless. She made herself plough on. A small part of her felt pity for him, after all, as a very small child she'd idolised him. But there was hardly any of that feeling in her now. He'd made sure of that, beaten it out of her and the rest of his family. The sooner she told him what had happened, the sooner she could leave.

"Yes, he disappeared. But, Father, they've found him."

His head snapped back to look straight at her. "What?" His tone was fierce. "I don't believe you."

"Why not? What do you mean?" The questions were out before she could stop them.

She waited for his answer, but none came. His shoulders sagged, and for a moment he looked like the defeated and confused old man that he was. But a moment later he straightened, grabbed the spade again and began to dig, and, for a few moments, the sound of it cutting and lifting the earth was the only thing to be heard.

Nerys waited, unsure how to go on, but the digging seemed to calm him, and finally he stopped and, still not looking at her, said, "He went away, deserted us."

"No, he disappeared."

The sound he made was scornful. "Tcha! He ran away, that's what he did, couldn't cope. Couldn't stand up for himself."

Nerys could no longer keep the anger out of her voice and she no longer had any desire to be careful of what she said. "They've found his body, Father, Caleb's body," she told him, her voice sharp and full of pain. "He's been dead for nearly ten years, and he was murdered, do you hear? Murdered!"

At first, she didn't think he'd taken it in, he just kept on digging, but gradually the cut and thrust of the spade grew slower and then stopped. He stood completely still, his body bent over his spade, then he swung round and the look on his face made her take a step back. She knew that look of barely controlled fury; it had haunted her childhood and still had the power to have her heart leap in her chest and a cold sweat break out on her body.

"Murdered?" he shouted. "Murdered! What nonsense. He ran away because he couldn't cope with being a man. He was no son of mine, d'you hear?" He turned his back on her and went on muttering, "No son of mine. I had to teach him a lesson. He was no son of mine!"

Nerys stood staring at him, aghast at the implications of what he'd said. Should she stay and try to tell her father more? Should she warn him that the police would be coming to speak to him? But no, it was no use. Abruptly she turned and trudged back through the allotments, moving faster and faster until she was running. She got to her car, fumbled with the keys, then pulled open the door and slumped into the seat. Breathing hard, she leant her forehead against the steering wheel, her body heaving as she began to sob.

Chapter 4

Fabia had arrived back home later than she expected on Thursday and, much as she'd tried, she hadn't been able to get through to Matt. That was often the way when he was deep into a new case, so she hadn't worried too much about it.

On Friday morning she was up and about early, busy in her garden, but not with the gardening. When she'd been at the artists' commune, a friend of Bella's had done a workshop on drawing with charcoal and Fabia was keen to try it out. She'd set up her easel on a small patch of lawn which was shaded by an ancient apple tree and was trying to capture the view in this new medium. In spite of the chill of a late March morning, the sun was bright, and it was good to be out in the fresh air.

How many times had she transferred this view to paper or canvas from one angle or another? She'd lost count. But it always raised her spirits, in whatever medium she chose. Some of the paintings she'd done had sold well in a friend's gift shop in Usk and others in a gallery in nearby Abergavenny. This one she was doing just for the pleasure of it – maybe she'd sell it, maybe she wouldn't, or she might give it to Matt for his flat. If he did sell the flat, as he'd talked of doing, it'd help if he had a few pictures on the walls when people came for viewings, wouldn't it?

Holding the stick of charcoal at arm's length, she turned it this way and that to check the perspective. Tall and statuesque, her unruly coppery hair tied back at the nape of her neck, she leant back and studied the landscape through half closed eyes. What she saw was a patchwork of fields, some dotted with sheep, and in the middle distance were some farm buildings nestled by a copse. Here and there bright patches of daffodils interrupted the greens and browns. There was an occasional dark glassy spread of water, witness to the flooding after the torrential rain and, in the far distance, the warm colours of the fields gave way to more moody tones, blue, grey and mauve, the lower slopes of the Brecon Beacons. This landscape is in my blood, Fabia thought, nowhere else matches up to it.

Her work was interrupted by the distant but insistent ringing of a phone. Without taking her eyes off her work, absentmindedly she rummaged in the pockets of her paint spattered overall. No mobile there. Then she realised the ringing was coming from the landline in the kitchen. She put down the stick of charcoal and walked quickly inside, stripped off the mittens she always wore while painting outside at this time of year, then searched around for a bit. She finally unearthed the handset on the kitchen table underneath a pile of magazines, most of them copies of The Artist.

"Hallo?"

"That took you a while. Where were you?"

Fabia's heart leapt. It always did when she heard Matt's voice unexpectedly, but she wasn't going to let him know that – she didn't want him getting a swollen head.

"I was in the garden, painting."

"Why didn't you have your mobile with you? I've tried it several times."

"I forgot. Anyway, stop nagging, Matt."

"Sorry, love."

"I haven't heard from you since Tuesday," she complained, then added, smiling, "So, Chief Inspector, what can I do for you, sir?"

But she could hear no smile in his voice when he replied, "We've got a case you might be able to help with."

This was not what she'd expected. "What do you mean, that I could help with? You usually don't like me getting involved, I'm not in the force anymore."

It was three years now since, suspected of corruption, Fabia had been compelled to retire from the Gwent Police. Three years ago, she'd been Superintendent Havard, tipped for Assistant Chief Constable in a few years if all went well. All had not gone well. But thanks to some friends and colleagues who'd stuck by her, and ultimately thanks to Matt, everyone knew now that she was not at fault; her name had been cleared and her pension reinstated. Now she was simply Fabia Havard, artist and illustrator, although, one way and another, she had been involved in a couple of cases that Matt had worked on, partly because people she knew had been involved. But this sounded different.

"I know that," he sounded irritated, "but this is a case you were in charge of years ago."

"How come? What sort of case?" she asked warily.

Matt didn't give her a direct answer. "You know that dig in Caerleon, on the banks of the Usk, just past the pub?"

"I do. I've heard about it from my next-door neighbour."

"I thought you might have—"

"He's an interesting bloke, Tony, I'm going to be doing some artwork for him."

"What sort of artwork?" Matt did not sound pleased.

"He wants me to do some sketches of the dig," Fabia said, ignoring his tone, "and of some of the artefacts they've discovered, for a new leaflet they're producing for the museum. We've been talking about it for a while, I thought I'd mentioned it to you. I'm really looking forward to getting to work on it."

"It sounds as if you're going to be spending a lot of time with him."

"Well, he is my neighbour, Matt."

Fabia grimaced ruefully. Matt was inclined to get a bit jealous, which sometimes made things difficult. She really should have a word with him about it, but this wasn't the time. "And I've been helping one of his daughters with her art homework as well, she's a talented kid, reminds me a bit of Amber Morgan."

"Oh, he's got kids, has he?"

"Yes, two daughters."

"What's his wife like?"

"I don't know, I haven't met her."

"How come?"

"Matt! What's with the interrogation?" Fabia protested. "You were telling me something about the dig in Caerleon, is this case connected to it?"

There was a pause and Fabia thought Matt was going to continue questioning her about Tony Vaughan, but he didn't.

"There was a mudslide just below the dig earlier this week," he told her. "Part of the riverbank disappeared into the Usk after that awful storm."

"I'm not surprised. The pond in Gwiddon Park has turned into a mini lake."

"The landslip has revealed some human remains," Matt said.

"But isn't that to be expected on a dig, finding human remains I mean?"

"That's what they thought at first, but not this time," Matt said. "These are relatively recent."

"Oh?" Fabia wondered what was coming next. "Tony hasn't said anything." Sod it, she thought, I shouldn't have mentioned him again.

"Well he wouldn't, would he?" Matt snapped, then he went on in a more reasonable tone. "He was there when the remains were found, but we asked them all to keep quiet about it, got Rees-Jones to pull a few strings, he's a friend of the vice chancellor at Cardiff and the dig's being done by their archaeology department."

"I suppose he has his uses," Fabia said, her tone sardonic. Rees-Jones was no friend of Fabia's either.

"When we questioned the students, we put the wind up them about talking to all and sundry, particularly the press, and it seems to have worked. Of course, the weather helped. They let it be known the bank was unsafe, so that stopped anyone getting too close. And the archaeological team agreed to tell the press pack no-one could be let in to take photos as it might contaminate the area of the dig. True enough, really. Anyway, that was a couple of days ago, but we're not going to be able to keep a lid on it for much longer, not with a crowd of students involved, someone's bound to start blabbing soon."

"I should imagine so." Fabia could just see them chattering away like a bunch of sparrows. "So, the remains definitely aren't Roman?"

"No," said Matt. "He's only been dead about nine years."

"He? Have you managed to make an identification?"

"Yes, partly because he was wearing one of those medical alert pendants. We also discovered his mobile phone where the back pocket of his jeans would have been, although that's pretty useless now obviously. Still, we've given the sim card to Aidan Rogers."

"Is he the computer geek who did all that trawling through computers and devices on the White Monk Abbey case?"

"Yes, that's the one. I'm hoping he'll be able to retrieve some of the information, but I'm not holding my breath."

"After all this time?" Fabia asked. "I wouldn't have thought that was possible."

"You're probably right, but it's worth a try. Anyway, a dental check confirmed his identity, it came through first thing this morning. He was a university student called Caleb Morgan."

"Oh Lord!" Fabia said. The name was familiar, and it threw her back into the past with a jolt. It had been a missing persons case she'd led when she was an inspector. Most successful cases faded in the memory, were put to bed and crossed off the list. But the unsolved ones, they were different. Fabia had always found that they lingered, niggling away, like a wound that never quite healed.

When Caleb Morgan had been reported missing, Fabia had been sure they'd be able to trace him quite quickly, but as the days and weeks went by, she'd become more and more frustrated by the lack of progress. Fabia remembered that she'd not taken to the father; he'd come across as a blustering bully who seemed to blame his wife for their son's disappearance. In contrast she'd been deeply impressed by the mother's dignity, and her obvious determination not to give up on her son. Although she had hinted at some conflict between them, in spite of Fabia's probing she'd not been specific about the cause. She remembered that his mother and twin sister had plastered Cardiff, Cwmbran, Newport and Caerleon with posters of Caleb, and done endless interviews begging for people to come forward. And his friends had used social media, posting message after message, but it was no use. He had just dropped off the radar.

Fabia had been determined to find him, partly because of his mother and sister's single-minded perseverance, partly because of the obvious distress of his friends. But another thing about the case had got under her skin. It was the face in the photos. Caleb's dark hair, the haunted look in his eyes, and his shy smile, everything about him had cried out to her. And now here was Matt telling her his body had been found within a few miles of where she lived.

"Fabia? Are you there?" Matt asked, sounding anxious.

"Yes, Matt." She took a deep breath. "I remember it all too well. Was the cold case unit still working on it?"

"Yes, but I wanted your input as well. I told Gerry Fairweather I'd have a private word with you, see if you could come up with anything."

Fabia gave a bark of laughter. "Foulweather on cold cases? I bet he's pleased about that."

Matt laughed. "He's a lazy bugger so I dare say it suits him well enough."

"What was his reaction when you told him you were going to contact me?"

"He looked a bit sour when I mentioned your name, but he had the wit not to comment."

Gerry Fairweather was one of the officers who'd believed the rumours about her three years ago. As with some others, she was pretty sure he'd have resented being proved wrong, and probably still believed she'd been guilty of corruption.

"He was delighted to point out that now we have a body," Matt told her, "or the remains of one, it's no longer a cold case."

"But it's linked to one," Fabia said. "Never mind him, what is it you want me to do?"

"Would you mind very much coming into my office? I've got all the information here from way back and I'd like your input."

Fabia's heart sank a little. She'd only been to the station a couple of times since her retirement and she found it difficult to go back, but she told herself not to be a coward.

"Okay, do you want me to come now?"

"Could you? I'd like to talk to you before we let out more details to the media."

Fabia glanced at the kitchen clock hanging above the cooker. A quarter past ten. "Here's an idea," she said. "It'll take me about half an hour to get to you at this time of day. We can go through the case notes, then you can treat me to lunch at the River's Edge."

"It's a deal," Matt said.

Chapter 5

Having tidied up her artist's paraphernalia, Fabia got going. From the house she'd inherited from her Auntie Meg, her route took her over the narrow sheep drovers' bridge. Fifteen minutes later she was on the outskirts of Caerleon, the ancient City of Legions. It was home to one of the most important Roman settlements ever discovered in Europe and had always been a source of fascination to Fabia, with the ruins of the vast amphitheatre and the beautifully restored Roman baths. She drove slowly through the town and, a few minutes later, was passing the remains of the tenth-century castle. She slowed right down as she made her way across the road bridge over the Usk, trying to get a glimpse of the archaeological excavation that Matt had mentioned. She craned her neck to look up the muddy banks, but the river curved away and she could see no sign of the dig. An irritable hooting made her speed up with an apologetic wave to the car behind her.

The traffic cleared a little as she passed by the Celtic Manor resort high above the road. Briefly she joined the M4, then left it to make her way through Newport. Once again, she was travelling alongside the meandering River Usk, past the great red circle of the Steel Wave, a sculpture dedicated to the steel industry, and a little further along she could see the elegant lines of the new footbridge. It was not long before she was parking near the building which had had such a profound effect on her life. Taking a deep breath, she got out of the car, straightened her back, and thought, okay, here we go.

In reception she asked for Matt, steeling herself for recognition to appear in the eyes of the young Sikh constable behind the glass panel, but it didn't. Stupid to go on worrying about it, she told herself, I should have got over all that by now. A few minutes later Matt came loping down the stairs to greet her.

With a glance at the man on the desk, he simply clasped her arm and smiled at her. "Come on up," he said, and she followed him upstairs. As they made their way through the main office, several people looked up from their computer screens and smiled a greeting. Fabia noticed Gerry Fairweather scowling at her from the far side of the crowded room and couldn't resist giving him a wave. "Hallo Gerry," she said, forcing herself to smile, "long time since I've seen you."

He just gave her a curt nod, then turned and walked off, scowling.

"That's me told," she said to Matt.

"Well, you did rather ask for it."

"True," Fabia said, "but not very kind of you to point it out."

Matt grinned at her. "Forget about him. Here's Dilys."

"Hiya, good to see you, ma'am," Dilys Bevan said, smiling warmly.

"Hallo, Dilys, you've cut your hair again."

"Yup," Dilys said, lifting a hand to her short curls, "too much trouble when it's long."

"Maybe I should try cutting mine."

"Don't you dare," Matt muttered, then turned to his sergeant. "Could you bring in those notes on the body found at the dig, Dilys?"

"Rightio, sir."

Matt waved her to a chair then sat down behind his desk, clicked away at his laptop and turned it to face her. On the screen was the photo of a young man, clean-shaven and pale-skinned, a gentle face, his grey-green eyes in striking contrast to his dark hair. It was the photo that his sister had used for the poster. Fabia studied it carefully. She remembered it so well.

"Do you remember his mother and sister gathered a positive army of family and friends to put posters up asking anyone who saw him to contact them or the police?" she asked.

"I do," Matt said.

"And the father refused to get involved. I didn't take to him one little bit, I thought he was a nasty piece of work. He didn't want them to draw attention to any of it. He seemed to care more about how the boy's disappearance would reflect on him than about finding his son. He kept telling his wife and daughter they were wasting their time, that it was up to Caleb if he wanted to... how did he put it?... if he wanted to bugger off with his fancy friends. He flatly refused to take the situation seriously, seemed far more angry than worried; that really stuck in my mind, but then, the whole case did."

"Why particularly?"

"I don't know. There was something about the way he looked, but I could never pin it down."

Dilys came back carrying a file. She opened it up and took out some papers, sorting through them. "I could have shown you these on my laptop, but I thought it'd be clearer if I printed them out," she said.

"How well you know me, Dilys," Fabia told her.

Dilys smiled and selected a sheet. "Here we are. This is the pathologist's report."

Fabia glanced down at it then up again, grinning. "Pat Curtis? She's still in charge, is she?"

"Yup," Matt said, "she's her same delightful self."

Fabia laughed. She knew the pathologist and her grumpiness of old. That said, she was very good at her job.

"Well, let's have a look at these," Fabia said. She picked up the report and began to read through it. After a few minutes she looked up at Matt. "She's sure about the cause of death?"

"Adamant," Matt said. "He was hit over the head, several blows, with such force that the skull completely caved in – death must have been instantaneous."

"And it couldn't have been due to a fall?"

"She says not. She says the extent and nature of the damage rules that out, something to do with how localised it is and also because it's the only evidence of damage to his body. If he'd fallen from a height, there would have been other injuries, broken bones, etc."

"Is there any way of telling, after all this time, whether or not he died where he was found?" Fabia asked.

"No, not really, at least the SOCOs haven't come back with anything yet. We've got on to the county surveyors' office and asked for information about the state of the Usk riverbank at the time, how different the course of the river was then. We're pretty sure the place he was found was a good deal further from the river at the time, but they haven't got back to us with confirmation yet."

"And what do you want from me?" Fabia's tone was wary.

"Whatever you can remember. It'd be useful to get as much information as possible before Chloe and I go and speak to his family again."

"Chloe?" Fabia wondered why Dilys wouldn't be going with him.

"Chloe's just finished her family liaison training," Dilys told her. "This is her first case going solo, so to speak."

There was something in the sergeant's voice that made Fabia glance at her, but her face gave nothing away. "Shall I give her a shout?" Dilys asked.

"Would you? She needs to be in on this," said Matt.

Fabia had met Chloe Daniels several times over the past year and had admired her enthusiasm for the job. She was small and brown-skinned, her curls usually done in a complex pattern of plaits, and she had endless energy. The only problem she could envisage was the fact that her new job would probably bring her into closer contact with Matt and there was no doubt that Chloe had a bit of a crush on him. Maybe that was what Dilys had been thinking about too. Fabia hoped he was aware of it, she wouldn't want the girl to get hurt, but she really didn't feel she could say anything. Best not to interfere, she told herself.

She looked up as Chloe bounced into the room, face bright and smiling.

"Hiya, Ms Havard," she said, "haven't seen you for a while, not since that business up at White Monk Abbey."

"Congratulations on your new job," Fabia said, smiling at her.

"Thank you, I hope I don't mess up."

Dilys glanced at her and said briskly, "You'll have to make sure that doesn't happen." But she smiled to soften the comment.

"You'll be fine," Matt told her. "You'll do a great job."

Fabia noticed the look that Chloe gave him, swelling with pride at his praise. Oh dear, watch out, Matt, she thought.

"Okay," she said, "so is there anything else for me to look through?"

"This is everything from the case at the time." She handed Fabia a file and, from the closed expression on Dilys's face, Fabia wasn't sure she was entirely happy with doing so.

Matt glanced at his sergeant then said, "Dilys isn't sure we should burden you with all this."

"It's not that... well–" Dilys reddened a little, looking embarrassed. "It was a long time ago," she added lamely.

"But I think the notes should jog Fabia's memory of the case, Dilys, since she was in charge back then," Matt said, turning back to Fabia. "I told the Chief Super that I'd be asking you about your part in it and he said it'd be okay for me to run things past you."

"How on earth did you persuade him?" Fabia asked, eyebrows raised.

"I made much of your fantastic powers of recall," Matt told her, grinning, "and anyway, he was a bit distracted at the time, something to do with an unsatisfactory game of golf, so I managed to slip it in without too much trouble. Obviously, I didn't tell him the extent to which you'd be involved."

Fabia thought she could understand Dilys's concerns, this certainly wasn't a conventional way of working. And she was a little surprised at Matt, who was a determined follower of the rules. She gave him an enquiring glance, but he just looked back at her blandly, so she decided not to comment.

"Shall I go and get some coffee from across the road?" Chloe said to Matt. "I know you can't stand the stuff the machine churns out."

"That'd be great, Chloe," Matt said. "Black for me, Fabia will have a latte."

The look Fabia gave him indicated that she could speak for herself, thank you very much.

"Sorry," Matt said, grinning.

"But he's right, Chloe, a latte would be great. Now let's have a look at these," Fabia said, opening up the chunky file.

* * *

There was silence in the room as Fabia sat and went through the notes. With many years of practice when she'd been in the police force, Fabia had learnt to skim read, so it didn't take her long to go through the records of the case. It came back to her so vividly that she felt herself back in that front room of the council house in Cwmbran, sitting in a shabby armchair opposite the parents of the missing boy, his sister on the arm of her mother's chair, a hand protectively on the older woman's shoulder. She remembered the angry glare in his father's eyes, the pain so evident in the faces of the two women, and Matt sitting to one side, quiet, concentrating on the family's reactions.

"There was something else the father said back then that stuck in my mind." She put a hand to her forehead, frowning in an effort to remember. "That was it. He was sitting on the side lines, not making much of a contribution, but I heard him mutter 'bloody poofter' at one point and I think he said 'if he wants to go, let him go, good riddance' at another. The sister reacted to that, turned on him and told him to shut up, but his wife just ignored him."

"I don't remember his muttering, but I'm sure you mentioned it to me at the time," Matt said.

"What a dreadful attitude for a father to have," Dilys remarked. "Do you think he had anything to do with his son's death?"

"I don't know," Matt said. "Hopefully something will emerge from the inevitable interviews, we haven't spoken to the father yet, we're doing that tomorrow morning. He's pretty frail now, apparently, lives in sheltered housing in Usk. His daughter told us he's in the first stages of dementia."

"Oh dear, that'll make things more difficult, for you as well as for the family," Fabia said. "I remember him well, there was a sort of suppressed violence about him, as if he was only just under control."

"Which could point towards him being responsible," Matt suggested.

"I suppose so, from a physical point of view, yes."

"But surely, his own son?" Dilys protested.

"It has been known," Matt said.

Chloe came back into the room with four cartons of coffee in a cardboard container. Once they were distributed, she sat down, all attention.

"And then there was that group of friends," Fabia said. "Do you remember this one?" She pointed to a name in the notes. "Iolo Beynam. I think he and Caleb were more than just friends, but no-one actually said they were an item. Not one of them mentioned that he was gay, not the friends nor the family; we just had that old-fashioned poofter comment from the father. There were two distinct sides in that family, father on one side, mother and daughter on the other." She paused, scanning the notes again. "This interview here, that was just with his twin, Nerys, and their mother. I made a note of the fact that at one point his sister said, 'Never mind what Father says, what do you think, Mam? It's pointless taking any notice of him'. That also made an impression on me at the time. And I got the impression the mother was reluctant, at first, to include his friends in the poster campaign, but his twin persuaded her. I don't know why she didn't want them to be involved, she just didn't seem very keen on them, particularly the ones that he shared his student house with."

The four of them went on discussing the case while Dilys made notes and Chloe sat taking it all in.

Sometime later, Matt sat back and stretched. "As you can see, the mother and sister live in Pontygwyn now."

"Oh!" She glanced back at the notes. "So they do. I missed that. Number 20 Morton Road, that's up past St Madoc's school on the way to Abergavenny, I wonder how long they've been there."

"Did you know they lived there?" Matt asked, his tone slightly accusing.

"No, of course not, why would I?"

"Well, you might have heard something about them on your very healthy grape vine."

"Well, I hadn't," Fabia snapped. "I've heard nothing about them between the closing of the case years ago and now."

Matt grinned at her. "Sorry," he said, "it's just that you're usually such a fount of information about Pontygwyn and its inhabitants."

"Maybe," she said, "but there are limits. It's not as if it's some tiny village, Matt."

"True."

"I know it's pushing the rules a bit, and I do understand your concerns, Dilys, but can I have copies of this lot to take home with me? I'd like to go through them in more detail."

Matt gave her a considering look, then said, "Oh, go on then, since I've actually asked you to become involved and had it approved by the boss."

Dilys's only comment was, "I'll go and get copies."

"You're a gem," Fabia said, smiling at her.

"What with all the cuts," Matt said, as Dilys left the room, followed by Chloe, "we need all the help we can get."

Matt was frowning across at Fabia as he pushed a hand through his hair. She wondered what was on his mind, that gesture always meant that he was worrying about something. When he did speak, it wasn't what she expected.

"Have you thought any more about what we talked about the other night?"

She knew immediately what he was getting at but didn't think this was the right time to talk about it. "Of course I have, Matt, but can't we talk about it at lunch?"

"I suppose. I just wondered—"

They were interrupted by Dilys's return.

"There you are, ma'am," she said, putting the file down in front of Fabia, who wondered if her use of the formal title was Dilys's way of putting things on a more official footing.

"Thanks, Dilys. I'll be sure to keep these strictly to myself."

"It'll be fine," Matt said airily, but Fabia wasn't sure Dilys was convinced.

She changed the subject. "I could do one of those mind maps that you're always so scornful about," Fabia said with a sly smile.

"I am not," Matt protested.

"Yes, you are."

"A mind map?" queried Dilys. "How would that help?"

"It'd help with your profiling. I find it concentrates my so-called little grey cells, what's left of them," Fabia said, grinning at her. "Look, let me show you." She pulled a piece of paper towards her and sat down, began scribbling as Dilys leant looking over her shoulder. "If you put the most important aspect of a case, say the name of the victim in the middle, and then you link that up to all the other aspects and people involved, their motivations, this and that about their personalities, etc., it creates a pattern that can show things up that simply reading case notes just doesn't do."

"That's tidy," said Dilys, "I might try that in future."

"Oh Lord, not you too," Matt protested.

"Stop being so grumpy," Fabia told him. "And it'll jog my memory, maybe there are other points I'll remember from the case as I go. I might have missed something at the time that'll come back to me."

"That'd be unusual," Matt said.

Fabia gave him a smile. "Thanks for the compliment, Chief Inspector."

Matt grinned then got up and shrugged on his jacket. "Fabia and I are going to go and have a bite to eat now, and I'll see you back here at two thirty, okay?"

"You're actually going out for lunch?" Dilys asked, her tone teasing.

"Yes," said Matt. "Why not?"

"You mean there'll be no sausage rolls and can of coke at your desk, sir?"

"Shut up, Dilys."

She grinned and said to Fabia, "You're a good influence, ma'am, keep it up."

Fabia laughed. "I'll do my best."

"And while you're out," said Dilys, "I'll get on with checking exactly where all these people were at the time of his disappearance and where they are now; maybe do a bit of tracking between the two timelines, what do you think?"

"Good idea, Dilys," Matt said. "See you later."

Chapter 6

By common consent, while they ate their lunch, Fabia and Matt hadn't spoken much more about the case as Fabia had wanted to know more about Chloe's new job, whose idea it had been that she should apply and where she'd gone to do the training. Then Matt had mentioned that his brother, Pierre, was coming over from Guernsey, where he was a local vicar, to a theological conference in Cardiff.

"When's he arriving? I'd love to see him again," Fabia said.

"The weekend after next."

"Is he going to be staying with you?"

"No way, he's not your sleeping on sofas type, my brother. The conference is at the All Nations Centre, and it's residential, but we'll be meeting up at some point."

"Is Jane coming with him?"

"No, she can't get the time off," he said. "She's just been promoted to something called a nurse manager at their hospital."

"Well done her, she's a force to be reckoned with, your sister-in-law."

"You could say that." Matt grimaced. "She's always scared the shit out of me."

"Don't be silly, Matt, she's just a bit brisk, that's all."

But now they were waiting for their coffee in silence, as Fabia gazed out the window at the river and the elegant arms of the white footbridge just upstream. When the silence had dragged out a little, Fabia looked at Matt and found him frowning across at her.

"You want to discuss it again, don't you?"

"What?"

"What you mentioned in the office, about us living together. That was what you meant, wasn't it?"

"Well, yes. You said you'd thought some more about it."

"I have, but I'm still not sure, Matt. And we really haven't time to – sort of – do it justice now. But there's something else worrying you isn't there?"

The expression on his face was difficult to interpret. "What's on your mind?" she asked.

"What? Oh, nothing."

She decided not to push him. "Where's that coffee?" she said, looking around for the waiter. "Don't you have to get back?"

He glanced at his watch. "I can afford a bit longer. It's not as if I often take time off for lunch. Dilys wasn't exaggerating."

He looked out of the window then back at Fabia, still frowning. The coffee arrived and he drank it almost in one gulp.

"Look, Matt," she said as she put her own empty cup carefully back in the saucer. "I can tell there's something gnawing away at you."

"What do you mean?" he asked.

"I know you too well. We've talked about Chloe and her new job, and we've talked about your brother, and I've said I'll help you with this investigation, and we'll talk about who's going to move where another time, I promise. So, what else is niggling at you?"

Yet again he pushed a hand through his hair in that familiar gesture. "It's nothing, really," he said, then contradicted himself. "It's just that – well, I was wondering about this Tony Vaughan bloke."

This wasn't what Fabia had been expecting. Now it was her turn to frown. "Tony? What about him?"

"Well, I was wondering what he's like. He seems to have appeared out of nowhere."

Fabia couldn't stop herself smiling. "He appeared, as you call it, about four months ago, when he got the job in Caerleon and moved in next door. Haven't you met him a couple of times when you've been round at mine?"

"I have, but I've no idea where he's from? He's got a family, hasn't he?"

"Yes, as I've told you. His two girls live with him during the week because they're at Caerleon Comprehensive, and his wife – they're separated – lives in Swansea, she's just taken up a job as a head teacher at a school down there. He's a nice bloke."

Matt scowled. "So, are they going to get a divorce?"

"I've no idea, at the moment they're just separated, and it's not the kind of question you ask. I've met his wife, Martha, a couple of times."

"And how much do you see of him?"

"What do you mean?" Fabia asked, beginning to feel irritated.

"Well, when I phoned last week you said you couldn't talk because you were expected next door."

"Yes, to help Rosie, his daughter, with her art homework."

"And then when I met him at the dig, he… he was talking about you as if you're close friends."

"Well, we are friends, and neighbours."

"Yes, but," Matt said, not looking her in the eye as he folded and refolded his napkin. "Do you – do you meet up often?"

"What do you mean, meet up?" Fabia's tone was chilly.

"Well, you know—"

"No, I don't, Matt."

His frown deepened. "It's just that, well I thought we were…"

At last he looked up at her, then stretched out and took her hand where it rested on the table. Fabia was surprised when he went off on what she felt was a tangent. "I know you don't want to get married, Fabia, you've been clear enough about that, but we are a couple, aren't we?"

"Yes, of course we are." She returned the pressure of his fingers. "I love you, Matt, you know that, but that doesn't mean I can't have other friendships, does it?"

"Of course not, but it just feels as if you're rather closer to this Tony Vaughan bloke than, say, John Meredith," he said, mentioning their mutual friend, a solicitor who'd been involved in a case they'd both worked on a few months before.

"Yes, John's a good friend, but he's got Anjali."

"And I've got you?" It was a question, full of uncertainty.

There was a pause before she answered. "We've got each other, Matt, but I value my independence, and you're always busy." She tried to keep the resentment out of her voice, Matt's job got in the way far too often. "And," she went on quietly, "you have to admit my previous experience of relationships has been pretty toxic, I don't want to screw things up again. Let's enjoy what we've got and take things slowly, that's what we said we'd do, wasn't it?"

Matt sighed. "That's what you always say."

"But you agreed, Matt." Fabia tried to lighten the atmosphere. "I thought I was the one who's meant to be impulsive."

He didn't smile. "You are, and that's what worries me."

"For goodness sake, Matt." She was angry now. "What do you think's going to happen? Do you imagine next time you turn up on my doorstep without warning I'm going to be next door shagging Tony?"

"Don't be crude."

"Bugger off, Matt."

"Fabia, I'm sorry, I—"

But she wasn't listening. She pushed her chair back. "I think this conversation is at an end. Thanks for lunch," she snapped as she hitched her bag onto her shoulder, then she strode out of the restaurant leaving Matt trapped by having to pay the bill.

* * *

When Matt got back to the office, Dilys was about to ask if he'd enjoyed his lunch but changed her mind after one glance at his face. That thunderous scowl spoke volumes.

She knew the history of their rocky relationship, how they'd been estranged for two years and how Matt had subsequently been responsible for clearing Fabia's name when they'd met up again. She wondered what on earth had happened at lunch, but she had the sense not to probe. She was still wondering when she sat back down at her desk.

Over the last few months there'd been such a positive change in her boss. He'd gone from an uncommunicative and rather solitary person to a much more relaxed and happier individual, and she'd become used to his mentioning Fabia constantly, talking as if they were a couple. In the end, one evening when they'd gone to the pub after work, she'd plucked up the courage to ask him direct.

"Are you and Fabia, sort of, together now?" she'd asked him, then felt her cheeks redden. "Sorry, sir, I shouldn't pry."

But he hadn't seemed to mind. "Together?" He'd grinned. "You could call it that, yes, you could definitely call it that."

53

"I'm glad. She's great, is Fabia."

"She certainly is," he'd said.

Now Dilys pulled her keyboard forward and told herself not to over-react, it was probably just an argument – they'd be fine. She really hoped she was right.

Chapter 7

Gaenor Baptiste let herself into her Newport flat and dumped her shopping bags in the hall, then picked up a copy of the Western Mail from the door mat; her elderly neighbour always passed it on when he'd finished reading it – he didn't believe in reading the news on line. She walked wearily through to her living room and put her briefcase, laptop and the newspaper on the coffee table, then stretched and yawned. What a day! Thank goodness it was Saturday tomorrow. Those first-year students could be very trying, half of them hung over after a night at the students' union, the other half far more interested in their mobile phones than anything she had to say. And she'd certainly have to deal with that objectionable lad and his snide comments. Nothing he'd said had been overtly racist or misogynistic, but there'd been an undercurrent, and a lot of whispering between him and his pal. Who'd have thought she'd still be having to deal with this kind of nonsense? But then she had to admit in the last couple of years it had got worse. A sign of the times perhaps. She sighed. She was more than ready for a drink, a meal and a quiet evening watching something mindless on Netflix. She picked up the bags from the hall and took them through to the kitchen but told herself she'd sort the shopping in a minute.

Lifting a glass down from the cupboard, she mixed herself a gin and tonic then wandered back into the living room and sat down on her ancient sofa, absentmindedly pulling the newspaper towards her as she did so. She took a long appreciative sip from her drink, began to leaf through the pages, then, a moment later, gasped and straightened.

"What the hell?" Sitting forward, she flattened the paper out on the coffee table and concentrated on a report on page three. Chewing at her bottom lip, she read through it again. "Oh lord. Poor, poor Caleb." Pressing a hand to her mouth, she sat wondering what to do, then grabbed up her mobile and scrolled down to the number she wanted.

After a few rings, she heard a familiar voice, "Hiya Gaenor, how's things? I've been meaning to phone you for ages."

"You always say that, Iolo."

He picked up on her tone of voice. "What's up? You don't sound too good."

"I'm afraid I've got some news." She hesitated.

"Afraid?"

"Yes, well, I've just been reading this report in the Western Mail and it seems they've found a body, they're doing a dig by the Usk in Caerleon."

"What? Roman?" Iolo asked, but he sounded distracted and Gaenor could hear a baby crying in the background. Iolo called out, "Rory! Lizzie needs her nappy changed." Then he was back with her. "Sorry, being a father of two is exhausting, and Rory's busy cooking dinner."

"How are they?" Gaenor asked, aware that she was putting off telling him the bad news.

"They're… well… great, delightful, amazing, a pain in the arse – sorry, I'm inclined to go on a bit when it comes to the kids, but after waiting so long, Rory and I can't believe our luck, having two gorgeous kids. As you know Dylan's a noisy little tyke, but Lizzie's calmer, quieter. We've managed to find a fantastic nanny, so we've both got back to work more or less full time, although I'm working from home quite a lot."

"I'm really looking forward to meeting Lizzie. She looked so sweet in those photos you sent me."

"But that's not what you phoned about, is it?" he said. "You were saying they've found a body by the Usk."

Gaenor paused for a moment then decided it was time for the direct approach. "It's Caleb, Iolo, they've found Caleb."

There was a long silence on the other end of the line. Gaenor wondered if they'd been cut off and said, "Iolo?"

"I'm here." She heard him take a long, shuddering breath. "Are they sure it's him?"

"It looks like it. I've just been reading about it in the Mail, they say he's been identified, and the next of kin have been informed." She looked down at the paper where it lay, on the coffee table, and ran her finger down the report. "The police think he's been dead for some years and the report says a murder investigation has been launched and they're appealing for information."

"Murder! Oh my God! How?"

"It doesn't say."

"Will they want to speak to us?" Iolo asked, and Gaenor could hear that he sounded worried.

"I should imagine so, after all, we were there when he disappeared." Gaenor took a deep breath. "I must phone Filly and warn her."

"I suppose so, she's back at home in Wales, isn't she?"

"Yes, she came home because her mam's getting very frail," Gaenor said. "We meet up quite regularly. And she seems to have had a few health problems lately, poor Filly. I've got a key to her flat because she had a horrendous bout of bronchitis a few weeks ago and I was doing all her shopping."

57

"You're a star, Gaenor."

"Well, she'd do the same for me."

"And what about Clare?" Iolo asked. "I suppose she ought to be told."

"But how? As far as I know, she's still in Australia, and it's not up to us really, we weren't exactly close."

"True. She was such a pain back then with her temper tantrums and her neediness."

"And the rest," Gaenor said sardonically. "Sorry. I still find it hard to think about those last few weeks."

"I know, love. And now this." For a moment there was silence on the other end of the line, then Iolo said, "But who would want to kill poor Caleb? He wouldn't have harmed a fly, and he'd had such a dreadful time before he escaped to uni."

"I know, it doesn't bear thinking about." Gaenor's voice was anguished, then another thought occurred to her. "Do you think I should get in contact with his sister?"

"No, leave it for now," Iolo said quickly. "The family will have enough on their plate."

"I doubt his awful father will care," Gaenor said bitterly. "He was a horrible man and he probably hasn't changed. But I liked his mum, in spite of her preaching, and his twin sister is a friend of mine on Facebook."

"Yes. Nerys was the only one in the family who didn't seem to mind about Caleb being gay. She's a good sort. When we were together, she was working in M&S in Cwmbran, often used to get us socks and stuff on discount, but she was doing an OU degree at the same time. It takes guts, that." He paused again, then said, "Look, if you contact the police maybe you should give them my phone number and e-mail address, best to show willing, don't you think?"

"They might well be getting in touch with you off their own bat, but I'll do that anyway."

He changed the subject and she sensed he was trying to lighten the atmosphere when he said, "How's the lecturing going, Dr Baptiste?"

She smiled. "I'm still not used to that title. Sounds odd, somehow."

"Are you enjoying being back in South Wales? It must be quite a change after London."

"It's always good to come home, and the job is great. I love the lecturing, although I've got a right bunch of first years to deal with this term."

"Worse than usual?"

"Not really, just a couple who're a tad racist."

"What the hell? I wouldn't have thought they'd dare with you." She could hear that he was smiling.

"I've mellowed, Iolo. I'm not as fierce as I used to be."

"I remember the way you used to stick up for Caleb." He was serious again. "Shit, Gaenor, this is such a lousy thing to happen, everything will be raked up again, all those questions, that probing. I'm lucky, I've got Rory and the kids. But you – you make sure you phone me if things kick off."

"I will, love, and I'm tougher than you think," she assured him. "Give my love to your husband."

"Will do."

As she ended the call she wondered if what she'd said was true. At that moment she didn't feel in the least bit tough.

Chapter 8

Clare Jeffreys had arrived back in Wales from Australia in early March. Her job in Sydney had come to an end, her cousin had got married and moved away, and she'd decided it was time to make a new start. She felt that coming back home to Wales had been a good decision. She'd found a job as a personal trainer and she was delighted with the small flat she'd found with its view of Belle Vue Park. It was minimalist, the pale grey walls uninterrupted by pictures except for an abstract painting on an unframed block board above the fireplace. The plain wood floors and Ikea furniture to her taste, and she'd chosen a soft leather suite in charcoal grey to blend in with the rest. It was a perfect one-bedroom bolt hole where she could recreate her life without reference to the past.

But there was one thing she always did which connected her to the world outside. As she had many times over her nine years away, she sat at her computer and checked the local news in South Wales on the BBC website. The police were asking for witnesses to a stabbing in Newport to come forward; there was a report of a serious accident on the M4 near Swansea; and, on a less serious note, a story about a six-year-old boy and his collie dog who had won an award for herding sheep on his parents' farm near Brecon. Then she saw it, a name she recognised. It gave her quite a jolt. She adjusted her glasses and leant forward, studying the screen more carefully. Caleb Morgan. Lovely Caleb. My God, that took her back! Back to the chapel youth group where they'd first met. Back to those days when she'd followed him everywhere. She read through the short report and felt suddenly sick. His body had been discovered during an archaeological dig in Caerleon. How on earth had that happened? She bit her bottom lip, leaving it with the imprint of her teeth. Maybe it wasn't the Caleb she'd known, but no, there couldn't be that many Caleb Morgans. It must be him. Caleb, she thought, my Caleb.

She pushed her fair hair from her forehead, leant back on the sofa and sat quite still for a moment. The conventional BBC words told her very little. She needed to know more, but who could she ask? She didn't think Gaenor Baptiste would take kindly to a phone call from her out of the blue after all this time; they'd never got on, and anyway, her mobile number probably wasn't the same as it had been back then. Who else was there? Iolo Beynam? No, she'd rather not call him. But there was one person she'd kept in contact with – Filly Jenner. She'd been the only one of those housemates who hadn't seemed to mind someone not connected with the university joining their social group. And Clare knew the number she had was current because she'd made contact a few weeks ago when she'd decided to come back from Australia. Yes, she'd give her a call. She picked up her mobile and scrolled down to the number she wanted.

It rang for quite a while. Clare listened to the ring tone in mounting frustration and she was just about to give up on the call when it was picked up and a hesitant voice said, "Hallo?"

"Hi, Filly? It's Clare."

"Oh, hallo, Clare, how… how are you?"

"I'm fine. I'm back in Newport."

"That must be very different to Australia."

"It is a bit, but I've landed a lovely job as a personal trainer in a gym, I'm really looking forward to starting that next week." She took a deep breath, desperately wanting to ask about Caleb, but not wanting to jump right in. "And how are things with you?"

"Okay. My mam's had to go into a home, but I visit her most days."

"Oh dear, that must be difficult for you."

"It's not so bad, really," Filly assured her. "Luckily the home's not far from my flat. Poor darling, she's quite frail now and she can't get around like she used to. It's horrid for her, but she's so patient, love her."

It struck Clare that if she was old and frail, Filly would be just the right person to have around. But this wasn't getting anywhere, she needed to guide Filly round to what she wanted to know. She opened her mouth to speak, but Filly was still talking.

"I've started a lovely new job at a health food shop and restaurant," she went on. "It's so good to feel you're doing the right thing, selling stuff that won't harm anyone; do you see what I mean?"

"I certainly do. It sounds like a shoo-in for you."

"Yes, it is, particularly as I'm a vegan now, and they have lots of lovely food that I can actually eat, gorgeous ready meals, and everything they sell is natural, no chemicals or drugs or anything."

"That's great," Clare said, trying to keep the impatience out of her voice.

There was silence on the other end of the line and Clare decided it'd be okay now to approach the reason for her call. "I was just getting up to date with the local news, Filly, and I wondered if you'd seen a report about a body being found in Caerleon."

"A body?"

"Yes, on the banks of the Usk, people on an archaeological dig found it."

"Oh, I see," Filly said. "I suppose it could be a Roman legionnaire, that'd be exciting."

"No, it's much more recent than that. Do you remember Caleb Morgan?"

"How could I forget?" Filly sounded agonised. "That poor boy. They never found out what happened to him, did they?"

Clare felt her impatience rising. Filly didn't seem to have made the connection between the body and Caleb. But then, she'd always been a bit vague and unworldly. "I'm afraid they've found out now, Filly," she said as gently as she could. "The body they've found is Caleb's." Her voice cracked as she said the name.

"Oh… my… God! Whatever happened? Is he dead?"

"Well, yes, love, he is," Clare said. "The article doesn't say a lot, just that his body was found and that the police have set up a murder investigation."

"But that's terrible!"

"I know. Apparently, the family have been told. It must be an absolute nightmare for them. They've probably spent all these years thinking he'll turn up again – people do, you know – but not like this."

"The poor, poor things." There was a catch in Filly's voice. "Oh dear, I just can't believe it. He and his twin were so close, she must be completely devastated."

"I know," Clare said, "but I suppose they'll have some kind of closure now. It must have been a nightmare all these years not knowing what happened to him. I wonder if I should contact Nerys."

"Do you think? Well, it might be a good idea." Filly didn't sound too sure. "I haven't spoken to any of his family for years, but I do see quite a lot of Gaenor, and Iolo's one of my friends on Facebook."

"I wonder if they know what's happened, should we contact them, do you think?" Clare asked, and waited for a response. She got the one she wanted.

"I suppose I could give Gaenor a ring to find out if she knows anything more."

"That's a good idea," Clare said, "I've sort of lost touch with them both, so I'm a bit reluctant to barge in, if you know what I mean."

"Of course, I do," Filly said, her tone sincere. She was always sympathetic to the problems of others.

"Perhaps you could let me know what they say, I'd really like to find out more, after all, Caleb was a particular friend of mine, we were very close for so long. I just can't believe what's happened."

"You poor thing," Filly said softly. There was a small silence on the other end of the line, then Filly added, "I suppose you were close, I mean. Do you want me to phone Gaenor now? She'll be so sad about it. She's such a kind person, she was really helpful when I was ill a few weeks ago."

"Good for Gaenor," Clare said. "Do you think you could phone her, Filly? I think she'd be a bit surprised to hear from me."

"Oh, I don't know…"

Clare smiled, trust Filly to deny the obvious. "I'd be really grateful if you would, Filly."

"No worries, I'll let you know what she says."

"And why don't we meet up for lunch, are you free tomorrow, or Sunday?" Clare asked, it'd be good to have some company.

"I can't over the weekend, I spend most of Saturday and Sunday with my mam," Filly said, sounding desperately apologetic. "I'm awfully sorry. But why don't you come to the café Monday, I can take my lunch hour and we can sit down and have a good catch-up, how about that?"

"That'd be great," Clare said.

Filly explained where the café was and, as Clare put the phone down, her mind went back to thoughts of Caleb. What would this mean? Would the police make contact? They'd probably be talking to all Caleb's friends from back then. She wasn't at all sure she wanted it all thrown open. On the other hand, deep inside, she felt an eagerness to talk about Caleb, to remember how it had been between them. She put her hands up to her cheeks and sat like that, her grey eyes wide and intent, going over her memories of him.

They'd met when they were both about eleven years old. Clare had been taken to the Jesus Brethren Chapel by her parents when they lived just outside Pontygwyn, and Caleb's mother had brought him and his twin along. All three of them had joined the youth club and, at first, Clare had made friends with Nerys, but soon it was Caleb who'd become her particular friend. As they grew older, she'd become more and more attached to him. He was different, not like the other boys, quiet and thoughtful, and she'd adored him. But things had gradually changed and although she'd thought of them as boyfriend and girlfriend, Caleb had never wanted to be open about it. She'd hung on, though, told everyone Caleb wasn't interested in any of the other girls. "He's my boyfriend" she'd insisted to anyone who'd listen, and gradually people began to believe her, all except Caleb who continued to keep her at arm's length.

But she'd continued to tell herself that they were together and tried to pretend she didn't hear the whispers behind their hands of others in the club, the grinning and giggling. She told herself they were just jealous and redoubled her efforts, telling people that his family didn't approve and that was why Caleb didn't show his feelings for her in public, that they had to meet up in secret. If the truth were known it had all become so real to her that, even now, part of her believed what she'd so desperately wanted to be true.

In the end Nerys had told her to leave him alone. Clare remembered how angry she'd felt about that. She'd thought Nerys was her friend. Even now she felt that old anger rising up inside her. But at the time Nerys had been so fierce about it that Clare had stepped back for a while. Then Caleb had gone off to university and, because Nerys and the rest of his family weren't around, Clare had decided to track him down, hoping that, away from their influence, he'd come back to her. She'd managed to do so by trawling round the pubs that the students from the Caerleon campus were known to go to. Finally, she'd got lucky and they'd met up again and she'd convinced herself that, in the end, he would give in, after all, she adored him and who could resist such strong feelings? How could it not happen since she wanted him so much? And she obviously knew him better than his other friends because she'd known him so much longer. But nothing she'd done had worked, and both Gaenor Baptiste and Iolo Beynam had warned her off in no uncertain terms. She blamed them entirely. They were just taking over where Nerys had left off. The only person who'd accepted her was Filly.

When she'd finally escaped to Australia, she'd tried her best to get him out of her mind, but now she was back, and she realised that, even though he was dead, he still had power over her. She desperately wanted to know what was going on. It occurred to her that there was nothing to stop her going back to the chapel. All those old biddies would be sure to be nattering away about this tragedy, and even if his mother and sister were still part of the congregation, she looked so different now that the chances were no-one would recognise her. She could always re-introduce herself to them when the time was right. She wondered if it was still the same pastor. She hoped so. She'd liked him.

Yes, going back to the chapel would be a good first step. On Sunday she'd go to the morning service.

Chapter 9

Fabia woke early on Sunday morning feeling conflicted. She was still angry with Matt, but she also felt a fool for making such a fuss. If she was honest with herself, she had to admit she was the one who'd laid down the rules about their relationship, it was her who had held back from moving in together, not Matt. Was she asking more from him than she was willing to give? It wasn't really surprising if he was a little insecure about it all.

Matt hadn't phoned her the day before, and she'd stubbornly refused to make contact herself. There had been one short text in the afternoon saying he wouldn't be able to make their usual Sunday lunch as he'd be working through the weekend, but he'd said nothing about their argument. Fabia's heart had sunk. She'd been hoping to be able to clear the air, but the fact that he'd simply texted her fanned the flames of her anger again, so she'd simply sent a text back saying, 'Okay, speak soon' and left it at that. She'd flung herself into an orgy of housework, something she usually avoided like the plague, then she'd gone for a long walk through Gwiddon Park, which was just down the road from her house.

She often walked there along the banks of the River Gwyn, a tributary of the Usk, but in the last couple of weeks she'd had to change her route, as part of the path that meandered along the riverbank was now under water and she'd no desire to go paddling in the chilly water where, in days past, they'd dunked poor women who'd been accused of witchcraft. Once through the park she'd walked on up towards the hills above her house and finally got back home, tired and no happier, as dusk was creeping in. She'd had a solitary supper in front of the fire, watched, but taken very little notice of, the latest episode of some hard-to-believe police drama, and climbed wearily up to bed with Matt still preying on her mind, feeling like a teenager in her first relationship.

What she needed was someone to talk to, preferably her closest friend, Cath Temple, who was vicar of St Cybi's Church in Pontygwyn. She'd be busy with services until later but there was no harm in giving her a ring to see if she was up for lunch at The Oaks pub later on. Fabia dialled Cath's number and was delighted when she picked up immediately.

When Fabia made the suggestion, Cath's initial reaction was, "But doesn't Matt come to you for lunch on Sundays?"

"He's busy," Fabia said, but she didn't elaborate.

"My last service is the ten thirty today," Cath said, "so I should be able to get to the pub by half twelve, is that okay?"

"That'll be fine. I'll phone and book a table. They can get pretty busy on Sundays."

"You sound tired. What's up?" Cath said, perceptive as ever.

"A couple of lousy nights. Matt and I had a bit of a row on Friday and I haven't heard from him since, well, other than a short text."

"Oh dear, is that why he's not coming around for lunch?"

"No, of course not," Fabia was quick to assure her. "As I said, he's busy with a new case. I'll tell you about it later."

"Sounds to me as if you're full of news."

"You could say that," Fabia said ruefully.

"I look forward to hearing all about it, but I must get going now, the church wardens want to speak to me before the service and I have a horrible feeling they've got something to complain about."

"Poor you. See you later." Fabia always felt better for talking to Cath, she'd know what she should do – she usually did.

* * *

Nerys Morgan didn't often go to chapel. It was a long time since she'd had any faith in the religion that was so important to her mother, but this morning Marion had begged her to go with her.

"Please, Nerys." She put a hand on her daughter's arm. "Cariad, it would be such a help to me to have you there."

"Okay, Mam, I'll come this time. Are you going to tell them all that Caleb's body has been found?"

"They'll know," her mother said wearily. "It was all over the news."

Nerys's heart sank. "Then wouldn't it be better to keep away and avoid the curiosity and the intrusive questions? Some of them are so nosey."

"But I need to pray for him, and they're not being nosey, they're being supportive. They care," her mother protested. "And I need to talk to Pastor Harris. He was such a help when Caleb disappeared, and I'm sure he'll be the same now. I just couldn't have coped without him over these last few years – a truly good man."

Nerys couldn't argue with that. Pastor Selwyn Harris had been there for her mother when Nerys's father had given her no support at all, and she had been deeply grateful for his care and his kindness. She looked at her mother, at the dark shadows under her eyes, the strain in her face, and wondered if she dared ask what was in her mind. But she had to.

"Do you know if the police have spoken to Father yet?"

"No, I don't. I suppose I should speak to him, but I find it so difficult. Half the time he doesn't seem to know who I am, and the other half he goes on and on about what a lousy wife I was and how I deserted him in his time of need. His time! What about him deserting us?"

"I know, Mam, but try not to upset yourself. I'll go and see him again later, check if they've been to speak to him yet. Let me go and put on something more appropriate than jeans and a jumper, I know you've always liked us to be smart for chapel."

The chapel in St Madoc's Road was an attractive wooden building which, from the outside, still looked like the village school it had once been. Inside the main hall were rows of wooden pews either side of a central aisle, arranged facing a dais on which was a table, and on the table an enormous bible lay open. Behind this table a high pulpit had been constructed with stairs mounting up on either side of it, and on the wall above the pulpit, in elaborate copperplate script, were painted the words 'Know that Jesus Christ is Lord'. To Nerys these words had always had an element of threat to them.

She and Marion had arrived just as the service was starting and Nerys was relieved to find seats towards the back. Several people smiled at them or lifted a hand in greeting, others turned to look at them – some looks tinged with sympathy, others showing blatant curiosity. Nerys knew they would be surrounded by her mother's friends after the service and dreaded all the prying and the questions. But for now, all she could do was let the familiar hymns and prayers wash over her as she sat there, unable to stop herself thinking back to when Caleb first disappeared.

At the time, she had been twenty and studying hard at her Open University degree. She'd not told her father about her studies; why do so when it would only have caused a row? He'd taunted and teased Caleb for taking up a place at Caerleon, "You should get a job in the steelworks instead of poncing about studying useless crap," he'd sneered. "Start paying your way, it'd make a man of you." But their aunt, who was Caleb's godmother, had put money towards his studies and, for once, their mother had stood up to her husband. Nerys had been glad for Caleb. It meant her twin could escape their father's bullying and it took the pressure off her and her mother that watching out for Caleb always entailed. She'd spent so many years protecting him, and not only from their father, but also from the gossip of her parents' friends and the mockery and bullying of kids at school, so when he left home it meant one less thing to worry about. But in spite of all that, for years she'd wondered whether he would have disappeared if he'd done as their father had wanted.

And now they knew the worst. He was dead. Murdered. The word seemed to fill her mind, heavy and dark. It felt as if all this was happening to someone else. But it wasn't, and she'd spent a sleepless night going over and over who might be responsible, and, at the same time, trying to avoid a horrifying suspicion that kept worming itself into her mind. She knew that, once again, she'd have to cope, do the supporting and comforting, and the only way to do that was to block out her own pain and grief.

It was exactly as Nerys had feared after the service. Several people gathered round them before they even managed to slip out of the pew.

"We're so very sorry to hear about Caleb."

"Dear Marion, how dreadful for you, please let me know if there's anything I can do."

"At least now you can lay your dear boy to rest."

Both she and her mother tried to respond, but Nerys couldn't help resenting the intrusion, although her mother seemed to find some comfort in their obvious care and interest. They were rescued by Pastor Harris who came up and, putting a hand on Marion's shoulder, addressed the people gathered round.

"As we did when Caleb disappeared, I shall gather some of our faithful and create a prayer chain. We shall pray for his soul, and for the soul of the perpetrator of this evil act," he said, "but now I think we need to pray that they'll be discovered and made to face man's and the Lord's judgement."

He put a hand under her mother's arm and guided the two of them from the chapel. As they got to the door, Nerys thought she saw someone familiar. But surely, she thought, she can't be here, she's in Australia. As she turned to get another look, she lost sight of the tall, fair-haired woman and decided she had been wrong. It must be all the memories being stirred up.

* * *

Fabia was very glad she'd booked a table as The Oaks was even busier than usual. Maggie Evans, the publican's wife, who also doubled as the pub's chef, was famous for her Sunday roasts and half the town seemed to have decided to indulge today. Just before one o'clock Fabia was settled in a window seat, two large gin and tonics in front of her. She'd been greeted by several friends as she'd made her way through the crowd to the table, but she now sat, lost in thought, oblivious to the chatter around her. Her mind picked away at her memories of Caleb's disappearance. If she concentrated on that she wouldn't brood about Matt. She'd been sitting there for about ten minutes when a cheerful voice from just behind her said, "Two gins! Things must be bad."

The woman who'd spoken was short and rounded, her curly, mouse brown hair cut close to her head, her blue shirt topped by a clerical collar.

Fabia grinned and got up to give her a hug. "One of them is for you, although I wouldn't object to drinking both, the way I feel."

"That bad?" Cath sat down opposite Fabia, pulled out the white, put it in her pocket then opened the neck of her shirt. "That's better. I didn't have time to change after church – I'd forgotten I had a baptism in the middle of this morning's service and that always stretches things out a bit – so I decided to come straight here." She took a gulp from her glass. "Phew! that's good, now, tell Auntie Cath all about it. What's Matt done?"

"How did you know it was to do with Matt?"

"You said so earlier, anyway, isn't it always?"

"No!"

Cath grinned. "So, tell me all."

"Not until we've ordered," Fabia said. "What'll you have?"

They bent to look at the menu together, both decided on Maggie's sumptuous roast beef and they chose a bottle of South African red to go with it, then Fabia threaded her way through the crowd to the bar to give the order. Once back in her seat she looked across at Cath who was almost bouncing up and down in her chair with impatience.

"I'll begin at the beginning," Fabia said.

"Always a good idea," Cath said, and the grin still lingered.

"Stop that smirking, you."

"Sorry," Cath said, now looking comically serious as she pulled at her ear lobes. "I'm all ears."

Fabia told her about Matt asking her to go into the station to talk about a cold case and went over the details. "Back then it was one of the first cases Matt and I worked on together. It's always stuck with me."

"Why? Because of Matt?"

"No, it was the boy himself; obviously I never met him, but the photos of him were – I don't know – I suppose poignant is the best description, he had such a sad, thoughtful face. And there was the family, there was obvious tension between them – quite apart from the disappearance. The father was a nasty piece of work, dismissive of his son, seemed not to care about him at all, and he kept telling his wife to pull herself together and stop making a fuss, which didn't help one little bit, just made things worse. She was distraught, as you can imagine, and kept on insisting she must talk to 'the pastor' – she was a member of the congregation at that Baptist chapel, you know, the one in St Madoc's Road."

"I know it well. It's called the Jesus Brethren Evangelical Chapel, quite a mouthful. It's very much independent of any larger organisation. They took over an old building that used to be a primary school, must have been about thirty years ago."

"I know. That's where my Auntie Meg used to teach."

"Did she? I never knew that. Anyway, the kids were all transferred to the new school in Gloucester Road. The building was pretty dilapidated at first, then, this must have been around ninety-nine, some old dear left Pastor Harris her fortune on condition that he put it into improving the building and the outreach done by the chapel." Cath frowned. "I could do with a rich benefactor to help with restoring the roof of St Cybi's."

Fabia nodded in sympathy. "His name rings a bell, but I can't put my finger on why. What's he like, this pastor?"

"A bit of an old stick, but harmless enough," Cath said. "It's not for me to criticise, really, as he does a lot of work with rough sleepers and the like. The charity committee we were both on used to meet at his house, it's one of those boring little bungalows with that awful paving instead of a garden, I hate that stuff."

"Never mind his lack of garden," Fabia said, aware that Cath could go on for ages about her rambling vicarage garden, "what was the charity doing?"

"We were raising funds for the night shelter, he worked damn hard on that. My trouble is he's got some trenchant views of the 'a woman's place is in the home' variety, and he's a bit of a homophobe too. I had a run-in with him about some gay conversion therapy he was advocating."

"Was he now? Caleb Morgan was gay. Anyway, I remember him saying they'd set up a prayer chain, whatever that is."

Cath interrupted, "It's when a group of people get together to pray about, or for, something specific. Some believe that it adds power to their prayers."

"Well, that's as may be, but the more his mother went on about this prayer chain, the more scornful her husband became. The only person who seemed able to stand up to him was the boy's twin sister. When she turned on her father and told him to shut up, he did."

"Were there any others in the family?"

"No other siblings, but I believe there was a godmother. I think she'd helped the boy escape to uni."

"You certainly remember a lot about these people," Cath said.

"Yes, I suppose I do, but I've also been reading through all the notes. Matt let me have copies of everything since I was involved back then."

There was a pause in their conversation as their wine arrived, swiftly followed by plates piled high with slices of rare beef, crispy roast potatoes, vegetables and Yorkshire pudding. The waitress brought them a jug of gravy and pots of mustard and horseradish then hurried off to deal with another order.

"Wow!" Cath said, "this looks good."

Fabia poured the wine and for a moment, as they began to eat, neither spoke. But Cath couldn't contain her curiosity for long.

"Obviously I'm interested in your cold case," Cath told her through a mouthful of roast beef, "but what's up between you and Matt?"

"Ah. Well, after I'd been to his office, we went and had lunch at that new place, the River's Edge, the food's really good, we should go there some–"

"Fabia!" Cath said, exasperated. "What about Matt?"

Fabia gave her an apologetic smile. "It all seems a bit silly now, but I've been worrying about it all day yesterday and all night." She paused. "You know my new neighbour, Tony Vaughan?"

"Absolutely. Nice chap."

"Well, Matt seems to have got it into his head that he's more than just a neighbour."

"What makes you think that?" Cath asked.

"He actually asked me how much I saw of Tony."

"So?"

"It's none of his business," Fabia burst out.

"Oh, come on, love, he's your lover, your partner – at least, that's how I think of him. He has a right to know if you're thinking of seeing someone else."

"But I'm not," Fabia protested. "And he's no need to be jealous of someone I just happen to live next door to. It's ridiculous to think of Tony as a threat to our relationship."

To Fabia's surprise Cath didn't pour scorn on the idea. Instead she said, "Is it?"

"What do you mean?"

"You do seem quite keen on Tony."

"Whatever gave you that idea?"

"Well, you've talked about him quite a lot, and you're quite close to one of his daughters, aren't you? What's more, his wife isn't around, so maybe he's looking for a relationship."

Fabia was about to argue, but Cath wouldn't allow her to do so.

"To add to that, Matt's been very busy lately and hasn't been dancing attendance as he did when you first got together before Christmas – at long last I have to say – so perhaps having an attractive bloke next door showing an interest has – sort of – filled the gap."

Fabia didn't respond immediately. She took a gulp of wine to give herself time to think, then gazed across at Cath wondering what on earth to say.

"Sweetheart," Cath reached across and patted Fabia's hand. "Don't look so stricken. You have been complaining that Matt hasn't been around that much, and you'd got used to him spending half his time at yours. You've also admitted that he wants more out of the relationship and you've been holding back, which is a bit of a contradiction now I come to think of it."

"I know, but–"

"I do understand your worries," Cath assured her, "given the shitty time you've had with men in the past, but don't you think it's time you put all that behind you? I think you should put your relationship with Matt on a more formal footing?"

"What? Wedding bells and all that malarkey?"

"Not necessarily wedding bells, but didn't you say that Matt wants the two of you to live together and you said no, at least, not yet?"

"I suppose, and he did mention it again on Friday. I know that's what I said, but now I think I'd like – well, lately I've been wondering if I should suggest he move to Pontygwyn."

"You mean move in with you, or find somewhere else round here?"

"Move in with me," Fabia said after a pause. Very carefully Fabia arranged her knife and fork on her empty plate and folded her napkin. "The thing is, Cath, that I've got so used to my independence, being free to come and go as I please, doing things my way, and if Matt moved in, I'd have to give all that up. On the other hand, if we lived together, I wouldn't have to spend so much time texting and phoning him to find out when we'll see each other next, it'd take the uncertainty out of things."

"I understand your feelings about being independent — who better — but I think you make too much of that. And think what you'd gain, a lovely man to keep you warm at night for a start." She grinned, but when Fabia didn't respond to this, she went on, serious now. "Take care of your relationship with Matt, he's not as tough as he seems, Fabia, and you're so well suited, perfect for each other. And as for this Tony chap, it may be flattering to have him making it clear he fancies you, particularly when Matt's a bit preoccupied, but remember Tony's still married, has kids, and who's to know that he and his wife might not get back together."

"But I'm not interested in Tony," Fabia protested.

"Good, just so long as Matt knows that."

"It's just Matt being jealous," she insisted dismissively.

Cath gave her a sharp look over her glasses. "Just make sure he doesn't have reason to be," she said.

There was a small silence, then Fabia admitted, "Oh, you're probably right." She gave Cath a rueful grin. "You usually are. Shall I get the bill?"

Cath smiled, "Yes, best to get going. I've got a confirmation class at four and I haven't done any preparation yet."

"I'll pay, it's my turn," Fabia said.

"I won't argue," Cath said. As they got up, she patted Fabia's arm. "Think about what I've said, and talk to Matt, don't shut him out."

Chapter 10

On Monday Fabia had plenty to keep herself occupied. In the morning she'd driven to the gift shop in Usk to deliver a few small pastel landscapes they'd bought, then gone on to a gallery in Abergavenny who had taken a couple of her watercolours. She'd grabbed a quick sandwich at lunch time then driven on to a friend in Pontypool to talk about a portrait she wanted Fabia to do for her daughter's eighteenth birthday. Having made arrangements for the first two sittings, Fabia went and did some food shopping at Spar in the high street.

During the day she'd checked and re-checked her mobile, hoping to hear from Matt – there'd been nothing. But this wasn't unusual. If he had a difficult case on the go, he often didn't make contact for a day or two, although surely this one was a bit different? He'd actually asked for her help, and yet there'd been little contact now since Friday.

She went into the kitchen and made herself a cup of tea, knowing she must find something to do that would distract her. Her mind went back to the case. What had happened to that boy? Who had hated or feared him so much that they'd smashed in his skull and buried him? She decided to make a start on the mind map she'd promised to do for Matt. At least, when he finally made contact, that would be something useful she could discuss with him.

In the dining room, which doubled as her office, she pulled forward the notes that Dilys had given her. First of all, she checked on all the profiling that they'd done of the people involved – the parents, his twin sister, his housemates and friends – and made notes of any points about each person that stood out. Then she listed some others who'd been hovering on the periphery of the investigation: his tutors, his godmother, the pastor who'd been at the family home when she'd first interviewed them. This done, she drew a large piece of paper towards her, gathered up a few different coloured pens, and began by placing Caleb's name at the centre of the paper. Using different colours for each person, she made a circle of the names of everyone else around him, some close, some further away.

After about an hour she sat back and looked at her handiwork: a colourful pattern of lines, scribbled comments and tiny sketches. As she stared at the name in the centre of her map, she did her best to bring Caleb alive in her mind. She'd been told he was gentle, stubborn, gay. A beautiful boy, his mother had called him, and his sister had said he was too kind for his own good. Fabia wondered now what she'd meant by that, and who she'd been thinking about when she said it.

There'd been those two housemates, the black girl, Gaenor, who'd become angry at the lack of progress in finding him and accused the police of slacking, and her jittery friend, Filly who had asked over and over again what could have happened and insisted that, in some way, it was all her fault. And there'd also been a young lad, Fabia checked the notes for his name, Iolo Beynam. His white-faced shock over the disappearance had struck Fabia as more than just worry over a friend. Then there'd been another friend, Clare Jeffreys, who'd seemed very eager to be interviewed and had implied that she and Caleb had been more than just friends, which was odd if he really was gay.

As she sat there staring at her handiwork, a vague pattern seemed to emerge. Would Matt allow her to be involved in questioning all of them again? He and Dilys, and probably Chloe, would be doing so, but would he let her poke her nose in? She doubted that he would.

So, there she was, back to wondering about Matt and what he was doing.

She sat down to watch the news on BBC Wales Today just in time to catch Matt and Dilys holding a news conference, appealing for information from people who may have known Caleb Morgan in the past. She could tell, as she studied his face, that Matt was feeling stressed. He seemed unable to hide his irritation at some of the questions asked by the gathered journalists. She doubted that anyone who didn't know him intimately would have picked up on that, but at one point she noticed Dilys glance at him and, with great skill, in Fabia's opinion, interrupt to answer a question herself. Bless you, my girl, she thought, you've got his back. But now it was nearly eight and she still hadn't heard from him, and when she punched his number into her mobile it went straight to voicemail. Half an hour later she was on her way out to the kitchen when her mobile buzzed. In her haste to answer it, she nearly dropped it on the floor, but managed to retrieve it in time, and gave a sigh of relief as she saw who it was.

"Hi Matt," she said, keeping her voice light, not wanting to give away how much she'd been longing to hear from him. "I saw you and Dilys on the news, has it produced anything?"

"Not a lot." There was a slightly awkward pause. "Fabia, look, I'm sorry, I– oh this is no use. Can I come round?"

She tried to control the wave of relief that swept over her and not to let it show in her voice. "Um, yes of course. Have you eaten?"

"No. Haven't had time."

"Not to worry. I did some shopping on my way home from Pontypool this afternoon, so I've got plenty of food in."

"What have you been doing in Pontypool?"

"Visiting someone I met when I had that exhibition at the Chapel Gallery." She explained about the daughter's eighteenth birthday portrait.

"Nice idea. Anyway, I'll get to you in about half an hour, is that okay?" He sounded ridiculously hesitant.

"That's fine. See you then."

Fabia couldn't help smiling to herself as she put her mobile down. However complicated their relationship, she always looked forward to seeing him. When he was with her life seemed complete, even when they were arguing and at odds. Maybe he'd be able to stay. A little voice in her mind said that if he lived there it wouldn't be an issue. Okay, she told it, I realise that, but I can't think about it now. She opened the fridge and got out mushrooms, shallots and parmesan, Matt loved a risotto and she had just about enough time to make one before he arrived. She reached for the jar of rice.

* * *

Iolo Beynam was looking forward to a beer and a meal when he got home rather late on Monday evening. His journey home to the house in Brixton that he shared with his husband and their children had been a nightmare. The production company he worked for had its offices a stone's throw from Oxford Circus, and his commute was forty minutes, but tonight there'd been an accident on the Victoria Line and it was now more like two hours since he'd left the office. He'd texted Rory to warn him of the delay, and knew that, by the time he arrived, Lizzie and

Dylan would be in bed. He hated to miss their bath and story time.

When he let himself in, he could hear the sound of music coming from the kitchen at the back of the house. Kicking off his shoes, he made his way through and found Rory there stirring something on the hob.

"That smells good," Iolo said. He hitched off his backpack and put it on the table, then leant over Rory's shoulder to inspect the contents of the saucepan.

"Since you had that business lunch, I thought I'd just do carrot and coriander soup. There's a fresh loaf to go with it, and some cheese as well if you need more. Lousy journey?"

"Yup. Did the babes go down alright?"

"Lizzie was a bit grumpy, I think she's got another tooth coming through. Dylan explained it, with that 'let's explain things to this idiot adult' look on his face. He said Lizzie's teefs are pushing and pushing." Iolo grinned at the description. "In the end they both settled quite quickly," Rory added.

"Bless him, he's such a little father." He went to the fridge to get out a bottle of beer, held it up with an enquiring look, and Rory said, "Yes please, I was waiting for you to come in before opening one."

Iolo opened the two bottles and handed one to Rory and, as he did so, his mobile set up a clamour in the pocket of his jeans. He pulled it out, glanced at the screen and saw that it was Gaenor. He frowned. Her last call had been on Saturday and she didn't usually phone him quite so frequently, but then, what with this awful business about Caleb, perhaps it wasn't that surprising. "Hallo, darling," he said, "what's up?"

"It's more who, you won't believe who's crawled out of the woodwork."

"Tell me."

"Clare! She's back in Newport."

He sat down at the kitchen table, leant his elbows on it and asked, "Did she phone you?" He found it hard to believe that Clare would have done so.

"No. I dare say she can't stand me after that last set to we had before she went off to Australia. She got on to Filly and Filly phoned me. Poor Filly, she sounded so stressed." Gaenor explained about Filly's mother. "She's rather trapped, and she always seems to end up being the one that's used by others. She's way too soft a touch to stand up to Clare. Do you remember that business when Clare wanted to get Caleb on his own and she made Filly set it all up, let him think he'd be meeting her at the pub when it was really Clare that pitched up? I was so angry about that."

"I remember it well. She was a bit of a pain, wasn't she? The trouble was, Caleb was just as soft as Filly. I was always pushing him to tell Clare to sod off, and to stand up to his awful father, but he never would."

"I wish he'd reported her for stalking."

"I don't know, Gaenor, it wasn't as bad as that, and they'd been friends since they were kids."

"I know," Gaenor sighed. "But then, I suppose back then he wouldn't have been taken seriously, and men are far less likely to report that sort of problem, aren't they?"

"I suppose."

"I can't help thinking that, if he had reported it, things might have been different."

"How do you mean?" Iolo frowned, wondering what was coming next.

"I don't know," Gaenor said, sounding exasperated with herself.

"You're grabbing at straws, love. If it was some random attack, what difference would it have made?"

"And that's what's getting to me," Gaenor said. "Who on earth would think of killing someone as harmless as Caleb? Christ, if I could think of anything that'd help find the bastard, I'd phone up that Lambert bloke immediately."

"I know, love, me too. And talking of it being random, the other thing that's occurred to me, Gaenor, is that it could have been a homophobic attack. There were some pretty shitty people around when we were at uni."

"I suppose. But that cuts out anyone from our social group, Clare included. Anyway, she was already in Australia when Caleb disappeared. Filly didn't know his body had been found until Clare told her," Gaenor said, "and now she's persuaded the poor girl to phone around to find out more on her behalf, although that's not how Filly put it, but then she wouldn't, would she?"

"But why didn't Clare get straight on to us?"

"Come on Iolo, think about it."

"Yea, I suppose it's unlikely," he admitted.

"Anyway, I doubt she's got our phone numbers. What do you think we should do, Iolo?"

He frowned, not entirely sure what she meant. "Do? What do you mean?"

"About Filly, I mean."

"Gaenor, she's a grown woman, you can't spend your life protecting people from themselves."

"I know, I know."

"Have the police contacted you yet?" he asked.

"No, will they?"

"Of course, they will," he said, sounding exasperated.

"Sorry," she said, "I'm not thinking straight."

"I understand. Don't beat yourself up about it." He took a deep breath. "Two of them are coming up to London to speak to me tomorrow and I'm not sure how much to tell them."

"Well, everything I suppose," Gaenor said.

"Do you think? Even that awful time he went through when he was a kid," Iolo asked, his voice anguished.

"I suppose, but that's hardly relevant, he was a child then."

"I think we should keep that to ourselves, not muddy the waters."

"You're probably right," Gaenor sounded doubtful but didn't pursue it.

"Poor Caleb, he did have a crap time of it. I wish I'd done more to protect him."

"Don't you start blaming yourself," she told him.

Iolo didn't respond to this as Rory came up and put an arm around him. "Soup's ready," he said quietly.

"Look, love, I've got to go," he told Gaenor. "Let me know if anything else comes up, and I'll call tomorrow evening, tell you about the third degree."

He ended the call and sighed. Rory looked at him, concerned.

"You alright?" he asked and put his arms round Iolo to give him a hug.

Iolo returned the hug, said, "I'm fine," but he wasn't. He was feeling thoroughly unsettled and wishing the past had stayed where it should – in the past.

Chapter 11

Fabia was just stirring the last handful of Parmesan cheese into the risotto when Matt arrived. Having let himself in, he came striding down the corridor to the kitchen and grabbed her in a bear hug, then kissed her hard.

Once she could get her breath she gasped, "What was all that about?"

"Just, well, I'm sorry for being a stupid git, and I'm sorry for neglecting you over the weekend. And anyway, I like kissing you," he said, and did so again, but after a moment she pushed him away.

"Matt, stop it, the supper will be ruined." She turned back to her stirring, just in time to stop the risotto sticking to the bottom of the pan. "Get the plates out, they're warming in the oven."

It wasn't until they were sitting down opposite each other at the kitchen table that Fabia noticed the dark shadows under his slightly bloodshot eyes. She frowned across at him. "Have you been working non-stop since I saw you on Friday?" she asked, her tone accusing.

"Just about, it's a difficult one, this case, and it's not the only thing I'm working on. I've had to leave Dilys and Chloe to get on with the Morgan case while I dance attendance on one of Rees-Jones's pals because they had their house burgled."

"Oh dear, who?"

"Some golf club buddy," he said, then took a mouthful of risotto. "Wow, this is good. I'm delighted you made enough for three. This is the first decent meal I've had in days."

"You're an idiot, Matt. A lousy diet and grinding yourself into the ground won't help you do your job properly."

"What makes you think I'm not doing it properly?" he asked, looking offended.

"Well, how can you if you're stuffing your face with crap food and hardly sleeping?"

"I sleep. Don't nag, Fabia."

Fabia pulled herself up short. This was no good, starting another argument was the last thing either of them needed. "Sorry, and of course you do a good job, but I worry about you."

"Bless you, love, I know you do. But I wanted to fill the time, otherwise I would have spent hours worrying about you." He gave her a twisted grin. "See? You haven't got the monopoly on worry."

She decided it was time to change the subject. "So, tell me how it's going. I can understand what you mean when you say it's difficult, what with the time gap. What's been going on over the weekend?"

Before answering her question, he asked, "Can I help myself to some more?"

"Go ahead." She waited as patiently as she could while he did so.

When he was sitting down again and had refilled their wine glasses, he looked across at her. "Let me see, when I saw you Friday, we'd only just got going. The SOCOs finished on the site late Saturday. They combed the area for metres around, but the whole landscape has changed so much over the last few years. According to the county surveyors, even the river's course has changed a bit, widened, particularly after all those weeks of rain. Climate change has got a lot to answer for, so they didn't really find much that was useful, just his mobile phone. Aidan says he's stumped, but he's not given up, he knows of an outfit in London that does this kind of retrieval of information, so we've sent the sim card up to them."

"Wow, that'd be quite something if they could find anything on it."

"It would, but I'm not holding my breath."

"What about the body itself?" Fabia asked.

"Because of the position of the body, Pat Curtis thinks he was pushed into the grave. It must have taken the killer quite a time to dig it deep enough." Matt finally pushed his empty plate aside. "As to identification, there was the medical emergency pendant round his neck, I told you about that, and a few studs from the jeans he must have been wearing. There was also a watch, at least the remains of one. It must have been quite an expensive piece of kit, and the back had been engraved. They're still trying to work out what the engraving was, so far they've found two lots of 'lo' with an 'm' in between."

"Given to him by his parents? Or maybe a boyfriend since he was gay. Do you think that's relevant to the case? Could it have been a homophobic attack?"

Matt sighed. "If it was, that widens the field somewhat, doesn't it? I grant that we could be looking at a whole range of thugs that might think it was a good idea to target him. But the nature of the injury indicates there were just one or two blows. There were no other signs of him having been beaten up, although any soft tissue damage is obviously no longer evident, but there were no other broken bones."

"You'll have to investigate that aspect," Fabia said, "whether or not he'd been targeted, when you do the interviews with his friends, won't you?"

"Of course," said Matt, sounding slightly impatient.

"Have you spoken to his father yet?"

"Yes, we went to see him on Saturday morning," Matt told her. "I'm glad his daughter warned us that he's suffering from the first stages of dementia. That could account for his behaviour, but I don't know enough about it to tell."

Fabia leant her folded arms on the table and frowned across at Matt. "What sort of behaviour?"

Matt thought for a minute. "When we told him who we were he said, well, shouted something about that bloody woman always complaining, called her a stupid old cow, and a whole lot else. We finally managed to establish that his next-door neighbour had complained about him putting his rubbish in the wrong bin. Anyway, once we'd explained that it was nothing to do with her, he calmed down a bit, but when we told him about the discovery of the body and that it was Caleb's, he told us he already knew, then followed that up by telling us Caleb was not his son."

"Oh dear."

"We went through it all again, said we'd spoken to his ex-wife and his daughter but he denied all knowledge of them too. Luckily Dilys has experience of dementia, her mother suffered from it."

"So, you didn't take Chloe on this one?" Fabia asked without looking at him.

"No, she was busy." He didn't elaborate. "We finally managed to get through to him and he accepted that the boy had existed and was part of his family, but he suddenly got up and started pacing up and down the room, muttering."

"What was he saying?"

"At first it was hard to work out what the hell it was," Matt told her, "then Dilys realised he was saying, 'I had to do it, it was the only way, I had to, I had to' over and over."

Fabia's eyes widened. "That doesn't sound too good."

"We weren't sure at first what he was talking about. Dilys was her usual patient and persistent self. She began walking up and down with him and quietly asked him what it was that he had to do. At first, he didn't respond, hardly seemed to realise she was there, then he turned and looked straight at her." Matt dragged a hand through his hair. "I was worried for a moment. He's an old man but he's big and powerful, and I could almost feel the anger pulsing through him, but suddenly it changed. He seemed to sag, slumped down into a chair, looked up at Dilys and said, 'I told him he'd disgraced us. I told him to go and never come back, never contact me or his mother again, but I didn't mean it, I didn't mean it.' Then the poor devil broke down completely, great heaving sobs. I couldn't help feeling sorry for him."

"Deep down you're a softy," Fabia said, smiling.

Matt didn't return the smile. "Not when it comes to work, I'm not."

She didn't think it wise to contradict him. "Do you think his memory is reliable, that he actually did what he said?"

"I think so," Matt said. "Dilys says her mother's memory comes and goes, and her memories of the past are clearer, apparently the short-term memory suffers most. Anyway, he seemed completely lucid at that point."

"And when was it he told Caleb to leave?"

"We managed to establish that it was a while before he disappeared, he was pretty definite about that. He says they met up without telling the rest of the family."

"And you're sure he's telling the truth?" Fabia sounded sceptical.

Matt didn't respond immediately. He sat with his chin resting on his clasped hands, gazing across at her, but Fabia thought he wasn't seeing her, he was going over the picture in his mind of Caleb's father and what he'd told them.

Time ticked by and she waited, then Matt said, "Common sense would indicate that we can't take his word for it, and of course, he could have gone further and hit his son, but I have a feeling that he's telling the truth."

Fabia smiled at him with a touch of mockery. "A feeling? Matt, are you telling me you're going on feelings now?"

"Nah," he said, grinning, "I leave that to you, but I do have to look at it from all angles, don't I?"

Fabia got up to clear the plates and put them in the dishwasher, then pulled the loaded fruit bowl towards Matt and asked him if he'd like some cheese. Silly question really, she thought, he never refuses cheese. She brought some out from the fridge and, leaving him to help himself, sat down again and poured more wine.

"Now tell me what else you've been doing over the weekend," she said, "other than dancing attendance on Charlie's pals."

"I didn't spend all weekend on that idiot, and obviously the team kept going, contacting the people we need to speak to, going over all the info from when he disappeared, and researching the personnel involved, profiling."

Fabia suddenly jumped up. "I'm an idiot, let me go and get that mind map I made."

"Have you done that already? Great, I'll have some more of this Caerphilly while you go and get it."

When Fabia got back, she pushed away all the food, including the cheese, sat down beside him and spread the large sheet of cartridge paper before them. Covered in its colourful pattern of lines, squares and neatly printed names, they both leant forward to study it.

Matt pointed to one of the names. "I've cleared it with the Met for Dilys and me to go and interview this chap, Iolo Beynam, and I've got to fix up to interview her." He indicated Gaenor's name. "So far we haven't managed to track down the others. Clare Jeffreys, she's the one who went off to Australia before he disappeared, I'm hoping to get some background information from her. Nerys Morgan told Chloe that she was a friend from way back, not one of the uni crowd, and we need to find the other housemate, Felicity Jenner – she's known as Filly. I'm hoping Beynam and Baptiste will be able to point me in the right direction for both of them." Matt noticed something. "Why have you doubled the connecting lines between Caleb and these two?"

"Because I think they're more likely to have wished him harm."

He frowned. "Why that one? That's a bit off the wall, isn't it?"

"One of the things I remember from the investigation into his disappearance was that abuse was mentioned."

Matt's eyes widened in interest and he asked, "I don't remember that. Who by?"

Fabia frowned. "You know when someone says something and you're concentrating so hard on getting a response to a specific question you've asked, that you, sort of, miss the important bits? That's what happened, I think. I have a strong feeling I lost sight of something someone said that might have been important."

"Tell me about it," Matt said with a rueful look. "Maybe you'll find something in those notes that Dilys gave you that'll jog your memory."

"But I've gone through them all."

Matt shrugged. "Go through them again."

"Slave driver. Okay, I will," Fabia promised. "It wasn't until much later that I remembered it had been mentioned Caleb might have been a victim of abuse, either before or while he was at university. Let's face it, there's a broad field – lecturers, older students. But by then, Charlie Rees-Jones was saying we had to wrap it up and he put me on to a different case."

"Sexual or just physical abuse?"

"I don't know," Fabia said, frustrated, "and, as I said, I just can't remember who actually flagged it up."

"I think it's quite likely he was beaten by his father," Matt said, "that qualifies as abuse, do you think that was it?"

"No," Fabia said, frowning. "I don't think so. And another thing, one of his friends, I think it was Gaenor Baptiste, mentioned that someone was stalking him, so that's why I put those two connecting lines as possible stalkers. I'll have to go through the records again to see if they jog my memory. I must be getting old. My memory definitely isn't what it used to be."

As she got up to put the food away, Matt stretched and grinned across at her, Fabia knew that grin.

"You? Old?" he said. "Come off it, that's not my impression, or my experience for that matter." He got up and reached for her hand, rubbing the palm with his thumb. "I think it's time for bed, don't you? Give me a chance to prove to you how far from old you actually are."

There was a grain of resentment inside her that he seemed to assume he would be staying, but she told herself not to be stupid. They were lovers, weren't they? Why couldn't she just relax and accept their new relationship. Yet again she was brought up against her conversation with Cath earlier on.

Matt's smile died. He'd picked up on her thoughts. "I can't drive home, Fabia, too much of that wine of yours. Don't you want…"

The crestfallen look on his face made her smile and she put her arms round him. "Of course you can stay," she said, pushing her doubts away. "But if you have to get going at crack of dawn tomorrow, you'd better creep out without waking me, I'm not one for early starts these days."

"It's a deal," he said, and kissed her.

Chapter 12

Dilys and Matt caught a train late on Tuesday morning and arrived at Paddington at half past one.

"I'm working from home tomorrow," Iolo had told her. "I could see you around three in the afternoon." He hadn't sounded enthusiastic, which she supposed wasn't really surprising, but he hadn't put obstacles in their way.

Since they had a bit of time in hand, they decided to pause for a bite to eat before getting the tube to Brixton. Sitting at a café in the station concourse, having ordered sandwiches and coffee, Matt told Dilys about the mind map Fabia had done for him. He described the connections she'd made, particularly the two that she'd highlighted.

"But why those two?" Dilys asked. "In one case it's pretty obvious, given the fact that he was gay and all that, but why the other?"

Matt tried to explain Fabia's thinking, but he could tell there was something else worrying Dilys.

"What's up?" he asked.

"Nothing really, it's just that..." She looked down at the remains of her tuna sandwich and picked at the crust.

"Come on, Dilys, spit it out."

"I was just wondering if it's fair to ask Fabia to become too involved," she said in a rush, then added, trying to be diplomatic, "after all, it was a long time ago and it will worry her if she can't remember things."

"Dilys! She's forty-two not eighty-two!" Matt protested. "She's got a very good memory, and anyway, she had the information from back then to go through, all that would have jogged her memory."

Dilys took a sip of her coffee before she responded. "I know, but I've been thinking about that, and what with all the new data protection laws, I was wondering whether you... whether we should have done that."

Matt was aware that anything that came near to breaking the rules always worried Dilys, and he himself had a niggling doubt about involving Fabia. He was fully aware that his reasons for doing so weren't entirely professional, but the fact that Dilys was pointing this out made him stubborn. He wasn't about to admit he'd overstepped the mark.

"Her input is pretty useful, Dilys," he protested.

"I know, I know. But I was just wondering what reaction the boss would have if he found out the extent to which we've involved her."

"I don't give a flying... whatever," Matt amended quickly, "what Rees-Jones thinks, and anyway, I'm not going to tell him."

"But others might."

Matt stared across at her, wondering what she meant, then the penny dropped. "Oh, you mean Gerry Foulweather? Don't worry, I can deal with him if needs be."

"I hope so, sir, he's a slippery bastard."

"Couldn't have put it better myself."

He didn't think Dilys was convinced, but there was nothing he could do about that now, and he was a little irritated with her for bringing it up. "Fabia knows what she's up to, Dilys," he said firmly, "and I trust her judgement, well, her instincts."

"Yes, of course," Dilys said and glanced at her watch. "We'd better be on our way. He said it's ten to fifteen minutes' walk from Brixton tube."

"I hate the tube. We should have come by car," Matt grumbled.

"What?" exclaimed Dilys. "And have me driving through London! Not a happy thought."

"Why do you think you'd have been doing the driving?"

She gave him a look over her glasses and he grinned. "Okay, okay. But such disrespect from a subordinate, I don't know how I cope."

Dilys thought it best not to respond to this.

They arrived at Brixton tube station just after half past two and came out on to the bustling, colourful Brixton Road in bright sunshine. Dilys looked around, eyes wide, and Matt smiled at her expression.

"Fabia tells me Brixton Market is a must see," he said, "every kind of spice and vegetable you could think of and lots of craft stalls and interesting eateries. Maybe we'll have time to have a look around on the way back."

"Maybe," she said, but she didn't sound over-enthusiastic. "I'm not a great one for spicy food."

Matt laughed. "You don't know what you're missing."

"Hadn't we better get going?" she said quietly.

"You're such a slave driver, but yes, we'd better."

Dilys took out her phone and brought up the directions Iolo Beynam had given her. "He said turn left out of the station then cross over at the second bus stop, then it's the first on the right and a few hundred yards further on we turn left again."

They did as she suggested and, just before three o'clock, came to a narrow, terraced house in a quiet street. It had a neat paved front garden, with large pots of newly emerging daffodils either side of the glossy green front door. Matt rang the bell and heard it buzz inside. After a few moments they heard footsteps and a child chattering, and a shadow appeared behind the textured glass of the door just before it was opened to reveal a tall, dark-haired man wearing jeans and a cashmere jumper. He was balancing a curly-haired child on his hip and trying to prevent her grabbing his glasses. She gave them a stare, then a shy smile before going back to her assault on her father's glasses.

"Good afternoon, sir," Matt said, trying not to smile. "I'm Chief Inspector Lambert, this is my colleague Detective Sergeant Dilys Bevan."

"Hi, come in." He stepped aside, saying, as he did so, "Lizzie! Will you please stop that?" He put her down and she waddled off in front of them. As they followed in her wake, he glanced back at Matt and said, "Haven't we met before?"

"Yes," Matt said, "I was one of the officers involved when Caleb Morgan disappeared, a sergeant then."

"Oh yes, I remember, and the person in charge was that red-headed woman with the deep voice, I can't remember her name. She didn't look like a police officer at all, well, not to me."

Dilys glanced at Matt but didn't comment.

"Fabia Havard," Matt told him, "she's retired from the force now."

"I hope you don't mind sitting in the kitchen," Iolo said as they arrived in a light and airy room at the back of the house which extended into a conservatory. "Lizzie's toys are in here so that should keep her occupied. Lilita, our nanny, has gone to fetch Lizzie's brother from pre-school, so we've got a bit of time before he erupts into the house."

The child flopped on to her bottom and began to empty a box of various toys, while Iolo indicated that they should sit at the table. "Coffee?" he asked.

"That'd be good," Matt said and Dilys too accepted the offer.

While he was switching on the kettle and getting out mugs, and milk from the fridge, Dilys bent to help Lizzie empty her toy box. The child handed her a Peppa Pig board book and came to stand leaning against her knee, waiting to be told the story.

"Don't let her pester you," Iolo said.

"Don't worry, I have a niece and nephew this age, I'm used to playing with them and joining in a conversation at the same time."

Matt glanced at her, this was an aspect to Dilys he'd not come across before, but then they didn't usually end up interviewing people with small children. He decided to get going, they didn't have that much time.

"Do you mind if we record our conversation?" he asked. "It would help a great deal and you can check through the transcript when it's written up, make sure you're happy with it."

Iolo turned and gave him a straight look, frowned and then shrugged. "Okay, go ahead."

Still holding the book for Lizzie, Dilys took out her iPad and placed it on the table, tapped away, spoke briefly to say who was present, then nodded to Matt.

As Iolo handed them mugs of coffee and pushed milk and a bowl of sugar towards them, he asked, "Has it been confirmed that the body they found is Caleb's?"

"Yes, I'm sorry to say it has," Matt told him.

Iolo took a chair at the table and dragged a hand down across his mouth, slowly shaking his head as if in denial as he looked across at Matt. "That is so awful. When he disappeared, I thought... I tried to persuade myself he'd just decided to go away, to escape the shit that was happening to him and start a new life somewhere else, but I knew, deep down, that wasn't likely, particularly when he didn't make contact. You see, his godmother had bought him a mobile phone so he could have got in touch. That nagged at me for years and years," he said, his voice anguished. "Now, of course, I know why he didn't."

"You say he needed to escape, why was that?"

"His father was giving him a whole load of grief on several fronts, calling him names and criticising him for going to uni, the old man hated that, said it was a waste of time and money. Caleb had actually talked about getting away, said he'd move to London, Edinburgh, anywhere that his father couldn't get at him."

"But what about the rest of his family?" Dilys asked. "Did he mention them?"

"He was close to his twin, Nerys, and he said she'd supported him when he'd suggested leaving, and that there were ways of keeping in contact without anyone else knowing. He also said he was worried that Nerys's support of him was getting her into trouble with his father and that was another reason to leave."

"And his mother?" Matt asked.

Iolo gave him a bleak look, his lips tightening. "She was a real Bible thumper. She used to go to some fundamentalist chapel, and she was completely in thrall to the crap they spewed out. When he told her he was gay, she was devastated, begged him to 'change his mind'. She blamed his friends, well, me specifically, for corrupting him, then hurried off to their so-called pastor to organise some kind of cure." He indicated speech marks with his fingers and his scathing tone made his opinion of this quite clear. "There was hell to pay when Caleb refused to co-operate. He hated that chapel, and he hated what it did to her, which was hardly surprising, but he loved his mother, far more than she deserved, I thought. He was really cut up by her reaction. Nerys tried her best to mediate between them, but it was no good. And as to his bloody father—"

"He reacted badly too?" asked Matt.

"Reacted badly! The old bugger – oh, sorry Lizzie, shouldn't have said that." He became calmer and lowered his voice. "We were living together at the time, in student accommodation. When Caleb told me he was going to speak to his father, I tried to persuade him not to, I knew what his father was like, bully doesn't even come close." He went off at a slight tangent. "Caleb was sure he'd been violent towards their mother, but he couldn't get her to admit it."

"And what exactly was his father's reaction?" Matt asked, trying to bring him back on track.

"Like I said, he'd been giving him grief about not being a so-called proper man, but when Caleb actually came out and told him he was gay, his father beat him up."

Dilys, busy turning the pages of another book for Lizzie's benefit, looked up at this, but it was Matt who reacted, saying calmly, "Can you tell us more about that?"

Lizzie had begun to demand attention from her father and Iolo bent to pick her up, sat her on his lap and stroked her hair. She leant back against him and pushed her thumb into her mouth, and Iolo looked at Matt over her head, his eyes bleak.

"Caleb came home late one evening and it was obvious someone had had a real go at him. His clothes were filthy, caked in mud, and one of his eyes was beginning to close up, it was bloodshot and bruised. When I went to touch him, he flinched, but I made him let me check him over. He had this awful bruising coming out on his back and down his arm. It took me a while to persuade him to tell me what had happened, but in the end he did."

Iolo was stroking his daughter's hair absentmindedly as he spoke, as if it calmed him. "His father had an allotment and, because Caleb had wanted to speak to him away from the rest of the family, he'd gone to the allotment when he knew his father would be there. Caleb told him he was gay and that he was in a relationship, and the old man – well, he wasn't that old then – went berserk, called him all sorts of awful names then punched him in the face. Caleb fell over and when he was crouched on the ground his father kicked him, can you believe it? He managed to stumble up and ran for it with his father shouting after him that he should never come back, and he'd make sure Caleb never saw his mother again. It wouldn't surprise me if he was responsible for Caleb's death."

"How long was this before Caleb disappeared?" Matt asked.

"A couple of weeks, I suppose."

"Do you know whether or not he made contact with his father again?" Matt asked.

"No, I don't, but he might have wanted, like, to give it another go. He was a gentle, soft sort of person but he was pretty stubborn with it."

"And what about you?" Dilys asked. "You must have been desperately worried when he disappeared."

"Of course, I was," he said sharply, "but what could I do? His mother contacted you lot, and we – Gaenor and Filly and I, and some others – asked around campus, we asked all the people we could think of. We helped Nerys put up posters of his photo asking for information, went all over the place sticking them up wherever we could. And those of us who were on Facebook posted stuff. None of us were using Twitter, it would have helped if we had, but we didn't. And then, of course, you interviewed all of us."

"Is there anything else you remember particularly," Matt asked him.

"Nothing came of the poster campaign and, after a while, we gave up." He shrugged. "What else could we do? I tried to convince myself he'd found somewhere safe to stay, I told myself he could have lost his mobile. I did go back to his sister a few times to find out if she'd heard anything, but every time I did, she got so upset that, in the end I thought it best to leave her alone. How is she now? I wish I'd kept in contact."

"In a way I think she's relieved that he's been found," Dilys said, "but obviously she and her mother are very upset."

"And that awful father?"

"He's not a well man," she said, but she didn't elaborate.

He seemed to accept her reticence. "In some ways, it seems like another lifetime, in others as if he disappeared just months ago." He gave a shrug and went back to stroking his daughter's hair as she sat, sleepy-eyed, on his lap. "So much has changed, particularly since Rory and I got married and had the kids. Life, sort of, goes on, doesn't it? You never forget, but, gradually, you become accustomed."

"That's about the sum of it," Matt agreed, knowing exactly what he meant, then he asked, "Was there anyone else in your social group who might know more about his disappearance? Someone else who was close to him?"

There was a pause. Matt got the impression he was considering how best to answer the question.

"Caleb had told me that there was someone who was pestering him," Iolo said, "but I didn't know the details."

"What sort of pestering?"

"Followed him around, kept texting him, wouldn't leave him alone, and wouldn't believe he wasn't interested."

"This was a woman?"

"Yes."

"What was her name?" Matt persisted.

"Clare Jeffreys. She wasn't at uni with us, but she, sort of, became part of our social group because she knew Caleb through the youth group he used to go to when he was a kid. So, she was a family friend, I suppose. She went off to Australia not long before Caleb disappeared, but I think she might be back in Wales now. I even thought at the time that he might have gone with her, you know, to get right out of the way, but that was just grasping at straws."

"Is there anything else that you think might be useful to us?"

"No," Iolo said slowly, "not really."

Matt was convinced there was more, but before he had time to pursue it, they were interrupted by the arrival of the nanny, a blond-haired woman in her forties, and a small, dark-haired boy of about three. He was chattering nineteen to the dozen. "Dadda! Dadda! You never guess what Lilita done! You never guess!" He pulled up short at sight of Matt and Dilys, frowned, and said, "Who they is?"

"These are… friends of mine, darling," Iolo said, with an apologetic glance at the two police officers.

"Why they here?"

"They have just come to have coffee with your dadda," the nanny said, giving Matt and Dilys a cool, straight look.

Matt took the hint and got up. "Well, we'll leave you to it. We'd better get going" – he glanced at his watch – "our train leaves in an hour."

Dilys picked up her iPad and switched it off, put out her hand and ruffled Lizzie's hair and the child gave her a sleepy smile around her thumb.

"I'll see you out," Iolo said, handing his daughter over to her nanny. "I'll be back in a minute, Dylan. Ask Lilita to give you your milk and biscuits, and don't forget to say thank you."

They followed him down the hallway to the front door and, as they stood on the doorstep, Matt said, "Please contact us if you think of anything else that might be relevant, however trivial it may seem."

"I will."

"We'll get back to you if we need to," Matt said.

"By all means," he said, but he didn't sound enthusiastic, then he seemed to change his mind. "I want whoever killed Caleb to be caught. He was… he was important to me."

"We'll do our best, sir," Matt told him, but if the truth were known at that moment, he didn't hold out much hope.

Chapter 13

Matt had asked Chloe to go and check on Caleb's mother and sister while he and Dilys were in London. Nerys Morgan had phoned the day before to tell her they were being pestered by a crowd of news reporters, and Matt had arranged for Tom Watkins and another constable to go along and move them on, but he wanted Chloe to check up on them again. Marion Morgan had been pathetically eager to see her, and they'd decided on four o'clock that afternoon. Although Chloe had warned her that progress was inevitably slow, she had a suspicion that Mrs Morgan hadn't really taken this in.

She was tidying up her desk, ready to get going, when Gerry Fairweather came sauntering up, hands in his pockets and a smile on his face. He was not a person Chloe had much time for, but it was best to try to keep on the right side of him as he could be vindictive if crossed.

The first thing he said was innocuous enough. "How's the new job going then, young Chloe?"

"Fine, I'm enjoying it."

"You're working on this Caleb Morgan case, are you?"

"Yes, supporting the family."

"The original investigation into his disappearance was a botched-up job," he said suddenly, no longer smiling. "I said so at the time, but I'm afraid I was ignored."

Chloe glanced at him but didn't comment.

"Did you know it was one of the first jobs your boss worked on when he was transferred to Gwent?" Fairweather asked.

"No, I didn't."

"Yea. His trouble was he didn't really know the territory, no local knowledge or experience at the time, so it wasn't really his fault."

He grimaced and Chloe wondered if it was meant to indicate sympathy, though she doubted he'd feel any such thing for Chief Inspector Lambert.

"Trouble was I'd got on the wrong side of the then Inspector Havard." His tone was scathing. "So, she gave him the job rather than me. Tragic, really, when you think about it. We might have found the boy and his killer nine years ago, and that poor family would have had closure. Of course, now it's going to be almost impossible to find out who was responsible."

Chloe felt anger rising at his criticism of Matt, but she bit back words of denial. She hitched her bag on to her shoulder, ready to leave and hoping he'd take the hint, but he didn't move out of the way.

"And now it seems he's dragged her back in?" This was more a question than a statement. He stood waiting for a response, but Chloe still said nothing, and he went on, "Very bad idea, you should warn him about that. People may think her name has been cleared, that she had nothing to do with that fraud, but I have my doubts, and I'm not the only one. Political correctness, that's what it was. If she'd been a man, she would have got what was coming to her, mark my words."

"But everyone knows Fabia was completely exonerated," she exclaimed.

"Ah, Fabia is it now?" he mocked.

Chloe ignored this. "Ms Havard is a friend of the Chief Inspector's—"

"We all know that," he interrupted, then added with a leer, "a very good friend, I gather."

Chloe allowed herself a scornful glance at his unpleasant face. "And since she led the original investigation into the disappearance," she said firmly, "I think it's quite reasonable for him to consult her. She has a very good memory. I really don't see how anyone could object."

"Ever the loyal young constable, I see," Fairweather said.

"And anyway, it's not up to me." She stepped past him as she said, "I have to go, I've got an appointment with Mrs Morgan." She hurried away, feeling angry and disturbed by this encounter. She wondered if she should speak to Matt about it but decided she'd rather not. She might, however, have a quiet word with Dilys.

As she drove out of town towards the M4 she did her best to calm down and push Gerry Fairweather's words out of her mind, but it wasn't easy to do so, particularly as she hadn't been entirely happy herself when Matt had called Fabia in. Loath though she was to admit it to herself, she was a little jealous of the older woman. Surely Fabia Havard was much older than Matt, wasn't she? Well, by about seven years anyway. She day-dreamed a little about what it would be like to be as close to Matt as Fabia was, but pulled herself up short. Stop it, she told herself. There was absolutely no point in going down that route. Much better to concentrate on the job in hand. For the rest of the drive to Pontygwyn she made herself go through the details of the case and plan what she would say to Caleb's mother.

* * *

Half an hour later Chloe was drawing up a little way down the road from the house. She was relieved to see no evidence outside of any broadcast vans or sharp-eyed reporters hanging round with camera or microphone in hand. Maybe they'd heeded the warnings given last Friday, although she'd be surprised if they kept away for long, or maybe they'd found a juicier story to follow up. Chloe hoped so. Hitching her bag on to her shoulder, she locked the car, walked along the pavement, and strode quickly up the path, past the glorious magnolia, to the front door. It opened just as she got to it and Marion Morgan stood in the doorway, she'd obviously been watching out for Chloe's arrival. She looked haggard and the dark shadows under her eyes were evidence of little sleep, but she tried to smile as she said, "Come in, dear, I've put the kettle on."

"Oh please, you shouldn't have bothered."

"It's no bother. Go into the sitting room, I'll get the tea."

Chloe went through into the pleasantly warm room where an open fire was chattering away in the grate. The large box of photographs that Marion Morgan had shown her on her last visit still occupied the coffee table, and she noticed some photos of Caleb had been propped up on the mantelpiece. She studied them, wished that if she asked him what had happened, he'd respond. But the still face just gazed back at her, a slight smile on its face, as if mocking her for being fanciful.

She turned as Marion came back carrying a tray with two mugs and a plate of biscuits on it. "Sit down, dear, do."

Chloe moved the box carefully aside and Caleb's mother placed the tray beside it. Once they were both settled, Marion looked over at Chloe, her expression a mixture of weariness and hope. "Have you got any news?" she asked, her hands clasped tense around her mug.

"Not much, I'm afraid, but it's early days yet. Chief Inspector Lambert is interviewing all the people that Caleb knew at the time, his housemates and other friends, and we're hoping they'll be able to give us some useful information."

"Are they going to talk to that Iolo Beynam person?" She almost spat out the name.

"Yes, they are," Chloe told her, surprised by her tone. "He was a close friend of your son's, wasn't he?"

"Friend! What kind of friend would do what he did? He corrupted him. My poor Caleb was a gentle soul, not weak but easily influenced, and that boy – well, I suppose he's a man now – persuaded him into dreadful sinful practices." She lowered her voice as she said the last three words.

"I'm not sure I understand," Chloe said.

"He made Caleb into a homosexual," she said, almost whispering the word.

"You mean Caleb was gay?" Chloe asked as gently as she could. She knew this already, but she wanted his mother to elaborate. Some useful information might come out of it.

"No! He was a good boy, a lovely boy. He would never have gone down that path if he hadn't been led there by his so-called friend."

Chloe felt a protest rising up inside her but bit it back. This wasn't the time to stand up to prejudice of this kind, and it wasn't really her place to do so.

"I tried so hard to tell him how wrong it was," Caleb's mother went on. "But he wouldn't listen, he wouldn't listen. That awful boy had such an influence on him. I wouldn't be surprised if he had something to do with – with what happened."

"In what way?" Chloe asked, keeping her voice as gentle as possible.

"I don't know, I don't know." She was wringing her hands and there were tears in her eyes. "But Caleb had that lovely girlfriend, Clare, her name was, they'd known each other for years from the youth group at chapel, but he pushed her aside when he went to university and all because he met up with that perverted boy."

Chloe decided to try to broaden out her enquiries, maybe there were others that they didn't know about. "And what about his other friends?" she asked.

"Well, there was the coloured girl, Gaenor Baptiste." She was calmer now and there was none of the vitriol in her voice that there had been. "I liked her, she was a kind, tidy sort. Nerys had posters made with Caleb's photo on them, appealing for information from anyone who'd seen him, and Gaenor helped us a lot with putting them up all over the place, and the other girl – what was her name? Felicity, I think, she helped as well."

"Did anyone contact you after seeing the posters?"

"Several people, but none of it was any use."

Chloe was about to ask if there had been anyone else Caleb's mother remembered from back then, when the doorbell rang.

"I'm sorry," Marion said, "I'll just go and see who that is."

"Perhaps I'll keep an eye out while you do so, just in case it's someone from the press."

"Oh dear, do you think it might be?"

"There was no-one outside when I arrived, but best just check."

Chloe stood in the doorway of the sitting room and watched as Marion went down the hallway. How sad, she thought, that Caleb's relationship with his mother had been so fractured at the end of his life. But at least Marion hadn't rejected him completely as she knew sometimes happened. Could such bigotry have caused Marion to lose control and attack her son? No, surely not, and how could she, such a slight woman, have had the strength to bury him, unless someone had helped her? No, Chloe told herself, that didn't seem likely. But the idea persisted.

She heard Marion greet someone, sounding pleased, and a man's voice responding. Chloe went back to her seat as they came into the room. The man who followed in Marion's wake was very tall with neatly receding hair, observant blue eyes and thin, smiling lips. He wore an open-necked blue shirt and a grey suit.

"This is Pastor Selwyn Harris from the Jesus Brethren Chapel. He's been such a support to us all these years. Pastor, this is Detective Constable Chloe Daniels, she's our family liaison officer."

He held out a hand and Chloe shook it. His handshake was firm but brief.

"Good afternoon, sir," she said.

"I'm glad to hear that you're helping Marion and her family. This is a terrible time for everyone, and we must all help as much as we can. Are you any further on with the investigation?"

"It's early days yet," Chloe told him, "but we hope to have some news soon."

Mrs Morgan said, "I've just been telling PC Daniels—"

"Please, call me Chloe."

"Telling Chloe about Caleb's problems with that awful boy." She was gazing at him with a look of appeal in her face. "Do you remember, Pastor? I spoke to you about it at the time."

"I do remember. Yes, poor Caleb had lost his way." His voice was sorrowful, and he frowned as he spoke. "But we mustn't judge, that is for the Lord to do. Comfort yourself with the fact that our prayers might well have been answered had Caleb lived."

"Yes, of course," she said, wringing her hands round and round as she spoke, "I must do that."

Somehow Chloe didn't think that would be happening any time soon. She decided there wasn't a lot more she could do while the pastor was there, so she got up, hitched her bag on to her shoulder, and said, "I won't disturb you any further. I'll keep you informed of our progress, Mrs Morgan, and please don't hesitate to contact me at any time you want to."

"You stay here, Marion dear, finish your tea," the pastor said, smiling, "I'll see the officer out."

He followed Chloe to the front door. "A very sad situation," he said, his tone sombre, "but we at the chapel will support the family as much as we can."

"I'm sure you will."

"We have a strong community spirit and we will pray with them."

"It's good that they have such good friends around them," Chloe said noncommittally.

"So, have you found out anything further?" he asked, looking down at her, eyebrows raised.

"No, I'm afraid not, but Chief Inspector Lambert is putting every effort into discovering the truth." She decided to ask a few questions herself, no harm in grabbing the opportunity while it presented itself. "Did you know Caleb well, sir?"

"Oh yes, ever since his mother started to bring him and his sister to chapel, they must have been about ten at the time. He was a quiet boy, quite different to his twin. We have a very active youth group and they were members for some years, although Nerys decided it wasn't for her when she was about fourteen, she had a mind of her own even at that age, and unfortunately she persuaded Caleb to leave at the same time."

It was obvious Nerys's decision had not pleased him. Chloe didn't comment, just waited for him to go on.

"When Caleb decided to go to university, his mother came to ask my advice as there was some trouble between Caleb and his father about his decision. I regret to say I suggested it would be a good idea which, given later events, I deeply regret. Given the problems between him and his father, I could understand his need to detach himself, it often happens with youngsters at that age, but it is very sad the way it all turned out."

"I suppose teenagers always want to rebel a bit," was all Chloe could find to say.

"Unfortunately, yes, though many return to the fold in later life, but with his tragic disappearance, that obviously didn't happen with Caleb. I'm afraid Marion is right about his group of university friends, they were definitely not a good influence. I think that's where you need to concentrate your enquiries."

"You knew them?"

"More by repute and from what Marion told me, and I did a bit of research myself. I had a few connections at the Caerleon campus in those days." He frowned and hesitated, as if considering whether to say what was in his mind. "They were somewhat wild, I'm afraid, and I'm pretty sure they were into drugs of various kinds, but don't quote me on that as it was only hearsay."

"Thank you for telling me, it might be relevant to our enquiries."

"Any help I can give, please don't hesitate to ask, but I mustn't keep you, I'd better get back to Marion."

Chloe was thoughtful as she walked to her car. Drugs? She hadn't come across mention of anything like that in the records of the investigation, but she could always have missed something. The sooner she could pass that on to the chief, the better.

Chapter 14

Iolo checked the time: nine o'clock. He subsided wearily into an armchair, picked up the remote and clicked through the channels, but there was nothing worth watching and, truth to tell, he couldn't concentrate anyway. He'd spent the time since the two police officers had left, going over and over the past that they'd raked up, and he'd thought of several things he could have told them but had failed to mention. On automatic pilot, he'd helped Rory feed the children, given him a hand with their bath time and putting them to bed. Even Dylan had noticed his preoccupation when Iolo had been reading his bedtime story.

"Dadda, why you stopped? You not reading right."

Iolo had apologised and hugged his son close, gaining comfort from the warm little body.

After their own meal, it had been Rory who'd suggested he sit down and watch some mindless television. "You're so tense, do try to relax," he'd said, sounding slightly irritated. "To be honest I'm glad I'm going out."

"Sorry, love, I know I'm not good company tonight. It's everything being raked up again. I feel, sort of, responsible."

"Why? It's not your fault Caleb was killed."

"I know, but what if there were things I missed? What if there were signs that he was in trouble and I missed them?"

Rory gave him a worried look. "Iolo," he said, "what do you mean? What are you thinking of?"

Iolo sighed, shaking his head. "I don't really know. I've gone over and over the people who were around then, and their behaviour. His father, the stuff that happened when he was a kid, Clare being so persistent, his mother and her obsession, and then I start wondering if it was some random lunatic that was responsible."

Rory had put an arm round his shoulders. "I do understand but giving yourself all this grief is not going to help. Why don't you give Gaenor a ring? Maybe she'll come up with something."

Now that Rory was out meeting his sister for a drink, Iolo decided to take his advice. He punched in Gaenor's number and was relieved when she picked up almost immediately.

"The police came today," he told her, "have they talked to you yet?"

"No, I'm seeing them tomorrow afternoon. I've got meetings in Newport so, when they phoned, I suggested I should go into the station once I'm done. What are they like?"

"Okay, very polite. The chief inspector was that elegant bloke who interviewed us way back, sort of quiet, dark-haired."

"Elegant?" Gaenor queried, surprised.

"Yes, don't you remember him? Definitely not your average plod. And the sergeant was small and sharp-featured and didn't miss a trick, in spite of the fact she was keeping Lizzie occupied while we talked." He went through what he'd told them. "They were perfectly pleasant," he said, "and the woman, what was her name? Dilys something, she was very good with Lizzie."

"So, that means she must be okay," Gaenor said, and he could hear she was smiling.

"Of course," Iolo said, smiling too.

But he was soon serious again when Gaenor said, "Oh Iolo, this is all so awful. To think he was there, so close to us all that time."

"I know, love. And I keep wondering if it was my fault in some way, if I'd looked after him better, he might–"

"Don't be silly," Gaenor said quickly. "How were you to know someone was going to kill him? You looked after him, just as I did, he was that kind of person, he needed looking after. I always felt he was born with a layer of skin missing. With Caleb everything was too near the surface and too... too vulnerable. And having that awful man for a father didn't help. The only one in that family who looked out for him was his sister."

"I know. She must be going through hell, poor darling. I must phone her, have you got her number?"

"Yes, I'll text it to you. Anyway, what else did you tell the police?" Gaenor asked.

"I told them about Clare and her stalking," he said, his voice harsh. "She made life very difficult for him for a while. I was so relieved when she decided to go off to Australia. So was Caleb, it was like a weight had been lifted."

"I remember. How much did you tell them?"

"About Clare? Just that she was pestering him, and that she was a friend, so-called, from his childhood, not one of the uni crowd."

"They'll probably get hold of her."

"Good luck to them."

They talked on for a while, going round and round but not coming to any real conclusion. When they ended the call, Iolo sat staring into space, unable to stop himself going back to those last few days with Caleb and the dreadful aftermath. It was only when Rory came home that he was able to push it all to the back of his mind.

Chapter 15

Matt had just got back from the inquest into Caleb's death when Dilys poked her head round his office door.

"You're back, sir. How did it go?"

"Straightforward, it only took half an hour. They've adjourned pending further enquiries, as expected, and the body's been released for burial."

"Good. That'll help the family. Were any of them at the inquest?"

"Yes, his mother and sister, but I didn't see the father."

"Now the body's been released it'll give them something to concentrate on, organising the funeral," Dilys said.

Matt remembered that Dilys's father had died recently. She obviously knew what she was talking about, but he thought it best not to say so.

"Did you need me for anything?" he asked.

"Yes, sir. There's someone in reception asking to speak to you, about the case."

"Who is it?"

"It's Clare Jeffreys, one of the people Iolo Beynam mentioned."

"So, she's back from Australia, is she? At least that'll save us having to get in contact through the Sydney force. Did she say what prompted her to contact us?"

"She told Karim Singh, who's on reception, that she'd seen a report on the TV news and thought she should come and talk to us as she has information that might be useful. Shall I ask them to fix her up in one of the interview rooms?"

"Do that," Matt said, "room two, and get someone to give her a cup of coffee or whatever."

"Will do."

Ten minutes later Dilys and Matt went down to the interview room which was on the ground floor.

A window, the lower half of frosted glass, looked out on the station car park, and the walls, painted a dull grey-blue, were bare except for a large map of the Newport area on the one facing the window. A table occupied the centre of the room, two plain padded office chairs faced one side, and at the end of the table was the usual recording equipment. On the other side of the table, carton of coffee in hand, sat a rather striking woman. She was powerfully built, tall, with a strongly featured face, high cheek bones and long, straight blond hair, held in place by an old-fashioned velvet Alice band. She looked up as they came in, studying them through large, dark-framed glasses.

"Miss Jeffreys?" Matt said.

"That's me, and you are?" There was a slight Australian twang to her accent.

"Chief Inspector Lambert." He indicated Dilys. "And this is Detective Sergeant Bevan."

They both sat down. "We'll be recording this interview, just routine," Dilys assured her.

"That's fine, go ahead," Clare Jeffreys said, smiling, while Dilys set up the machine and recorded who was present. Once this was done Matt leant forward, his crossed arms on the table.

"I understand you have information for us with regard to the discovery of Caleb Morgan's body."

"Yes, well, I knew Caleb very well when we were teenagers." She bit her lower lip and then took a deep breath. "I was devastated when I heard about his disappearance all those years ago, but by then I was already in Australia so there was little I could do to help."

"When did you leave for Australia?" Matt asked.

"Let me see." She half closed her eyes in concentration. "It was in May 2010, a week before my 21st birthday, so that would be the 16th or 17th."

"And what made you contact us now?" he asked.

"Well, I was really upset when I saw the news about his body being found, and since I was so close to him back then, I thought I'd better come and talk to you. I thought I might be able to shed some light on what was going on at the time and the people he was involved with."

Matt didn't comment, he just waited for her to go on.

After a pause during which she glanced from Dilys to him and back again, she did so. "I wouldn't like you to think I was accusing anyone in particular," she said, with a worried frown, "but Caleb was in with a very cliquey crowd at university and two of them were very much in control – of him, I mean."

"How do you mean, in control?" Matt asked.

"Well, they had a great influence over him, persuaded him to detach himself from all his old friends." She pressed her lips together and there was a bleak look in her eyes. "Including me," she added.

Dilys took over the questioning. "Which friends, exactly, do you have in mind?" she asked.

"Iolo Beynam and Gaenor Baptiste," she said, "they were the, well, the ringleaders I suppose you could call it." There was a twist of her lips and her voice became harsh as she said their names, as if the words tasted unpleasant, but then she took a deep breath and went on more calmly.

"Caleb wasn't very strong-minded, he was easily influenced, and I think they had rather a hold over him."

"What sort of a hold?" Dilys asked.

She glanced at Dilys and gave a little shrug. "I'm afraid they didn't like me being around, they knew I really disapproved of drugs of any sort, and I think they were into experimenting, you could call it. And it was as if they didn't want anyone from his past interfering in their university life. Apart from my feelings about drug-taking, maybe they thought I wasn't the right sort of person to be part of their social group because I wasn't at uni. Anyway, they persuaded him that he should no longer go out with me."

"You were going out together at the time?" Matt asked, his tone neutral.

"Oh yes, we'd been together since we were – what? – thirteen, fourteen. Kids' stuff at first, then it got more serious, although Caleb always wanted to keep it quiet." She smiled a little ruefully. "I think that was because his parents were very strict, although his mam knew about our... our friendship."

This didn't match up with what they'd been told by his sister, or by Iolo Beynam, who'd said he and Caleb lived together as a couple. He wondered whose version of the story was closest to the truth. Unless of course, as often happened, Caleb had used his friendship with Clare Jeffreys as a way of pulling the wool over his parents' eyes until he went off to university, and Clare could have been taken in as well.

"And you believe his friends were the reason why your relationship ended?"

"I'm afraid so. They actually warned me off."

"How exactly?" Matt asked.

"I was doing my best to keep contact with him, for his sake as much as mine. I used to text him a lot, went to the pub when I thought he'd be there, that sort of thing. Like I said, I was really afraid they would persuade him to get into drugs and stuff like that, so I felt I needed to keep an eye on him."

Dilys frowned. This mention of drugs matched up with something Chloe had reported back. She could tell that Matt had picked up on it too as he leant forward a little, studying Clare Jeffreys' face intently as she went on.

"Iolo Beynam told me that what I was doing amounted to stalking Caleb." The expression on her face showed how ridiculous she thought this was. "I mean, what nonsense, and so offensive. He said Caleb didn't want to hear from me again and if I tried to contact him, they'd call the police. What good that would have done them, I cannot imagine. It was so insulting, don't you think?"

Neither Matt nor Dilys chose to answer this question, and, after a moment, she went on. "I desperately wanted to find out from Caleb what was going on, so I kept going around to the house to try and see him, and that's when that bloody Gaenor woman got involved. She had a real go at me. She was way out of order, said the most dreadful things."

"Do you know what Caleb thought of all this?" Matt asked.

"No. In spite of everything I did to make contact with him, I never managed to do so after that last time. All this happened not long before I went to Australia. I had a job lined up and my flight was already booked and everything, and my cousin was expecting me as I was going to stay with her to begin with. I just couldn't hang around. I had to accept that if Caleb had wanted to see me, he would have found a way to do so, so I gave in. Of course, originally both Caleb and I were going to go, but he'd pulled out. I'm pretty sure they were responsible for that decision too."

"He was planning to go to Australia with you?" Dilys asked, this was a new angle nobody else had mentioned.

"Of course," she said, giving Dilys a smile tinged with sadness. "We were a couple so, obviously, we both would have gone. We'd talked about it for, oh, years. We'd fantasised about making a new life away from the constraints his family put on him, and away from his memories of things that had happened in his childhood, things that had really hurt him."

"What sort of things?" Dilys asked.

"Oh, you know, his abusive father, his weird mother and there were, well, other things. All that was before he got together with that clique and they did their work on him and scuppered our plans. Like I said, I think part of the reason might have been because one or other of them was providing him with drugs, and of course, people like you, in the police, will know how addicts become dependent on their suppliers."

"I realise that several years have passed since all this happened," Matt said, "but do you have any proof that they were dealing in, or taking, drugs?"

"Actual proof?" she asked, frowning across at him.

Matt felt as if she wasn't quite sure what he had in mind, then her face cleared.

"Oh, you mean texts and stuff like that?"

"Yes, anything of that sort."

"Well, no." She gave an apologetic shrug. "That's the problem, I'm just sure in my own mind that that was the case, partly because of the change in Caleb. He went from being this lovely chap I'd known for so long, my gorgeous boyfriend" – there was a catch in her voice and tears in her eyes as she spoke – "to this stranger that would no longer have anything to do with me."

"It must have been very hard for you," Dilys said with real sympathy in her voice.

"Y-yes, it was." She turned to rummage in her handbag which she'd hung on the back of her chair, brought out a tissue and blew her nose. "I'm sorry, I was determined to keep it together, but this is all so upsetting."

"Don't worry," Dilys said, "we understand."

"You told our colleague on reception that you had information you thought might be useful to us," Matt said, attempting to bring the interview back on track. "Was it the information about the suspected drug-taking that you had in mind?"

"Yes… no… well, it was mostly that. I thought you ought to know what happened back then and–" she hesitated again and both Matt and Dilys waited quietly for her to go on.

She leant forward with her elbows on the table, hands clasped below her chin. "The thing is, Caleb was a good person, an honourable person, and if he threatened to, say, go to the police about the drugs, do you think one of them, or maybe both, could be responsible for his death? They could have wanted to shut him up."

Matt leant back in his chair, looking across at her, his expression non-committal. "At the moment," he said, "we're keeping an open mind, but we will certainly consider what you have told us."

"I really wouldn't put it past them," she insisted.

"As I said, we'll definitely make some enquiries with this in mind," Matt assured her.

"That's all I ask," she said. "I want whoever is responsible to be brought to justice, I want them to answer for what they did to my poor Caleb." She put up a hand and rubbed at her eyes then took a shuddering breath. "Please, please don't give up on him. Someone killed the only man I've ever really loved, and I want them found."

Soon after, they brought the interview to a close and Dilys escorted Clare Jeffreys out of the building while Matt took the recording upstairs. He wanted to listen to it again. A few minutes later, Dilys came back upstairs and appeared in the doorway of his office.

"What do you think of all that, sir?" she asked.

Matt frowned and ran a hand over his hair. "I'm not sure," he said slowly, "but she seems sincere enough. She certainly wants to find out what happened."

"This business about drug-taking, she's the second person to bring that up. Pastor Harris mentioned drugs to Chloe, which adds some weight to what Ms Jeffreys said."

"Yes, it does, we must definitely do a bit more digging into that."

"Do you want me to ask Aidan Rogers to do some research? And we could maybe find out from the drug squad if there's anything useful on their records."

"No, don't give it to Aidan, he's got that sim card to concentrate on, ask Dave Parry to have a go."

"Will do," Dilys said.

"I don't remember mention of any kind of addiction when Caleb disappeared. Surely his mother or sister would have said something at the time?"

"Maybe they didn't know," Dilys pointed out, "or they didn't want to get him into trouble, after all, they didn't know then that he was dead."

"Yes, of course, I hadn't thought of that. I'll ask Fabia if she remembers whether drugs were mentioned." He sat back in his chair, frowning across at his sergeant. "And what did you think of Clare Jeffreys?"

Dilys sat down, took her glasses off and rubbed at the lenses with a small cloth then stuffed it back in her pocket and replaced them. Matt was used to these short silences while she organised her thoughts, and simply waited for her to respond.

"Well, sir, at first I wasn't that impressed. I don't know exactly why, but I felt as if, on one level, she was enjoying the attention we were giving her. It was as if she was telling a story rather than giving us an account of something that actually happened. Do you know what I mean?"

"I think so."

"But then," Dilys went on, "when she got a bit upset, that seemed genuine enough. It must have been very difficult for her. And when she mentioned the drugs, that was entirely believable."

"I agree. Why don't we listen to the interview again and see if either of us picks up on something that we missed."

"Good idea."

Chapter 16

"I can't believe your father didn't come to the inquest. I just can't understand it. Why do you think he didn't?"

Nerys was used to this pattern of behaviour from her mother. She would remark on something her father had or had not done, often say she couldn't believe it, then follow it up with questions to which there were no easy answers. Nerys always wanted to ask her why she was constantly surprised by the thoughtless and abusive behaviour that was all too familiar to them both. But however often she pointed this out to her mother, there would always be the apparent surprise and shock followed by questioning. Nerys's training had given her a partial explanation; she thought it might be down to a deep reluctance to admit that the person her mother had loved and married could have turned into such an abusive individual, but it still managed to irritate her each time it happened.

Now she leant her elbows on the table and dropped her head in her hands, at all costs she must control this urge to snap at her poor mother. After a moment she lifted her head and, her voice full of weariness and thankfully devoid of irritation, said, "I don't know why you thought he would, Mam," she said. "He said he wasn't going to and that's that."

If the truth were known, Nerys was glad he hadn't been there. If he had been, she wasn't at all sure he would have remained calm and quiet, and the thought of him making one of his scenes at such a time and in such a public place was more than she could bear to contemplate.

She thought back to that crowded room. Chloe Daniels had met them in the car park behind the courthouse in Newport and, with two of her uniformed colleagues, had escorted them through the press mob and the crowd of sharp-faced bystanders, eyes avid with curiosity. They'd been led down a long corridor, ushered through imposing double doors into the court and taken to seats in the front row. Nerys had been glad of that as they had their backs to the rest of the people crowding into the room, but it also meant they couldn't see who was there. As they waited, she'd wondered how long it would take. The atmosphere of the place made her feel chilled to the bone.

Unable to resist, and feeling many eyes boring into her back, she'd glanced round. A tall woman with curly red hair and strong features had just sat down towards the back of the room, hadn't she been one of the police officers who'd been involved when Caleb disappeared? Nerys wasn't sure.

It had seemed like ages before the coroner entered the court. Nerys was surprised that she was quite a young woman, but she had an air of authority and conducted the proceedings with cool efficiency. From then on, things seemed to move fast. Witnesses were called. First there was someone from Caerleon museum and a professor from the university, both had been there when Caleb's body was discovered. Nerys glanced at her mother while they were being questioned, but Marion had sat like a stone, hands clasped tight in her lap, staring straight ahead. A woman with a closed-in face and straight fair hair was questioned, it turned out she was the pathologist who'd done the post-mortem. While she was speaking Nerys tried to block out what she said, but it was impossible to do so completely – "a severe blow to the head", "fractured skull", "death would have been instantaneous". Please, God, let this be over soon, she'd thought. Chief Inspector Lambert gave his evidence firmly and asked for an adjournment pending further enquires. This was granted. Then the coroner looked straight at her and her mother and expressed her condolences to the family. Nerys had clenched her teeth hard over her bottom lip to stop herself crying out, and she'd put an arm round her mother, but Marion didn't seem to have registered the coroner's words.

As they were bustled out to the car, she'd noticed Pastor Harris in the background. He'd smiled and lifted a hand in greeting, but he hadn't approached them. The red-haired woman had passed them without acknowledgement and Nerys had noticed her approach the Chief Inspector and speak to him.

When they arrived at the car, Chloe Daniels had said, "Are you alright to drive? I can always have you driven home."

"No," Nerys had said. "That's okay. I'll need the car later, and I just want to get Mam home as quickly as possible."

"If you're sure."

"Yes, we'll be fine, and thank you for looking after us."

She'd managed the drive home by concentrating hard on her driving – let in the clutch, change gear, slow down, indicate, check the mirror, speed up. She hadn't allowed herself to think of anything but the route she was taking and the other traffic on the road, and half an hour later they were back home in Pontygwyn where she'd ushered her mother inside, worried that Marion still hadn't spoken.

Now she looked across at her mother. "At least Caleb's body has been released for burial, so that means we can start arranging the funeral. We can give him a really good send off, Mam," she'd said, but this didn't get any response from her mother; so she went on, "Do you want me to contact Pastor Harris? He was there at the inquest, so he'll know already."

"Was he? I didn't see him. I didn't really notice anyone."

Nerys reached across to clasp her mother's hand. "That's hardly surprising, Mam."

"I suppose." Her mother's flat and expressionless voice wrenched at her heart. Almost she'd prefer some show of emotion. Nerys took a deep, steadying breath. She must stay strong. She must.

Getting up, she switched the kettle on and there was silence in the room while she made tea for them both. When she came back to the table she looked across at her mother and asked again, "Do you want me to give the pastor a ring, check on the arrangements?"

"Would you? He told me when he came round yesterday that if Caleb's body was released, he'd be able to arrange the funeral for Saturday morning."

"That soon?" Nerys said, feeling a reluctance to make it all so final. "Will he put us in touch with the undertakers?"

"I expect so. He suggested I choose a photo of Caleb to put on the order of service. And he said that, if we could choose the hymns we want, he'll look after everything else." Suddenly she stretched out her hand to grasp Nerys's fingers. "Nerys, I think it's very important that you tell your father he should be there, at the funeral. Can you persuade him to come? He should be there."

"I'll try, Mam, but you know how it is with him." She frowned across at her mother. "Why do you feel it's so very important?"

Marion stared at her daughter for a moment, her lips working before she burst out, "He's Caleb's father, your father!"

"I know, I know, but he's not behaved like a proper father for years, and he certainly didn't before Caleb disappeared... died," she said bitterly.

"But now we know what happened" – her mother's voice broke on the words – "your father must show... must prove–"

"Prove what, Mam?"

"That he wasn't – that he didn't–"

Nerys felt a chill creep into her body as she realised why there was such urgency in her mother's voice, realised what she was thinking. She pushed the thought out of her mind and interrupted her mother. She didn't want her to put into words what Nerys guessed was in her mind.

"I'll do my best, Mam," she said, and got up to clear their mugs away, unable to stay still any longer.

Chapter 17

When Matt got back to his flat later that evening the first thing he did was get himself a well-earned beer, it had been a long day. Next, he put a pizza in the oven and once he was settled with his second beer and the pizza, he phoned Fabia.

"I forgot to tell you earlier, we interviewed Gaenor Baptiste this morning."

"I remember her as being a quietly confident person, unflappable," said Fabia. "Although she was obviously upset at the time. What's she doing now?"

"Dilys did some research on her before she came in to speak to us. She's got her doctorate and she's a lecturer in business studies at Cardiff Uni. I got the impression she holds things pretty close to her chest, very cool and self-possessed, although that slipped a bit when she was talking about Clare Jeffreys. She obviously wasn't a fan, said she and the others – that's the other housemates – were delighted when she went off to Australia."

"Poor woman, to be disliked that much," Fabia said.

"You're always one to sympathise with the underdog," Matt said. "We saw her too today, she came in off her own bat this afternoon, said she'd seen on the news that Caleb's body had been found."

"All these women seem pretty keen to come and talk to you."

"Must be my magnetic charm." He heard a derisive snort from Fabia and smiled. "As to Clare Jeffreys, at least she was clear about when she went off to Australia, which is useful, although we'll have to double check on the exact date."

"What was your impression of her?" Fabia asked.

Matt pushed his empty plate away and sat back in his chair. "She's not easy to read. Dilys thought that on one level she was enjoying the attention, but I'm not so sure. She seemed genuinely upset that he was dead."

"For obvious reasons I didn't meet her during the original investigation. Is there any way I could meet her, and the others, now?"

"I don't see how, Fabia."

There was a pause and Matt began to think they'd been cut off. "Fabia? Are you still there?"

"Yes. I've had an idea. How about—" She sounded cautious and a little unsure of herself. "How about," she repeated, "you co-opt me because of my involvement originally? You could make it official, have me sworn in as a special constable."

"Now that, my love, is a wicked idea," Matt said, his mind racing.

"But what do you think?"

"I don't think anything like that has been done before," Matt said cautiously.

"Why don't you run it past Charlie Rees-Jones? He's already given you the okay to talk to me about the case, and you know well enough how to press his buttons. He's probably still smarting because he screwed up so royally over my so-called retirement. I know it's a while, now, but it might work. You could point out that it wouldn't cost anything, after all, it wouldn't be salaried. If I have some kind of official status, I could be much more helpful to you."

Matt laughed. "You are a witch. You know that, don't you?"

"Absolutely, the witch who lives next door to Gwiddon Pond, what could be more appropriate?"

"You know, I'm beginning to think it's not that bad an idea. Why didn't I think of it before?"

"Because you're wedded to the rule book and this is a bit off the wall."

"Probably, and about obeying rules." He lifted a hand and dragged it down over his mouth, wondering if he should take the risk of going on. Sod it! Why the hell not? "Fabia, can we talk about our own, well, rules, and not about work?" He heard her take a deep breath but plunged on. "You know I hate my flat, don't you?"

"You have said something of the sort, yes."

"And I spend a lot of my time at yours, don't I?"

"You do." She wasn't giving anything away.

"Would it be presumptuous of me to ask if we can make it permanent and I can move in with you?"

"Presumptuous? You're such an old-fashioned idiot, Matt."

"Shut up." He went on quickly before she could interrupt again. "We have discussed it, briefly, and you didn't completely reject the idea, you said you'd think about it. We are a couple, aren't we? We should be together, and this backing and forthing between Newport and Pontygwyn wastes so much time. We could do all the legal stuff, draw up a lease, I could pay you rent, whatever. I want to be with you, I want to come home to you. Fabia, I—"

"Oh Matt," she said with a crack in her voice.

"You're going to say no, aren't you?"

He heard her give a slightly shaky laugh, but she didn't give him a direct answer. "Cath was having a go at me on

Sunday, said I should snap you up before anyone else does."

"What on earth? There's no-one else likely to snap me up, as you call it, and anyway, I'm not interested in anyone else."

"I'm glad to hear it."

"And what about that Tony bloke from next door, he's more likely to do any snapping up that goes on."

"Shut up, Matt."

He had the sense to change the subject. "But never mind what Cath says, what about you?"

"You should mind about what Cath says," Fabia told him. "She's all for us making things official."

"I knew she was on my side," Matt said, grinning.

"Bless you, darling, she's your number one fan! But let's talk about this next time you come round. It's definitely a bottle of wine conversation, maybe two."

"Not only a witch, but a boozy witch at that."

"Thank you very much, Matthew Lambert!"

"My pleasure," he said, but the next moment he was serious again. "I'm really glad I've plucked up the courage to broach the subject, and I'll get on to Rees-Jones about that special constable business. Speak tomorrow?"

"I shall wait with bated breath, and Matt—"

"Yes?"

"Love you."

"And I you, my darling." He cut off the call and leant back in his chair, shaking his head a little, a smile on his face. That certainly wasn't how he'd expected the conversation to go.

Chapter 18

Fabia had slept very little. Like a hamster in a wheel, her mind had gone over and over the events of the previous day – the inquest, the possibility of becoming a special constable, Matt moving in, all melded into a confused drumming in her head as her thoughts slipped from one thing to the other. When she finally slept in the early hours, the confusion continued in her dreams and she woke to the chatter of the dawn chorus, feeling exhausted.

After a mug of hot, strong coffee and some toast and marmalade, she felt a little better, but she knew it would be pointless trying to do any work. That was another thing to worry about – she should be getting on with those sketches for Tony Vaughan's leaflet, but not today, she wouldn't be able to concentrate. She decided to walk up to the high street, there were a few odds and ends she needed, and it would help if she stretched her legs and got some fresh air. Since it was chilly, and rain was threatening, she wrapped up warm in her Puffa jacket and, with umbrella in hand, she set off.

She'd been to Spar and Reynold's cheese shop and was about to turn for home when the heavens opened and it began to rain old women and sticks, as her Auntie Meg would have called it. Instead of battling on with her meagre umbrella, she ducked into the newly opened Hywel's Coffee Shop. Until recently it had been Beynon's Cafe which had been run by the ancient Beynon twins: plump, rosy cheeked and always wearing identical overalls, they'd presided over the café-cum-bakery for decades, but recently it had changed hands. It was now run by a young couple who supplemented their income with self-catering for weddings and other events, but they had kept the bakery going, although their cakes and breads were a little more adventurous than the Swansea buns and Welsh cakes that the twins had baked. They also sold excellent coffee and Fabia decided a latte and a slice of their cranberry flapjack was just what she needed.

The place was crowded, and it was obvious she wasn't the only one who had decided to escape from the rain. Virtually all the tables were occupied but, as she stood waiting at the counter, Fabia noticed a table for two in the window occupied by only one customer. When she realised who it was, her mind began to race. Surely that was Caleb Morgan's sister, what was her name? Nerys, that was it. She was sitting gazing out of the window, her hands clasped round a tall mug. Fabia dithered, should she intrude, or should she leave the poor woman alone? But this was such an unlooked-for opportunity, and if Nerys made it obvious she didn't want company, Fabia would leave her alone.

She picked up her tray and wove her way across the room towards the window. When she got to the table she said, "Do you mind if I take this seat? Everyone seems to have come in here to get out of the rain."

Nerys looked up. Her eyes were bleak, and Fabia got the impression she was coming back from some faraway place, but then she gave a slight smile and said, "Of course, please." She waved a hand to the opposite seat, and, as Fabia settled herself, frowned across at her. "We've met, haven't we? I think I saw you in the court yesterday, the inquest..."

"Yes." Fabia smiled at her. "I'm Fabia Havard. I'm so sorry to hear about your brother."

"Thank you." She frowned again. "When I saw you yesterday, I thought I'd met you before. Weren't you one of the police officers who was around when Caleb disappeared?"

"I was," Fabia said, there was no point in denying it. "But I retired a couple of years ago. Your brother's disappearance is one of those cases that I never forgot. I was desperate to find him for you and I've always regretted that I didn't."

"But he was dead anyway."

Her voice, full of pain, wrenched at Fabia's heart.

"And now we know that he was murdered. But, of course, you know that, don't you? You were there in the court." Nerys gave a little shake of her head, as if to clear it. "Do you know the officers that are investigating the... the case?"

"Yes, I do, very well."

"What are they like? Are they likely to stick at it?" Nerys asked, then rushed on, "I work in child protection, so I realise how stretched the police are."

"I'm sure they'll do their very best," Fabia replied, thinking as she said it what an empty phrase it was.

"Are they good at their jobs?" she asked. "Sorry, I expect they are, but I just want to know how determined they'll be to find Caleb's killer. I want whoever killed him caught. I want them punished." Her voice was low and shook with the intensity of her feelings.

Fabia chose her words carefully. "From what I know of Chief Inspector Lambert, he certainly won't give up easily; nor will his sergeant, Dilys Bevan. They're both very good officers, they'll do their best to keep working away until they make an arrest." She hoped she was right and that Matt and Dilys were allowed to stay on the case, you never

138

knew how much money Charlie Rees-Jones would be willing to plough into an investigation. This one had no high-profile locals to encourage him to keep going – always an advantage with him.

For a moment they sat in silence. Fabia sipped her coffee and picked at the flapjack, wondering if she should tell Nerys that Matt had asked for her help. It might be a good idea. Caleb's sister might feel more inclined to talk to her if she knew she had a close connection to the investigating team. On the other hand, she could think Fabia was interfering and clam up completely. What to do? Nerys's coffee mug was empty and any minute now she might get up and leave.

"Nerys… can I call you Nerys?"

"Of course."

With her elbows on the table and hands clasped, Fabia took the plunge. "Chief Inspector Lambert contacted me when your brother's body was found because he remembered that I was involved when Caleb disappeared. He wanted to know if I could recall anything that'd help with the present investigation." Do I have to sound so formal, she wondered. Yes, probably best. "Since then he's kept me informed, and that was the reason I was at the inquest. I want to help as much as I possibly can. I feel that I failed you all when we didn't find Caleb all those years ago."

Nerys was looking across at her, her expression unreadable. For a moment they both sat in silence, then Nerys said, "I don't blame you. I blame whoever killed him then buried his body." Her voice cracked slightly on the words. "From what you remember, have you any idea who might have done this to him?"

"I'm afraid I don't, not as yet, but Matt Lambert and I, and his team, will do our best to find out, I promise you."

"Thank you." There was the buzzing of a phone and Nerys turned to rummage in her coat pocket. She looked at the screen, then gave Fabia an apologetic glance. "I'd better take this, it's my mother."

"No worries, you go ahead."

"Mam? Yes… no I haven't yet, I'm having a coffee… I know Mam, I'll be going straight there after… Mam, don't worry, I've got the list of hymns, I'll organise it all… yes, I won't be late so don't worry, okay? I know, love you too." She ended the call and gave Fabia a rueful look. "She's worrying about Caleb's funeral. It's on Saturday. I'm on my way to see Selwyn Harris, he's the pastor at the chapel. He's been so kind, he's pulled out all the stops arranging the funeral so soon, and he's such a support to my mam. I really must get going, I mustn't keep him waiting."

She got up and shrugged on her coat and Fabia rose too. "If there is anything I can do to help, or if you just need someone to talk to, please, please don't hesitate to contact me," she said. "Let me give you my mobile number."

Nerys tapped it into her phone as Fabia dictated it then held out her hand and Fabia took it between both of hers. "Look after yourself," she said, and stood watching as Nerys wove her way through the crowded room and out on to the high street.

Soon after, Fabia followed her out and, relieved that the rain had let up, she made her way swiftly along the high street, deep in thought. She was just about to turn right into Morwydden Lane when she stopped dead, causing some muttering from a couple who nearly cannoned into her. "Sorry, sorry," she said distractedly. She stood there, memories flooding back into her mind. It had been an abuse case. A young man had accused the minister at his church of abusing him. She remembered the person who'd made the accusation had had run-ins with the police, mainly due to his use of cannabis, and he hadn't been a reliable witness. Far from it. In the end, the case had been dropped and the minister had been completely exonerated. And that minister's name had been Selwyn

Harris. Why hadn't she picked up on it when Cath had been talking about him on Sunday? But Cath hadn't mentioned his first name, and Harris wasn't that unusual a name for this part of Wales.

Striding down the lane towards her house at the other end, her mind racing as she walked. She wondered if this could be the answer. Was this man an abuser? It would be a familiar story, given the number of cases of abuse by ministers and priests that had crawled out of the woodwork in the last decade or so. But still, maybe that poor boy had been telling the truth. And, if so, had Caleb too been one of his victims? Had Caleb threatened to expose him and... Bloody hell, she thought, I really need to get hold of Matt. This could throw the case wide open and lead to the most awful repercussions for Caleb's family. Hadn't Nerys said that the pastor had been a great support to her mother?

Fumbling for her key, she pushed open her front door, dumped her shopping in the hall then stood there tapping out Matt's number on her phone. It rang and rang, then went to voicemail.

"Oh, sod it," Fabia exclaimed, then added, "Sorry love. I need to speak to you. I think I've got something really useful, please phone back as soon as you can."

There was nothing she could do now but wait.

* * *

The meeting with Pastor Harris hadn't taken long and now Nerys was on her way to visit a family in Usk, just a brief check to see how they were getting on with a teenager who'd gone seriously off the rails. She'd tried to concentrate hard on work for the last few days; being busy pushed out the suspicions her mother had opened up, but she couldn't stop herself going over and over that conversation in the kitchen. It wasn't that her mother had actually said she suspected their father of having anything to do with Caleb's death, but she had implied it, hadn't she? A nagging voice in her mind kept telling her she should go and check on her father again, but the very thought made her stomach churn. Why should she? But there was an easy answer to that, he was a confused old man, not the violent bully that he had been in the past.

The home visit hadn't been far from the sheltered housing in Usk where her father lived. She checked her watch, half past one. She could just pop in quickly before going back to the centre, so she made her way to his flat, parked outside and, taking a deep breath in an effort to stop her heart hammering, made her way up the path. The flats were in attractive two-storey red brick buildings, four to a block. Her father's flat was on the ground floor to the right of the main entrance; to the left was the front door of another flat where, Nerys knew, a Mrs Hutchins lived. Her father had complained about his neighbour, said she was 'a nosey old bat', always on his case about the rubbish bins, but he would probably see interfering where only kindness was meant, she thought bitterly. She'd liked Mrs Hutchins when they'd met and got the impression that she kept a quiet eye on him.

She knocked on her father's door and waited, but there was no sound of footsteps from inside. She knocked again, called out, "Father, it's me, Nerys," but still there was no response. Maybe he was at the allotments. Damn, she thought, that'd mean another half an hour and I haven't got the time to go now. Turning, she was about to leave when Mrs Hutchins' door opened.

"Hallo, Nerys love, I thought I heard someone," Mrs Hutchins said. Nerys noticed that she was looking a little worried. "Are you looking for your da?"

"Yes, I was, he must be at the allotment."

"No, lovey, he's not. He told me he was going to the police station, in Newport."

"What? Why on earth?"

"He was in a bit of a state, poor man. I came home as he was leaving, about an hour ago, maybe a bit more. I asked him how he was, you know, just passing the time of day, and he gave me such a look." She pressed a hand to her plump chest. "He was saying the most... well... peculiar things, about having to make a confession. I couldn't really understand what he meant."

Nerys felt a chill creep over her skin. A confession? Oh God. "He gets a bit confused, Mrs Hutchins," she said, trying to keep her voice calm. "Did he say what kind of confession?"

"No, dear, but – well, I'm not being funny, but what with everything that's happened lately, you know... he worried me. I'm not wanting to interfere, but I was wondering whether I should phone you so I'm glad you've come around. I wouldn't want anything bad to happen to him."

"You're very kind, particularly as he can be a bit of a pain at times." She glanced at her watch. "I'd better get going now. Thank you for keeping an eye on him, you're a good neighbour."

"That's no problem, dear, we all have to look out for each other, don't we?"

Nerys made herself smile and then lifted a hand as she hurried off down the path. Once in the car she sat for a moment, thinking. What should she do? But she knew already. She'd have to follow her father to the police station. The bus journey would have taken him at least half an hour on a good day, probably a good deal longer, depending on the timetable, so by the time she got there the chances were that he'd still be talking to the police about... about whatever had come into his mind.

Quickly she called her boss, gave her a brief explanation, then she set off through Usk and Caerleon, heading for Newport.

Chapter 19

Fabia had tried several more times to get hold of Matt, but he still wasn't picking up. She'd done her best to distract herself by making some preliminary sketches for the museum leaflets, but then pushed them aside. She couldn't concentrate. At this rate, she told herself, he'll cancel the order and find some other artist. The trouble was she couldn't keep still. She collected a pile of newspapers and put them into the recycling, put several wine bottles into the appropriate bin, telling herself, as she always did, that she must cut down on her alcohol intake. She followed that by putting a pile of washing into the machine but noticed, half an hour later, that she'd forgotten to turn it on.

"For goodness sake, woman," she muttered to herself. "Just concentrate on your work and stop running around like a headless chicken."

But she still tried Matt one more time and, at last, he answered.

"Hi, can I phone you back?" he said. "I'm up to my ears and my battery's nearly out."

"But Matt, I think I've found out something really important, I bumped into–"

"I'm sorry, love, I'm just on my way to interview someone. I can't stop just now."

Fabia could hear voices and footsteps in the background and Matt's voice echoing against concrete walls. It sounded as if he was on his way down the stairs. She growled in frustration. "Okay, but please phone me as soon as you can."

"I'll do my best," he said. "Caleb's father's asking to speak to us. I don't know what he wants, but he's in a bit of a state, he—"

The phone went dead.

Caleb's father? What kind of a state? "Damn, damn, damn," Fabia muttered.

But there was no point whatsoever in sitting and wondering. She would just have to make herself get back to work and wait to hear from Matt. But then it occurred to her she could do some research into the abuse case – there was sure to be some interesting stuff on the net. Sitting down at the kitchen table, she opened up her laptop.

* * *

As Matt's phone cut off, he swore quietly and thrust it back in his pocket. Dilys glanced at him.

"Forgot to recharge it, sir?" she asked, suppressing a smile.

"Yet again," he said grumpily. "She says she's got some information."

"Fabia?"

"Yes, remind me to phone her when we've finished downstairs."

"Will do."

They were making their way down to the interview room where they had spoken to Clare Jeffreys the day before, but the person they were on their way to talk to was a very different proposition, although, like Clare Jeffreys, he had turned up at the station unannounced.

When Matt had been told that Caleb's father, Len Morgan, was asking to speak to someone, he'd wondered what on earth his reason could be, but suspected it might be in order to berate them about not having found his son's body immediately after he disappeared. When they'd spoken to him a few days ago he'd aggressively denied any knowledge of what had happened to his son. He'd dismissed Caleb as a waste of space and, at one point, told them he had no son, then ordered them out of his flat. They'd been unable to get any more out of him, but Matt had put him on the list of those people they'd need to talk to again.

When they entered the room, Morgan was pacing up and down, muttering to himself, obviously agitated.

"Good afternoon, sir," Matt said quietly, "I am Chief Inspector Lambert, this is Detective Sergeant Bevan. If you remember we spoke to you a few days ago. Please take a seat and tell us how we can help you."

Morgan glared across at him for a moment then threw himself into the chair, causing it to scrape across the floor. "Help me?" he growled. "No-one can help me, no-one."

Dilys switched on the recording equipment and said who was present.

"What you doing that for?" Morgan snapped at her.

"We always record interviews, sir. Simply routine," she said.

For a moment she thought he might protest, but after opening his mouth to speak as he frowned across at her, he clamped it shut and there was silence in the room. Below his bushy eyebrows, he continued to glare at them. Matt and Dilys waited and the silence stretched out, so after a few minutes Matt asked, "Would you like to tell us what has brought you to the station, sir?"

"I want to make a confession." The words were snapped out.

Matt felt Dilys stiffen beside him, but he didn't look at her, just asked quietly, "A confession, sir? About what?"

"I killed my son, I–"

Matt held up his hands and interrupted quickly. "Mr Morgan, before you say anything further I must warn you that you do not have to say anything, but it may harm your defence if you do not mention when questioned something which you later rely on in court. Do you understand?"

"Of course, I do, d'you think I'm *twp*? I'm not stupid."

"And would you like to have a solicitor present before we continue to question you?" Matt asked.

"What the hell do I need a solicitor for? All they'll do is bleed me of money I can't afford. Just take my confession and let's have done with it."

"It's not quite as simple as that, sir."

"Why?" He put a hand to his face and dragged it down across his features. "I hit my son, he died. I didn't realise at the time that he was going to die, but now you've…" He took a shuddering breath. "Now you've found his body, I know I must have killed him."

"And where was this?" Matt asked. He gave Dilys a quick glance, wondering if she too was remembering what Iolo Beynam had told them. He could hear the quiet, intense voice saying, *"Caleb came home late one evening and it was obvious someone had beaten him up… He had this awful bruising coming out on his back and down his arm."* But Iolo had said nothing about a blow to the head, and according to the post-mortem the blow had cracked and indented the skull, an injury no-one could have survived.

"What?" Morgan demanded, his large hands clutching at the table edge. "What do you mean where was it?"

"Where were the two of you when you hit him?"

For a while he just glared across at Matt again, his mouth working but no sound coming out. Matt sat back and Dilys took over. "Mr Morgan, we need to know a few more details about what happened. Can you remember where you and Caleb were when this confrontation took place?"

"I– er… I met up with him. It was… it was…" He frowned down at the table, drummed his fingers on it and said no more for a moment, then added, "He'd upset his mother. I was angry."

"I understand that, but we need to know where you were," she persisted gently.

He jumped up, causing his chair to rock back and forth behind him, and Matt braced himself, but Dilys just went quietly on. "Please, Mr Morgan, sit down and let's try to sort this out. Why don't we go back a bit? In what way had Caleb upset his mother?"

The old man subsided into his chair, leant back and crossed his arms. "All that crap about being gay. No son of mine's going to be a damn queer, is he? Nonsense it was, and his mother didn't like it, didn't like it at all. She was… she is religious, see, and she knows it's wrong. So, I told him, I did, not to come home until he'd sorted himself out. But when I told Marion, she went doolally, screamed and ranted at me, told me I had no right. No right? Course I had a right, he was my son. But she wouldn't have it, she told me I had to take it all back."

"And how long was this before you had the confrontation with your son?" Dilys asked.

"I don't know," his voice was quieter now. "How should I remember all these years later? Days, maybe weeks." Then all of a sudden, he was shouting again. "Why won't you accept my word for it all? Get this over, arrest me!"

"That's not how it works, sir," Matt told him quietly. "We need a good deal more information before we can take such a step."

Calmer now, Morgan went on, "He came to the allotment, pussy footing through the mud as if he was too good to be there. He always thought he was better than the rest of us, poncing off to university as if he was above doing an honest day's hard work. What did a lad like him need with a university degree? But his mother encouraged him, and that bloody godmother of his, Marion's Auntie-bloody-Delyth, she gave him money the rest of us could have done with, what with the steelworks going down the pan and people being made redundant."

He crossed his arms again and sunk his chin on his chest. Matt and Dilys waited for him to fill the heavy silence, and, when he started speaking again, it was more quietly, so quietly in fact that it was hard to hear him. "I lost it, see, and that's why he died, but I shouldn't have hit him, I know that now."

"Was it when he was at the allotment that you hit him?" Matt asked.

He glared up at Matt under his brows. "You deaf or something? That's what I said, wasn't it?"

"And where were these allotments?"

Again, there was silence in the room, and it looked as if the old man was making a great effort of memory as he frowned in concentration, rubbed his hand across his forehead, and said, "The allotment? Not the one I use now, no."

"And this was nine years ago."

"Yes, wasn't that what I just told you?" he muttered, looking at Matt as if he was stupid. "We were living in Cwmbran, so the allotments must have been by there. Yes, on the Usk Road."

"But his body was found down by the river in Caerleon."

Morgan ignored this, just went on muttering, "So maybe I punched him harder than I thought. That must be it. And he fell and – oh God – and died later, maybe days later." There was deep pain in his voice.

"I don't think that's possible, sir," Matt said, then leant forward in his chair and went on gently. "Mr Morgan, your son's body had been buried, and he was killed by one or two blows to the head with a sharp object."

The man's head jerked up and he stared across at Matt, slowly shaking his head. It seemed this information was new to him. But before he could say any more, they were interrupted by a knock on the door. It opened and Chloe slipped into the room. "Sir?" she said, "could I have a quick word?"

Matt got up and went over to her. There was a whispered conversation which Dilys couldn't catch, then Chloe left, and Matt came back to his seat.

But before Matt could say anything, Len Morgan went on as if there'd been no interruption. "So, you're telling me that he didn't die because I beat him up?"

"It would seem so," Matt told him.

"Are you sure?"

"As sure as I can be, sir."

Once again, he rubbed his hand down across his face saying, "Duw, duw," as he did so, and when he lowered his hand Matt noticed that there were tears in the old man's eyes.

"My colleague just came in to tell me your daughter is here, sir," Matt told him.

"My daughter?" It was if he didn't know he had one, then he said, "Nerys? What's she doing here?"

"She said she's come to pick you up, sir."

He looked from one to the other of them. "You… you don't think I was responsible…" His voice faded and there was silence.

"No, sir. I accept that there were times when you were violent towards your son," Matt said. "That is between you and your conscience."

"I had to teach him a lesson," he said, his voice raised now.

"I don't think the beating you gave him," Matt told him, his voice as neutral as he could get it, "had anything to do with his death."

"Then, can I go?"

"Yes, sir, although we might want to speak to you again at some point."

Matt and Dilys got up and watched as Morgan, with his hands flat on the table, pushed himself up from his seat. It was as if it took him a great effort to stand and Dilys wondered if she should go round the table and take his arm, but decided against it. He might not want any acknowledgment of what he would probably see as a weakness.

"My son, Caleb," he said, his voice shaking a little, "he was Nerys's twin. She... I think she still hasn't forgiven me for what happened. She's always thought, she has, that it was my fault that he disappeared. She blames me."

"But now you can explain to her that it wasn't your fault, sir," said Dilys quietly.

He gave her a strange look, as if this hadn't occurred to him until now. "I suppose I can." He took a deep, shuddering breath and nothing else was said as they escorted him from the interview room to reception where Nerys was waiting.

* * *

Nerys didn't get home until six, after she'd dropped her father off, as she'd gone back to the office to write up the report on her home visit earlier in the day. Once again, her boss suggested she take compassionate leave, but she insisted she'd rather keep working, doing so seemed to keep the nightmares at bay. She knew she could have waited to write it up the following day, but she'd preferred to get shot of it while it was fresh in her memory, particularly as the rest of the day had been so stressful and her mind was crowded with memories and emotions.

Her father had seemed very subdued on the way back to Usk. She'd asked what he'd confessed to and he'd just grunted, "It doesn't matter now. They tell me I have nothing to– that I'm not responsible for Caleb's death."

"Of course, you aren't," she'd told him, not entirely sure that some of the responsibility didn't rest with him, but she wasn't going to tell him that as he sat there, slumped in the seat, looking so old and defeated. "What made you think you were?"

There'd been silence in the car for a while and Nerys thought he wasn't going to answer her question, but then it all came out in a quiet, intense stream: that he'd beaten Caleb, that he'd told him to go and never come back, told him he was no son of his, that he'd called him as many damning names as he could. "I may not have been the one to strike the blow, that's what that police officer said, but I can't help thinking it was my fault in the end."

Nerys couldn't believe what she was hearing. She'd never known her father like this. Maybe it was to do with the dementia, facing the fact that soon he'd have lost the person he was used to being, or maybe it was the shock of finding out that Caleb had been dead all this time, she had no idea, but part of her preferred this father to the one she'd been used to for so long.

"Da" – she'd hardly realised she'd used the affectionate diminutive – "I'm afraid Mam did wonder if you had something to do with it."

She'd been amazed when he said, "I don't blame her. The way I was with him, why wouldn't she?"

"But haven't the police just told you that you can't have been responsible? Isn't that what the Chief Inspector said?"

"I know, but–"

"Please," she'd interrupted, "hear me out. Mam was really worried, she worries about everything, and she's in such pain I don't believe she's thinking straight at the moment." She didn't tell him that she too had had a niggling suspicion that he might have been involved. "Now we know that it's not possible, just to put Mam's mind at rest, come to the funeral, please, it would look so bad if you didn't."

For a while he'd sat with his head turned away from her, staring out of the car window, but she was sure he wasn't seeing the fields to either side, then the river to their right, the petrol station to their left, as she turned on to the ancient bridge over the Usk and on up the high street. It wasn't until she slowed down to turn into the road that took them to her father's flat that he spoke again, but all he said was, "Tell your mam I'll be there, tell her not to worry."

Nerys had watched as he stumbled up the path to his front door, hunched over with his hands deep in the pockets of his coat, a sad, beaten old man. She'd swallowed hard to stop herself crying, she'd done too much of that lately, then started up the car and driven slowly away.

Chapter 20

Fabia sat back, stretched her arms above her head and groaned as her stiff muscles reacted. She'd been staring at the screen of her laptop for what seemed like hours. Beside the laptop was a pad covered in scribbled notes where she'd jotted down some of the information she'd found, anything that she thought might be useful to pass on to Matt.

She'd started her search by going onto the Western Mail website and searching for the reports on the abuse case. She found the name of the boy who'd made the accusation, Tom Beddoes; then put his name into Google and came up with a few more links, including one about him being arrested for possession of cannabis with intent to supply. He'd ended up in Parc Young Offenders Prison in Bridgend with a sentence of six months. But then she came across another, quite different, link. It was a YouTube video about a boxing club in Newport, which was helping youngsters who'd been in trouble with the police turn their lives around, and the person who appeared to be in charge of the club was a man called Tom Beddoes.

Fabia went back to a photo of him at the time of his arrest: a sullen, scrawny boy with acne and a downturned, resentful mouth. Quite a contrast to the man in the video who was full-muscled, confident, smiling, his boxer's nose evidence of his activities, but she was sure it was the same person. He said that, originally, he'd gone to the club because he wanted to find some purpose in his life. Once there he'd found he had a talent for the sport and stayed on, and now he was managing the place and helping young men and women who'd lost their way, as he put it. "I've been there myself, see, and I know what it's like, and because of that they'll listen to me." He also had a blog aimed at "kids like me" as he put it. Good for you, Fabia thought, he'd certainly made something of his life after a rocky start.

But she wanted to know more. How had Beddoes ended up going to the youth club at the Jesus Brethren Chapel? Had he been telling the truth about the abuse? And why had he left it till years later to make the accusation? If he was telling the truth, had Harris's abuse included others, such as Caleb Morgan? Had Caleb been killed to stop him talking? A university student from a supposedly good family might be believed where a kid from the back streets of Newport or Cwmbran would not. Where to go next? Cath. Maybe she'd know something.

She took up the handset and punched in the number, one of the few she remembered without having to look it up or scroll down to find it on her mobile. Cath picked up almost immediately.

"Hi Fabia," she said, "I haven't spoken to you since Sunday. How's Matt?"

"He's fine as far as I know, up to his ears in this Caleb Morgan case."

"Oh yes, has there been any news on that?"

"Not so far. I spoke to Matt earlier on and he said Caleb's father had come into the station in a state, but he got cut off before he could go into detail, bloody frustrating."

Cath laughed. "Oh dear. Have you any idea what he wanted?"

"No," Fabia moaned, "and Matt hasn't got back to me. I'm desperate to talk to him because I bumped into Nerys Morgan, the boy's sister, this morning and on the way back home I had this sudden thought. I really wanted to pass it on to Matt, but so far – well, I'll just have to wait."

"What sudden thought?"

Fabia didn't give her a direct answer. "You know we were talking about Pastor Harris at lunch on Sunday?"

"Ye–es."

"Well," Fabia hesitated. Now that she was actually going to put into words what was in her mind, it suddenly seemed too far-fetched. "Do you remember a child abuse case a few years ago? I think it was 2006 or thereabouts."

"Before my time, I came to the parish a couple of years later."

"Yes, of course."

"Who was accused?"

"It was Selwyn Harris." Fabia heard Cath gasp on the other end of the line.

"Good Lord! That doesn't seem very likely, Fabia," Cath said. "Who accused him?"

"It was one of the kids who'd been in the chapel youth group, the same one that Caleb was in. He was a bit of a disturbed child, totally dysfunctional background, into cannabis and probably more later on, earned himself a few months in the Parc at Bridgend. When he accused the pastor, that wasn't long after he was released, he was sent off with a flea in his ear for wasting police time, and the pastor was completely exonerated."

"But what's put you on to it now? There has to be more to it if you're so desperate to tell Matt about this."

"Well, what a great cover for that kind of abuse, pillar of the community, working with vulnerable children, it's happened again and again, and if this Tom Beddoes, that's the boy's name, was actually telling the truth, maybe he wasn't the only victim, maybe Caleb Morgan was abused as well." Fabia frowned. Her doubts were increasing. "But I'm beginning to think I'm letting my imagination run away with me. I just wondered, since you know the pastor, what you would think."

"I'd say it's highly unlikely," Cath said. "And if what you suggest is the case, and you think he might have something to do with Caleb's death, well, that's even more unlikely, isn't it?"

"Yes... no, oh I don't know, Cath. I just had this thought that it might explain things. I suddenly remembered the case on my way home this morning and... nah, forget it, I'm being stupid."

"Not stupid, Fabia," Cath said, and Fabia could hear that she was smiling, "but maybe grasping at straws. Talk to Matt, see what he thinks."

"No, I don't think I will, he'll just laugh at me."

"Surely not," Cath said, and she was laughing now.

"Well, you are!"

"Sorry, love. I do think it's highly unlikely from what I know of the man. I'd put it out of your mind."

Once she'd ended the call, doubts or no doubts, she knew she'd not be able to let it go. She didn't think she'd talk to Matt about it, though, but there was someone else she could talk to – Tom Beddoes. But she'd have to think of a very good reason for doing so. How on earth could she get to talk to him? She sat racking her brains, then grinned, yes, that would do it.

* * *

The boxing club in Newport where Tom Beddoes worked was named after Shaftesbury Park nearby. On Friday morning, Fabia managed to find a parking space a few metres down the road, by the park railings, and, feeling a little nervous, she approached the building. In

157

another life it had probably been a warehouse of some kind, two storeys of red brick with the ground floor windows high off the pavement, protected by wire grills. She approached a pair of double doors above which was the legend 'Shaftesbury Boxing and Fitness Club' and below that, in a flowing script 'Find your strength, no fear, no limits'. Never mind my strength, I need to find my courage, Fabia thought ruefully. Then she told herself off for being a wimp.

She wished now that she'd told Matt what she was planning to do when he'd phoned the night before. He'd told her all about Len Morgan's supposed confession and the outcome. "I felt quite sorry for the man, he's obviously confused and I'm pretty certain that he blames himself for the boy's death."

"I remember him as a big bull of a man," Fabia had said, her tone unsympathetic. "Aggressive, and he seemed completely oblivious to what his poor wife was going through."

"The aggression is still there to a certain extent, but he's sort of diminished now. His daughter told Chloe that he's in the early stages of dementia, which could account for it. Anyway, what did you want me for earlier?"

She'd explained about bumping into Nerys in Hywel's Coffee Shop and went on to tell him how she'd suddenly remembered, on the way home, about the abuse case, but now she'd had time to think more about it, and having spoken to Cath, she knew she didn't sound as sure of herself as she would have earlier.

"I think that's a bit far-fetched, don't you think?" Matt had said, echoing Cath's reaction. "After all, would he risk his career and his position in the community? You say he was completely cleared of the charge and the kid who accused him was a bit of a tearaway."

"I know, but that doesn't mean he was lying, does it?" Fabia had said, stubbornly trying to hang on to her theory. "You're getting cynical in your old age."

158

"No, I'm not," he'd protested. "Look love, I'll get one of the lads to do some research, find out what this Beddoes—"

Fabia had interrupted him. "I've done my own research. Seems he's turned his life around and now he runs a boxing and fitness club. There's a YouTube video about him, and he does a blog as well, aimed at kids like him who had a difficult start and encouraging them to sort themselves out."

"Good for him," Matt said. "I'll do some digging. Leave it with me."

In the end Fabia had ended the call without telling him what she planned to do. Sod it, she'd go it alone and then, if she found out anything useful, she could present it to Matt on a plate.

Chapter 21

But now, as Fabia stood on the pavement looking up at the rather forbidding building, she was regretting that decision. Although she felt she had a good cover story – she was going to tell whoever she managed to see that she was an artist and wanted to do a series of drawings of boxers in action – she had no idea how, if she managed to speak to Tom Beddoes, she'd introduce the abuse case and ask him about it. Play it by ear, that was the only thing to do.

Fabia pushed open the door and found herself in a foyer with a noticeboard on her left and stairs rising up to her right. Opposite her were two swing doors and, from the noises she could hear, she thought that might be where the main activity was going on. Pushing them open, she found herself in a large room that seemed to take up most of the ground floor of the building. To the left there was a boxing ring where two young women, wearing helmets and boxing gloves, were prancing round each other. Along the back wall there were several different exercise machines, some in use, some not, and punch bags hung from the ceiling. To the right there was a sitting area with drinks and vending machines. The place was full of noise, the beat of background music, people talking and shouting and the hum of the machines, and it smelt of a mixture of hot rubber, chalk, liniment and sweaty bodies. She stood there for a moment looking around and thought maybe it wouldn't be such a fiction, this idea of doing those sketches. Her cover story could actually be an interesting project.

By the ring a young man, full-muscled and stocky, was leaning on the ropes calling out instructions to the two women. "Keep moving, keep moving. Gloves up, Dion, that's it, elbows in." Then, a moment later, he said, "She got you there, see, cos you'd let your guard down." He jumped up into the ring and put an arm round each of them. "That was a good bout. Now, go and get a drink, the two of you, and an energy bar, you deserve it."

The two women jumped down from the ring, the man turned, and Fabia recognised him. What a bit of luck! It was Tom Beddoes. Quickly, before he could disappear, she walked across to him.

* * *

Later that morning, when Fabia got home, the first thing she did was leave a message on Matt's voicemail asking him to phone her as soon as possible. The second thing she did was to phone Cath. The meeting with Tom Beddoes hadn't gone quite as she'd planned, and she desperately needed to talk things through with someone.

"You'll never guess what I did this morning," she said as she clattered around making herself a cup of coffee.

"That sounds ominous. What did you do?"

"You know that Tom Beddoes I was talking about yesterday?"

"Ye—es."

Fabia rushed on, "Well, I didn't tell you yesterday that I'd trawled through the net and found out what happened to him. He seems to have turned his life around, he runs a boxing and gym club now and it looks pretty successful."

"How do you know?" Cath asked.

"I went there to talk to him," Fabia admitted.

"Fabia! Just like that?" Cath's voice had risen in disbelief.

"No, I had a good cover story."

"You are hopeless," Cath said, but Fabia could tell she was smiling. But she probably wouldn't be doing so when she heard the rest.

"So, what was this cover story?" Cath asked.

"I told him I wanted to do a series of drawings of boxers in action, and I have to tell you, I think I will. I've got quite keen on the idea, and he seemed really interested, although maybe he won't be so much now that– anyway, we talked about it for a while and I slipped in that I used to be a police officer."

"What was his reaction? From what you told me yesterday, I wouldn't have thought he'd be that keen on police officers, even retired ones."

"He cooled right off and glared at me."

"Oh dear, but that's what I would have expected, hardly surprising, is it?"

Fabia took this question as rhetorical. "I tried to bring him round. I came clean and told him I was involved with the investigation into Caleb Morgan's disappearance and had been asked to help with the current case, and I did manage to establish that he'd been a friend of Caleb's way back, at the youth club, but when I tried to find out more, about the abuse and stuff, he said it was none of my business."

"He's right, you know."

"I suppose, but he did add that that was all in the past and… what was it he said? Oh yes, he said anyway, no-one believed him so why should I. I told him I'd like to know his side of the story, but he clammed up and told me he didn't want to 'go back there'. The thing is, I have this feeling that he was telling the truth."

"That's as may be, Fabia, but you can't push him. He's right when he says it's none of your business. Raking it all up may do more harm than good, to him I mean. And I don't think Matt's going to be awfully pleased with you, is he?"

"But Cath," Fabia protested, "Matt asked for my help, so I thought talking to Tom was exactly that, helping."

"You're incorrigible, Fabia, and a great loss to the force, I have to say."

"Thank you, love," Fabia said, "I think that's a compliment. Anyway, I just couldn't get him to talk about it all, not even as a way of helping to find Caleb's killer. The only thing he said was that Caleb believed him and that he was a good friend. But then something happened, well someone happened."

"What? Who?" Cath sounded worried now.

"Do you remember me mentioning someone called Gerry Fairweather? Matt and I used to call him Foulweather."

"Wasn't he one of the officers that made things difficult for you? Believed all the crap about you being involved in corruption?"

"Yes, awful man," Fabia said. "Back then he hated the fact I was promoted, and he wasn't. He was there when I went to the station last week. I thought then that I wouldn't put it past him to make trouble about Matt asking me to help out, and, knowing the efficiency of the gossip machine at the station, he's almost certainly found out all the details. The fact that I was there the other day probably had him sniffing around for information immediately after I'd left."

"But what's he got to do with your visit to the gym?"

"He walked in, when I was there!"

"Oh, for goodness sake, Fabia." Cath sounded really worried now.

"I know, I know. The bloody man came slap up to Tom and clapped him on the shoulder, then turned to me

163

and said, 'Doing your usual snooping around are you, Fabia?' Fabia, he called me, can you believe it?"

"Whoa!" Cath protested, not responding to this last question. "Let me get this straight. You mean he knows this Tom bloke? Did you get the impression they were, like, good friends?"

Fabia thought about it for a moment. "Well, I wouldn't exactly say good friends, Tom scowled at him and looked a bit wary, and he called him Mr Fairweather, not Gerry, so perhaps he's just keeping Gerry on side. Tom Beddoes probably knows how much trouble the awful man could make for the gym if he chose to. He's such a poisonous toad. I wouldn't put it past him to take kick-backs for turning a blind eye if, say, Tom got into drugs again."

"What did you do?" Cath asked.

"It was a toss-up between going all Superintendent Havard with him or behaving as if he was just an ordinary colleague from way back."

"And you chose?"

"Sort of halfway between the two, I suppose. I had to think fast. Anyway, I just nodded, said 'Hallo Gerry', then I turned my back on him and said to Tom that I'd get back to him about the sketches, thanked him for his time, and left."

"Good for you, but Fabia…"

"Yes."

"If this Gerry idiot has got it in for you," Cath said, "do you think he's going to tell Matt that he bumped into you at the gym?"

Fabia sighed. "Almost certainly, and he'll put the worst light on it, believe you me, and Matt is going to be really pissed off with me. But how was I to know that shit had anything to do with the gym?"

"Unfortunate, to say the least." Cath sounded as if she was smiling now.

"It's not bloody funny, Cath!"

"No, I know it isn't. You'll just have to grovel, or, alternatively point out to Matt that he asked for your help, then feed him well and take him to bed."

"You, my friend, are a wicked woman," Fabia told her. "And I'm still going to suggest to Matt that he goes and talks to Tom Beddoes, once he's stopped tearing a strip off me for interfering, that is. I think that boy may well know stuff he's not telling."

Cath laughed at this. "Good luck with that. And while we're talking about Matt, when's he moving in?"

"Shut up, Cath. After this lot, probably never! And anyway, I haven't seen much of him the last few days, he's been too busy." Fabia changed tack before Cath could say any more about Matt. "By the way, I was planning to ask you, are you going to go to Caleb's funeral tomorrow? It's at the chapel, at eleven."

"Well, no, I wasn't. Why?"

"I'm going to go, mainly to – well – to see if there's anything or anyone that jogs my memory, but I feel I might be less conspicuous if there's someone else with me, and I don't want to be with the police contingent, so would you come?"

There was a pause, then Cath said, "Okay, I suppose I could go as part of the community, a fellow minister and all that, but do you think the family will mind?"

"I doubt that they'll notice."

"You're right, funerals usually go past in a daze for the family, poor loves."

"I think it's going to be pretty full," Fabia told her. "That chapel isn't very big, and the snoopers and gossips will be out in full force."

"And that doesn't include us?" Cath's tone was sardonic.

"Cath!" Fabia protested. "I'm trying to help."

"Sorry, I know you are. Forget I said it."

"Okay, and thanks. Shall I meet you there about a quarter past ten?"

"That'll be fine. And let me know what Matt's reaction is to your activities. You know I'll be here to pick up the pieces when he goes completely ape shit."

"I've just gone right off you," Fabia said, and heard Cath laugh as she cut off the call.

Chapter 22

When Fabia arrived at the chapel on Saturday morning there was already a crowd of reporters and a few sightseers gathered in the road. They were being held back by several police officers, but before she could join Cath, who was already standing to one side of the porch, a dark-haired, sharp-faced young woman approached her.

"Ms Havard?" she queried.

Fabia, taken by surprise, frowned and said, "Yes?"

"You used to be Superintendent Havard of the Newport Police, I believe."

Fabia's heart sank. "I did."

"I'm from the Newport Evening News, I wonder if I could have a quick word about your past involvement in the disappearance of—"

She got no further. The look Fabia gave her was one that would have had an incompetent young constable rooted to the spot and shaking with dread. Unfortunately, it didn't seem to have that effect on this woman.

"No," Fabia said, icily, "you may not."

"It won't take long," the woman persisted, smiling and taking a phone out of her pocket. "Can you tell us if you feel you did all you could at the time?" She held her phone up near Fabia's face ready to record her response.

Fabia ignored her and looked across at a police officer who was standing a few feet away. She was pleased that she recognised him. "PC Watkins, Tom, isn't it?"

His head snapped round at the sound of her voice, and he strode over.

"Good morning, ma'am."

"Do me a favour," she said without looking at the reporter, "escort this... person away from the chapel door. She says she's a reporter. Whether or not she is, I've no idea. We really don't want the family upset by individuals like this when they arrive."

"Will do, ma'am," he said. "Okay, miss," he said to the young woman. "Best to stay over there with your colleagues, don't you think?"

Her eyes narrowed, and she flashed Fabia a venomous look. "I am simply doing my job, and I only wanted a quick word," she insisted.

Fabia didn't wait to hear the rest of the exchange but walked rapidly away, seething with anger as she joined Cath by the chapel door.

"What was all that about?" Cath asked.

"Some nasty little hack from the Evening News, she seemed to know who I am, damn it. God, they make me angry, bloody leeches."

"Well," Cath said quietly as they entered the chapel, "they do have a job to do."

"That's more or less what she said, but sorry, I had quite enough of them when I had to retire, ghastly bunch of parasites."

"Not all of them. I thought you said that Chloe's brother, Gareth, works for the News, and he was quite useful on the Amber Morgan case, wasn't he?"

"Why do you always have to be so reasonable?" Fabia muttered.

They entered the chapel and were handed an order of service by one of the undertakers. Fabia glanced at it, the photo of Caleb stared back at her, a head and shoulders shot of a dark, delicately featured, serious young man. What a waste, she thought; what a dreadfully tragic waste.

Once they were settled in a pew at the back, Fabia noticed that the coffin was already placed on the dais at the front. Behind it was a table, Fabia supposed this served for an altar, and behind that was an imposing pulpit. The coffin seemed dwarfed in comparison, and it was almost completely swamped by the flowers that covered its top.

The chapel was already filling up with people, some standing around talking in low tones, others already sitting in the pews, bent in prayer or looking around. The organ was playing softly, but Fabia didn't recognise any of the music. She too looked around, curious to find out if there was anyone that she knew and she did recognise a few acquaintances, all people who lived in Pontygwyn, but no-one she knew well.

As she sat there, she was overwhelmed with a feeling of deep sadness for Caleb and for his family. The encounter with the reporter had shaken her and now she felt anger rising alongside the sadness, but it was impotent anger, for what could she do now? She had no rank, no position from which to act. She tried to express how she felt to Cath, who put a hand on her arm.

"Don't be silly," Cath said. "Matt's asked for your help, hasn't he?"

"I'm not sure he will again, he's pretty pissed off with me."

"About your visit to the boxing gym?"

"Yup," Fabia said shortly.

"I was afraid he would be. What did he say?"

Fabia thought back to the evening before. Matt had phoned quite late and, without giving her a chance to say anything other than 'hallo love', he'd asked, "What on earth did you think you were up to, Fabia, going to talk to Tom Beddoes?"

"Well, I thought it might help."

"Help? For goodness sake, woman, what on earth made you think that?"

"Don't you woman me, Matthew Lambert," Fabia had told him, even more angry because deep down she knew she was in the wrong.

He ignored this and, just as angry as her, said, "I had Gerry Fairweather prancing into my office looking all smug and dead pleased with himself. He was ever so apologetic, but he thought I ought to know that he'd walked in on you interrogating Beddoes and wondered if, perhaps, I should warn you–"

"Warn me?" Fabia had finally managed to interrupt. "Bloody cheek. Warn me about what?"

"About interfering in an on-going case that has nothing to do with you."

"Bugger that, Matt! Of course I've got something to do with it, I was involved in the original investigation and you co-opted me on to this one."

"I know, but I'm beginning to regret it."

"Thanks a bunch," she'd snapped. "Anyway, have you forgotten I was the one who failed, yes failed, to find out what happened to Caleb when he disappeared?"

"It wasn't just you, Fabia, it was the whole team, me included."

"But I was in charge."

"I know, and I realise how that makes you feel," his tone was softer now. "But listen, love, I've already got Rees-Jones breathing down my neck about involving you. He's flat out refused to consider the special constable business. The last thing I want is bloody Fairweather dripping his poison into the boss's ears."

Fabia knew exactly what Matt meant, but she wasn't going to admit it. "Sod Gerry. I don't care what he does."

"But I do, and he could make a lot of trouble – for both of us." He'd paused, then said in a calmer voice, "You should have told me what you were planning, Fabia."

For a moment she'd struggled with herself then said, "I know, I'm sorry, Matt, but I did have a good cover story, and I think I'm going ahead with it."

"And what was that?" Matt asked warily.

"I've asked Tom Beddoes if I can do a series of drawings of boxers in the ring, I'm really keen on the idea. And if I do, he can use them to promote the place, it could be good publicity for him."

"Granted, but not until this case is over, understand?"

Her anger had subsided, but she still felt hurt by his attitude. "If you say so, sir," she said, her tone acid.

"Fabia, look darling," he'd said wearily. He hardly ever called her darling. "I do appreciate your input, honest, but you must realise I have to be careful. You know about the politics in this place – who better – and Dilys thinks Gerry has really got it in for you."

"Oh? So Dilys knows all about this too, does she?" She'd felt her anger rising again.

"For goodness sake, Fabia, what does that matter? She's one of your biggest fans. Anyway, she was there when Gerry came into my office." There'd been another loaded silence, then Matt had asked, "So, did you get anything out of Tom Beddoes before you were interrupted?"

For a moment Fabia had considered saying no, but then she relented; that would be just plain petty. She'd taken a deep breath and told him about her conversation with Beddoes, that she had a feeling he was telling the truth and that she thought he wasn't very keen on Gerry Fairweather. "There was an atmosphere, he was wary, as if he didn't want Gerry there but couldn't tell him to go. I don't know. I think Gerry might have some kind of hold over him."

"Maybe it's just the police he doesn't like, that could explain it."

"I suppose, but I felt there was more to it than that."

"Another of your feelings, Fabia?"

She could tell he was smiling now. "Sod off, Matt."

"I must, actually, I'm still in the office with piles to do before I leave."

Fabia had been tempted to ask him to come to Pontygwyn, but she'd pushed the idea away, best not when there was so much potential for argument, they'd both better calm down first. But she'd found it difficult to sleep, missing Matt's warmth beside her. Having been estranged and then held him at arm's length for so long, she now had to admit she wanted to make up for lost time.

* * *

In the car on the way to the funeral, Dilys, sounding diffident, asked Matt, "Have you spoken to Fabia about her visit to Tom Beddoes, sir?"

"Yes," he said, his tone grim, as he negotiated the series of roundabouts that would take them out of the centre of Newport and onto the M4. "She told me she had a cover story, as she called it."

"Oh?" Dilys sounded amused.

Matt told Dilys what it was and was slightly surprised at her reaction.

"Sounds like a good idea," she said.

"That's as may be, but it didn't stop her questioning him about accusing Selwyn Harris of abuse. When we go and speak to him, which we'll have to, her interference means he'll be forewarned. She can be such a pain!"

Dilys didn't comment on this statement.

"And then Gerry waltzing in – Fabia just doesn't seem to realise how much trouble he could stir up."

"I'm not so sure," said Dilys. "I think she might know very well, but she's just defiant about it; won't be bullied."

"That's all very well, but she's not the only one who's going to suffer the consequences."

"Maybe not now, but she did in the past, didn't she?"

Matt knew he was being unfair. "You're right, Dilys, sorry, it's just that, well, I find her input useful and Charlie Rees-Jones could so easily put the kybosh on it. And anyway, I worry about her."

"I know you do, and why wouldn't you? She's your partner after all." What Dilys said next sounded as if she was going off at a tangent. "Did I ever tell you about that young constable, Lois Le Feuvre? I worked with her a few years ago."

"I don't remember you mentioning her, and I would have because it sounds like a Channel Islands name."

"I think she might have come from Jersey. Anyway, she moved to the Pembrokeshire force a few years ago, I don't think you ever worked with her."

Matt glanced at Dilys, wondering what this had to do with the conversation they'd been having. "What about her?"

"Well, we were quite good friends. I'd just been made sergeant and we'd been working on a domestic together, a pretty nasty one. Anyway, we decided we'd go to the pub after work, get the taste out of our mouths. Both of us were pretty stressed, but Lois was in more of a state about it than I was. She went off on one about abusive men, and men in general really, and what made me sit up and take notice is that she mentioned Gerry Fairweather."

"In what context exactly?" asked Matt, giving her a sharp look.

"It turned out he'd tried it on with her. Amongst other things he told her he could help with her promotion if she was 'nice' to him, bloody slimeball."

"Did she report him?"

"No. She said she didn't want the hassle," Dilys said, sounding exasperated. "And she'd already applied for a transfer, which would obviously put a stop to his crap because she'd no longer be around, but I persuaded her to give me all the details, the wheres and the whens, and I kept notes of it all, actually I recorded some of what she said, sort of for future use."

"Dilys!"

"Look, Matt."

It wasn't often she called him by his name. He realised this was something that meant a lot to her.

"I've watched that shit play this game with a lot of young PCs. He's never tried it on with me, but—"

"Probably wouldn't dare," Matt said, grinning.

"Maybe, although he has thrown the occasional 'why don't you like men?' nonsense at me, and I once caught him muttering something about 'that bloody dyke' as I went past."

"And you didn't challenge him? Report him?" Matt demanded.

"I've been waiting," she said, and her voice was hard and cold, "biding my time."

"If I was Gerry, I'd be afraid, very afraid."

"Yes, well, if he starts stirring things up for Fabia, I might decide to throw this particular load of shit at the fan and make sure Gerry's standing right in the firing line."

Matt laughed aloud. "I've never heard you talk like that before. Never mind Gerry being afraid, you're certainly scaring me."

There was silence in the car for a while and then Matt said, "Dilys, thank you."

"No problem, sir. I like your Fabia and I can't stand Gerry – is it Foulweather you two call him?"

"Yes."

"Very appropriate," said Dilys.

Chapter 23

On arrival at the chapel, Matt and Dilys saw the media crowd and, with Tom Watkins' help, managed to side-step them. He muttered to Dilys that he supposed he'd have to speak to the press again at some point if things didn't move on, but this definitely wasn't the time to get involved with 'that shower' as he called them. Once inside, he noticed Fabia and Cath but didn't go to speak to them, although Fabia turned and gave him a quick smile. He and Dilys also sat at the back, but on the opposite side to Fabia, and they too studied the congregation as they arrived.

"There's Gaenor Baptiste, sir, just come in," Dilys murmured. "Do you know who that is with her?"

"It could be the other housemate from back then, Felicity, or Filly, Jenner. She looks vaguely familiar. We'll have to speak to her sooner rather than later."

"And there's Clare Jeffreys, she's just joined them." Dilys's eyes widened as she saw Gaenor's reaction to Clare, who was settling herself next to Filly. "Doesn't look as if Dr Baptiste is particularly pleased to see her."

"No," Matt said, "it doesn't. Interesting."

"I wonder if Iolo Beynam will come," Matt said.

"I doubt it, given how the family feel about him. I'd put him down as quite a tactful person, wouldn't you?"

"Yes, I think you're right."

The chapel was crowded now with some people standing around at the sides. Just before eleven o'clock there was a hush as the family arrived, escorted down to the front pew by one of the undertakers. As they made their slow progress down the centre aisle, Marion Morgan seemed completely unaware of the congregation either side of her, although Nerys, supporting her on one side, nodded to a few people. On her other side walked the stooped figure of Len Morgan and another elderly woman, tall and grey-haired, who Matt didn't recognise. Chloe, who had come with the family, mainly to protect them from the press pack, slipped into the pew next to Matt and Dilys.

"I'm glad his da has come," Dilys murmured.

"I think Nerys persuaded him," Chloe told her.

"Do you know who the woman is walking beside him?"

"That's Caleb's godmother, Delyth Gwynne," Chloe said. "I've only met her today, she seems a pretty formidable woman. Mr Morgan is certainly a bit in awe of her."

"I suppose that's no bad thing," Matt said, remembering that Len Morgan had spoken of her angrily when they'd interviewed him.

A moment later Pastor Selwyn Harris walked down the aisle accompanied by three men and a woman. He was dressed in a long black robe with a deep purple stole round his neck, on which was embroidered a black cross on either side. The four people with him wore sober dark suits but no vestments. The service began with a hymn, followed by prayers and more hymns, and a lengthy address by Harris as he stood in the pulpit above the coffin. Matt hardly listened to any of it. For him it was all platitudes and empty words which brought back too strongly memories of his sister Bethan's funeral. He could imagine all too clearly how Nerys Morgan was feeling, the deep physical pain of grief, the anger and the constant questioning. Who did this? Why? At least, with Bethan, he knew the answer to the first question, but he'd never managed to answer the second. He looked around at the people gathered in the pews and asked himself, is Caleb's killer sitting in this chapel? He knew they could be, and that they could also be showing no sign whatever of their guilt.

As he sat there, his determination to find the killer crystallised. Whoever it was, they would not get away with it, not if Matt Lambert had anything to do with it. He glanced across at Fabia and found her looking at him and gave her a half smile and a nod, convinced she knew exactly what he was thinking.

* * *

The family had left for the crematorium but Fabia and Cath, Matt and Dilys waited in their respective pews, studying the congregation as it made its slow way out of the chapel. Chloe had slipped out to join the family, saying that they'd asked her to go with them to the crematorium in case the press followed them there.

When they finally emerged, there were a few people still lingering by the porch, three of whom were Gaenor Baptiste, Filly Jenner and Clare Jeffreys, and as Matt and Cath came out into the weak April sunshine, they could tell there was a confrontation going on. Gaenor and Clare were facing each other, both rigid with anger, their raised voices clearly audible to all around. Filly seemed to be trying to calm them both down, but she wasn't having much success.

"Do you think we ought to intervene?" Dilys asked Matt.

Matt watched and listened for a few moments as Fabia and Cath joined them.

"What do you bloody mean, you have a right to be here?" Gaenor demanded. "You were no friend of Caleb's."

"I was his closest and best friend, and you know it." Clare spat out the words. "I knew him long before you did. He was my boyfriend, I loved him."

"Please, you two…" Filly faltered, but the others ignored her.

"Boyfriend!" Gaenor exclaimed scornfully. "Don't be ridiculous. He was gay, Clare, gay! And you made his life hell hounding him like you did. I'll never forgive you for that."

"Hell? How dare you say that?" Clare's voice had risen to a screech and the few people who still lingered were watching them in avid interest, disapproval writ large on some of their faces.

"This is no good," Cath said to Fabia, "we should intervene."

"You two go," Matt said. "It's not a police matter." Fabia and Dilys both glanced at him, surprised. "You and Cath might be able to find out what the row is about, how it started, and that could be useful to us." He sounded a little embarrassed, but then added, more firmly, "If Dilys or I get involved they'll probably all clam up."

Fabia didn't need any further encouragement. She strode over to the three women, followed closely by Cath.

"Excuse me." She was ignored, so she said again, a little louder, "excuse me."

At last all three of them looked round at her.

"I really don't think this is appropriate behaviour at the moment, do you? You seem to be attracting an awful lot of attention."

Gaenor's eyebrows rose, cold and rather haughty as she looked from Fabia to Cath, and then glanced behind them. Clare turned sharply to stare at Fabia, then at Cath and her eyes widened as she noticed Cath's clerical collar. Filly looked from one to the other of them with guilt written all over her face. She was the first to speak.

"I know. I'm so… um, so sorry, I tried, well, to tell them, but…" she trailed off.

"I realise that," said Fabia, and smiled reassuringly at Filly, who seemed to be the sort of person who would apologise willy nilly, even if their behaviour was no fault of hers.

Clare's eyes had narrowed as she looked at Fabia. "I recognise you. You're with the police."

"Not anymore," Fabia said, "but yes, I used to be, and I was involved in the search for Caleb Morgan when he first disappeared."

"Not a very successful search," Clare said, her tone sharp.

"I'm afraid not," Fabia responded calmly.

"I'm sure it wasn't your fault," Filly said.

Fabia smiled at her again, then turned to Gaenor. "It's Dr Baptiste, isn't it?"

"Not doctor back then," Gaenor said, flushing a little.

"No, I suppose not," Fabia said. "I saw something in the Western Mail about your appointment in Cardiff and I recognised the photo. And I remember interviewing you at the time of Caleb's disappearance. You were one of his housemates, weren't you?"

"I was, and so was Filly." Gaenor had turned her back on Clare, effectively cutting her out of the conversation, and Fabia noticed a blaze of anger in Clare's eyes. "We helped the family put posters up all over. Caleb's boyfriend" – there was a slight emphasis on the word – "Iolo Beynam, and several others helped us."

"Boyfriend," Clare spat out scornfully, and Gaenor turned on her.

But before they could start up their argument again, Cath said firmly, "I think it would be best, if you really want to continue arguing, for you to find somewhere more appropriate to do so. After all, this is a place of worship and Caleb's funeral has just been held." It was a rebuke, spoken softly, but clear in its intention.

All three women turned to look at her. Gaenor looked embarrassed, Filly flushed to the roots of her hair and Clare looked angry. How different they were, thought Fabia.

A second later Gaenor said, "You're absolutely right, and I have no desire to continue arguing. I have to get home." She turned to Fabia, gave her a stiff little smile, and said, "Good to have met you again," which seemed rather inappropriate in the circumstances, but Fabia just smiled.

Gaenor turned to Filly. "Can I give you a lift, Filly?"

But, at this, Clare pushed forward, "Filly came with me. I can take her home, thank you very much, Gaenor."

Gaenor ignored her. "I'll give you a ring later," she said to Filly. "Maybe come round. Will you be home this evening?"

"Yes, after I've been to see Mam, I usually get back about half seven."

"Well, if I can, I'll pop in."

Fabia watched as Filly shot a nervous glance at Clare, then said, to Gaenor, "Yes, that would be nice." Then she turned to Fabia and gave a strange little nod sideways, took a few steps away from them then looked back. Fabia took this as an indication that Filly wanted to speak to her, but away from the others, so she gave Cath a quick look, hoping she'd get the message. Cath did and turned to the other two women.

Fabia didn't hear what Cath said as she placed a hand on Filly's arm and walked down the path a little, glancing back as she did so to see that both Gaenor and Clare were watching intently as they moved away.

She turned to Filly. "You wanted to speak to me?" she asked.

Filly clutched at Fabia's arm and lowered her voice. "Can I… would you mind if I talked to you, privately?"

"About Caleb."

"Yes, yes, sort of."

"Is it something you should tell the police?"

"I suppose, well, I don't know. I'd rather not. At least, I'd like to ask your advice first."

"You can, but…" Fabia made a decision. She could always insist that Filly talk to Matt if she thought it necessary. "Okay, I'll give you my mobile number, but if what you have to tell me is relevant to the investigation, it will have to be passed on to the police," she insisted.

Filly nodded and said, "Well, I suppose – of course," but she didn't sound very happy about it.

Fabia dictated her number and Filly tapped it into her phone. "Now I must get going," Fabia said, "and I think your friend is anxious to leave." She could see Clare staring across at them.

"Oh, yes, right, I must go."

Fabia wondered if she always spoke in this jerky way. Poor woman, she seemed to be in a permanent state of jittery nerves. "Give me a ring any time," she said. Fabia watched as she made her way back to join Clare and, a moment later, she saw them drive off in a brightly coloured Fiat.

Frowning a little, she turned back towards where Matt and Dilys were standing, deep in conversation. She walked over and Cath joined them.

"Phew!" Cath said, "that was interesting. I thought we were going to have a full-blown fight on our hands at one point."

"So did I," Fabia said.

"And?" Matt asked, impatient. "What did she want? Did you get anything useful?"

"Possibly," Fabia said, giving him a challenging look, then she relented and told him what had been said, and added, "If Filly Jenner comes up with anything you need to know, I'll persuade her to come and speak to you."

"You better had," Matt said, with a twisted grin.

"Sod off, Chief Inspector," Fabia said, returning his grin. "Anyway, you pushed us into talking to them."

"She's not wrong, sir," Dilys said.

"I know, I know."

"I was going to suggest a spot of lunch," Fabia said. "I've got plenty in for all four of us."

"Sorry, Fabia, that's such a tempting idea but I'm halfway through my sermon," said Cath apologetically, "I really must get back to it."

"I'd love to, but we really have to go back to the station," Matt said. "We've got a pile of paperwork to deal with and some interviews set up."

He looked as if he wasn't sure he should say what was in his mind. Fabia noticed Dilys glance at him and she could have sworn she was hiding a smile. What was going on here?

"Oh yes?" she said. "Who with?"

He paused a moment, then said casually, "Tom Beddoes, hopefully," adding quickly, "okay Dilys, let's get going. I'll phone you later, Fabia," he said as he strode away, followed by Dilys.

"Don't forget!" Fabia called after him. She ignored Cath giggling away behind her.

Chapter 24

Fabia was surprised to hear from Filly later that afternoon, she hadn't expected her to call quite so soon. The breathy, hesitant voice was instantly recognisable when she picked up her phone.

"Ms Havard? It's Filly Jenner. I was wondering, could I come around before I drive home?"

"Yes, of course you can, where are you now?"

"In Newport, Clare and I have just finished lunch. It won't take me a moment to pick up my car and I could be back in Pontygwyn in half an hour."

"That's fine," Fabia said, and gave her directions. Filly said she knew Gwiddon Park and would find her way from there. She arrived just before four and Fabia offered her tea or coffee.

"Coffee would be lovely, black please. I don't drink milk, it's like theft, isn't it?"

Fabia gave a non-committal response to this and turned to make the drinks. As she did so she studied her visitor, who'd taken a chair at the kitchen table. Her face was pale, and her forehead creased with worry as she twisted a lock of frizzy, mouse brown hair round a finger.

Fabia pushed a packet of digestive biscuits towards her and said, "Help yourself."

"Oh, no, thank you, I'm vegan you see," she said apologetically.

"Would you like some fruit then?" Fabia asked.

"No, no, I'm fine."

It took Filly quite a time to come to the point. At first, she asked how long Fabia had lived in Pontygwyn, then she remarked on how pretty she thought it was, although she would find it more difficult to get to work if she lived out here. "I work in that lovely café and health food shop, you know, in Market Arcade, which means I can walk to work, it only takes me about twenty minutes." Then she went on to talk about her mother and her worries about her frailty and wondering how long she'd be able to live in the home, which was rather expensive. Fabia responded to all this, then decided she would have to ask direct what it was that Filly wanted from her.

"When we spoke earlier today you said you wanted to talk to me about Caleb," she said when Filly seemed to have run out of small talk. "What is it that's worrying you?"

"Yes, well, yes, I suppose it is about him that I wanted to, um…"

"Was it something about his disappearance?"

"No, not exactly."

"Filly, can I call you that?"

Filly nodded.

"Look, I think it would be best if you told me exactly what's on your mind. I can't help you if I don't know, can I?"

Filly smiled and her cheeks flushed a little. "I do go on a bit, don't I? My mam says I talk like a pepper mill."

Fabia smiled, then said, "So, how can I help you?"

Filly chewed at her lip for a moment then plunged in, talking quietly as if she didn't want to be overheard. "I'm that worried I don't know which way to turn," she said, "and this morning I thought, since you'd been in the police and you knew about Caleb disappearing, it would be a good idea to talk to you, that you'd understand." She took a deep breath and then went on. "It's just that I think Caleb was being... had been, abused, and I wondered if it had anything to do with... with what happened to him."

Fabia waited for more, but as the silence lengthened, she asked, "What made you think that? Did he tell you so?"

"Sort of. It was when we first moved into halls, very early on, before we moved into the house with Iolo and Gaenor. Back then it was just him and me. The block we were in had five, sort of, study bedrooms and we shared a kitchen and living room with the others. Caleb and I were particular friends then, and we used to sit up till all hours talking." A shadow of pain crossed her face. "He was such a kind, soft-hearted person and I was pretty homesick. It was the first time I'd been away from home and, well, it was difficult, but he helped me so much. I've always kept a diary, you see, and when I heard about his body being found, I went back to look at what I'd written in it, just to try and remember him better."

"And he told you, about the abuse I mean?" Fabia asked gently.

"Not in so many words, but yes, I'm sure that was what he meant."

"And what exactly was it that he said?"

"It was this one time when we'd been drinking a bit, I don't anymore, it's not good to put anything in your body that would cause harm, is it?"

Fabia smiled but didn't comment.

"Anyway, we'd bought this cheap cider, it was all we could afford, really. We weren't drunk exactly, but, you know, a bit tipsy, but I still remember it very clearly. It was the first time he'd mentioned being gay, and he asked me if I thought people could be made to be gay because of stuff that had been done to them."

"What sort of stuff?"

"Well, to do with their up-bringing and things, I suppose. His father used to beat him, I knew that, and he told me about his mam wanting him to go for therapy because she thought it was some great sin or some kind of illness to be gay. He said he used to go to this youth club at the chapel they went to – that's where he met Clare."

"Did she have anything to do with what he was talking about?" asked Fabia.

"Oh no, that wasn't it. No, he said that while he was at the youth club, he had to hide what he was, gay that is, and he implied that being friends with Clare helped him do that. It was only later he told his mam, just before he went to university – that he was gay, I mean. Anyway, he told me – how was it he put it? He said things had happened to him when he was first going to the club."

"Did he go into detail?"

"No, but he did tell me it went back to when he was younger, about eleven or twelve. He said there was one particular person, he wouldn't tell me who, but I got the impression it was a man, and this person–" she stopped, her cheeks reddening.

"Go on, Filly. There's not much I haven't heard before, one way and another," Fabia assured her.

"This person used to make Caleb do things" – her voice dropped almost to a whisper – "sexual things, to him – with him."

"And Caleb had never told anyone?"

"No. I asked him that, but he said he couldn't, that he was told he must keep it a secret."

"I'm afraid that's pretty much the pattern these things follow," Fabia told her.

"I suppose," said Filly. "It's awful, isn't it?"

"It certainly is. In the past I had to deal with many a case of abuse, and the hold these people have over their victims is beyond belief. But tell me more about Caleb, did he ever give you any idea who it was, even the slightest clue?"

Filly looked at her, unshed tears in her eyes. Fabia didn't comment but pushed a box of tissues towards her, watched her take one and blow her nose hard, then she went on, "No, he wouldn't. And he seemed to think that it was because of what had happened that he was gay, which is so cruel, poor boy. I remember, oh so clearly, telling him that was nonsense, that it was just the way he was born, but I think he'd been brought up to think that it was so wrong and he was – well – bad, you know, bad inside and that he'd chosen" – she wiggled her fingers to indicate speech marks – "to be gay. Yes, he definitely thought that what had happened to him, the abuse, was his fault."

"Could you not even make a guess at who the abuser was?" Fabia asked, clutching at straws.

"Not really, and he never said. But what I was thinking is, once Caleb was with Iolo and had accepted that being gay was okay, which I think he did, more or less, and Iolo sort of looked after him, he was definitely the stronger of the two in that relationship…" She trailed off, seeming to have lost her thread, but then she went on, "Like I said, once Caleb decided it was okay to be the way he was, maybe he decided to tell someone about that person doing what he did to him. And maybe, just maybe, that person was the one who killed him if Caleb told them he was going to, well, throw it all open, you know, go to the police or whatever."

"It's possible," Fabia said.

"Wouldn't you say more than possible?"

She seemed very anxious to convince Fabia that her theory was correct. But Fabia wasn't going to tell her what she thought, she'd rather keep that to herself for now.

"Of course, there are other things that happened back then that might have something to do with it," Filly said, almost as if she was speaking to herself.

"What sort of things?" Fabia asked rather too eagerly.

Eyes wide, Filly gazed across at her, but Fabia didn't think she was seeing her. There was a look on her face that was hard to interpret. She opened her mouth to speak, then closed it, then she said, "Oh, I don't know, ignore me, I was just thinking– no, never mind."

"Anything you can remember could be useful, you know."

"But there isn't anything else," Filly said firmly. Abruptly she got up from the table, wound her scarf round her neck and buttoned her coat, avoiding Fabia's eye as she did so. "I must get going, get back home. Thank you so much for listening. I've done what I said I'd– I've told you all I can, I think."

She held out a hand and Fabia noticed that it was shaking slightly. Fabia clasped it firmly in both of hers. "You know where I am if anything else occurs to you, please don't hesitate to give me a ring. And it would be a very good idea if you told the police what you've told me, it could be helpful."

"Do you think so?"

"Yes, I do," Fabia said firmly.

"I–I'll think about it."

"Filly, I really think you should," Fabia urged.

"I know, I know, but it's so difficult," Filly said, sounding anguished, and Fabia noticed that there were tears in her eyes, but the next moment she was smiling and saying, "Thank you so much for seeing me, I'm just being silly."

"I don't think you are," Fabia said, reluctant to let her go, but Filly was walking down the hallway towards the front door now. Fabia knew she couldn't force her to stay or reveal what else was on her mind.

"I tell you what," Fabia said as they got to the door. "I'll give you a ring in a couple of days' time, just to check how you are. Then, if you've thought of anything else that'd be helpful, you can tell me, okay?"

"Of course, of course," Filly said, but she seemed determined to leave and Fabia was forced to allow her to do so.

As Fabia made her way back to the kitchen, she was pretty sure Filly wouldn't go to the police. One thing she was sure of, though, was that there'd been more that Filly could have told her, but she'd changed her mind. How frustrating, Fabia thought. I must pass all that on to Matt.

* * *

"She came round much sooner than I expected," Fabia told Matt when she phoned him later that evening. She'd brought him up to date on what Filly had told her, but she added, "I'm sure there was something more that occurred to her as she was sitting there."

"What do you think it was?"

"I've no idea, Matt. She said something about having done what she promised she would, but I don't know what she meant. Promised who? And what? It's really getting to me, but I'm not sure why. Maybe her jitteriness is catching."

"Or maybe your famed intuition is working overtime."

She could hear that he was smiling.

"I told her I'd phone her in a couple of days, just to check up. I think I'll make it sooner rather than later."

"It's worth a try."

"Have you and Dilys got any further today? How did it go with Tom Beddoes?"

"We didn't catch him today," Matt told her, "but one of the trainers told us he'll be in tomorrow so we're going around in the morning."

"Let me know what he tells you."

"Will do."

Chapter 25

Matt and Dilys had spent some time the day before going over the evidence and court reports from the abuse case involving Tom Beddoes and Selwyn Harris.

"These character references for Mr Harris," Matt said to Dilys, "have you noticed that one of them was provided by Neville Breverton? He was the MP involved in the Amber Morgan case and we both know what happened to him."

"We do indeed, sir," Dilys said, a note of satisfaction in her voice.

"And this other one is from someone called Henry Phillips. Now, that rings a bell. Wasn't he that teacher from the boys' school, saint something or other, who was had up last year for messing around with one of his pupils?"

Dilys frowned in an effort to remember, then said, "Hold on, sir, I'll just do a bit of searching." She tapped away at her laptop and then gave a cry of triumph. "There we are, you're absolutely right. It was Saint Derfel boys' school, he lost his job, got a six-month suspended sentence and was put on the sex offender register for life. That's a fine pair to choose for your character references."

"Ah, but this was before either of them screwed up, wasn't it? And look at this, Dilys." Matt pointed to something on his screen and Dily pulled her chair round to look. "It seems that Beddoes had no representation and the barrister defending Harris was some hot-shot from Cardiff. The boy didn't have a chance, particularly as it looks to me as if the investigating team didn't exactly do a good job. Makes you ashamed, doesn't it? It was handled very badly even if Beddoes wasn't telling the truth."

"Times have changed a bit since then."

"I bloody hope so," said Matt. "Oh, by the way, Dilys, Fabia told me yesterday that it'd be worth our talking to Filly Jenner sooner rather than later, can you set that up?"

"Will do, sir. Did she say why particularly?"

"Filly went round to Fabia's on Saturday, after the funeral, and she implied that she knew Caleb was abused, and Fabia also got the idea there was more she might have told her but, after she mentioned the abuse, she clammed up. Hopefully she'll tell all when we speak to her."

"Let's hope so," said Dilys, "could be useful."

"That's what I thought." He pushed his chair back from the desk and put on his coat. "Let's get going, I'm even more interested in what Beddoes has to tell us now."

* * *

They drove across town to the Shaftesbury Boxing Club mid-morning on Sunday having checked on the website for the opening times. They hadn't made contact beforehand, preferring to turn up unannounced, although they were pretty sure the trainer Dilys had spoken to would have told Beddoes they'd be coming.

As they walked along the pavement towards the red brick building, Matt said to Dilys, "The research Dave Parry did may not have turned anything up when it comes to this particular establishment, but I've got this niggle in the back of my mind that we had a report about trouble at one of these clubs, something to do with illegal use of steroids."

"I think that was the one over by the Ironworks industrial estate," Dilys told him, "this one's clean as a whistle as far as we know."

They got to the double-doored entrance and Matt pushed them open and followed Dilys into the gym itself. There was little activity, but Matt supposed that was unsurprising on a Sunday morning. The ring was devoid of the soft shuffle and thump of boxers' feet and only two of the exercise machines were in use. At the end of the room, by the drinks machines, two men were deep in conversation, one tall and dark-skinned with his tightly curled hair cropped close to his head, the other stocky, his head shaved, with one arm covered in intricate tattoos and his white tee shirt, with its Puma logo, stretched across bulging muscles.

Dilys leant towards Matt and said quietly, "That bloke over by there, the stocky one with the tattoos, I think that's Tom Beddoes."

Matt looked across the room, studied the man for a second. "Good," he said, and they made their way over to the two men who both looked round as they approached, wariness in their eyes.

"Mr Beddoes?" Matt said.

"Who wants to know?" Tom Beddoes asked, his voice curt.

"I'm DCI Lambert, this is DS Bevan, Newport police. Could we have a quick word?"

The wariness in his eyes became sharper. "What about?"

"We're investigating a case you may be able to help us with," Matt said.

"Helping the police with their enquiries," he sneered, "I know what that means."

"Sir, we do need your help," Dilys told him. "It won't take long."

He gave her a hard look then glanced at his companion, who was standing quietly taking all this in. "Okay, Linford, get yourself sorted and I'll be with you in half an hour."

"Rightio, boss," the other man said, giving them a backward glance as he walked away, obviously reluctant to miss anything interesting.

"Come into my office," Beddoes said and strode towards a door the other side of the drinks machine. Matt and Dilys followed him.

The room wasn't large, and it was crowded with bits and pieces of equipment, weights and wheel rollers, skipping ropes hanging from hooks on the wall, and two shelves groaning with trophies of many different sizes. There were advertising posters on the walls as well and a shelf of books, all of which seemed to be about exercise, boxing and nutrition. There was only just room for a desk and the pair of plastic chairs that faced it.

Beddoes went around the desk and sat down, waved a hand at the plastic chairs, then leant back in his black leather office chair and crossed his arms over his powerful chest.

"So, what's all this about?"

Matt gave Dilys a glance as they sat down, and she took the hint. "Mr Beddoes, we're investigating the death of Caleb Morgan who disappeared nine years ago. You might have seen in the media that his body had been found in Caerleon?"

His eyes had widened in recognition, but all he said was, "I might."

"And did you recognise the name as someone you used to know?"

"What? You're accusing me of being involved or something?"

"No, we are not," Matt said patiently, deciding it was time he joined the conversation. "But, as you probably know, if you've seen the reports, we're now treating this as a murder enquiry. There's no doubt in our mind that he was unlawfully killed, and we're going back to all those people who knew him years ago – his university friends and people he knew as a teenager, as well as his family – to find out if they can tell us anything that will be useful, maybe provide information that will help catch his killer."

Beddoes didn't respond to this and Dilys took up the questioning once more. "We believe that you and Caleb were friends when you both went to the Jesus Brethren Youth Club in Pontygwyn, is that correct?"

Beddoes pressed his lips together, glaring across at her. "So, you sent that ex copper to pick my brains thinking she'd get something out of me."

"What ex copper?" Matt asked, knowing perfectly well who he meant.

"That bloody Havard woman, came snooping round here with some story about doing drawings of people in the ring, my arse. Can't you do your own dirty work?"

"Ms Havard is actually an artist now and no, we did not send her to see you, that was her own idea, because she was in charge of the search for Caleb when he disappeared," Matt said tightly. "I apologise if you felt she was snooping. But can we get back to the matter in hand? You did know Caleb back then, didn't you?"

For a moment Matt thought he wasn't going to get an answer, but then Beddoes seemed to come to a decision, leant forward and rested his crossed arms on the desk.

"Yes, we knew each other, but not particularly well."

"How old were you when you attended the club?"

He frowned. "How old? What's that got to do with it?"

Matt leant forward too and rested his elbows on his knees. "It's just that we're trying to build up a picture of Caleb's past life in order to give us some background, it helps to get to know about a victim's life, and any friends he had back then might be able to help us do that, which is why we've come to see you."

"But how did you know I was a friend of his?"

This was the crunch question and Matt knew he'd have to answer it honestly, it was the only way to get to the reason for their questioning. "His sister, Nerys, told us that they both went to the youth club and—"

"And she mentioned me?" There was a touch of relief in his voice as he interrupted.

"No, not exactly," Dilys said. "While we were researching Caleb's past, we came across some information about the pastor from the chapel."

At this, Beddoes sat back and pushed his chair away from the desk. Dilys and Matt could see that his fists were suddenly clenched. "That bastard," he muttered.

"What makes you say that?" Dilys asked gently.

"For fuck's sake, don't give me that! It's obvious you know bloody well." He gave a twisted, humourless grin and stood up, leant on the desk and glared across at them. "All this fucking research you've been doing, it's turned up reports on that court case, hasn't it? How I got screwed over by that so-called pastor with his influential cronies? How no-one would believe me because I was just a working-class kid from a sink estate, a druggie. Oh, he's been in trouble with the cops, he's done time; no way you can believe a word he says, kick him down the road and forget about him. I know how it works, I do. And now I'd like you to get out of my gym, mine, do you understand? I've made something of myself and I don't need you lot shitting on my patch."

Neither Matt nor Dilys interrupted him and, when he finally came to a halt, neither moved.

After a moment Beddoes subsided back into his chair and Matt said, "I sympathise with what you went through. We would, however, like to go back to that case and hear your side of the story."

"What for?"

"Because we want to find out if Caleb would have backed you up had he been around at the time," Matt told him, his voice quiet and matter of fact.

There was a moment of complete silence in the room as Beddoes took this in, glaring across at them without saying a word. Matt and Dilys waited. They could hear the sound of exercise and effort coming from the gym, the constant thump of music that had been in the background since they arrived, the occasional snatch of conversation, a burst of laughter. Then, all of a sudden Beddoes' body sagged. He leant back in his chair, closed his eyes for a moment and swallowed hard.

Matt looked across at Dilys and gave a little nod. She didn't need any further encouragement.

"Mr Beddoes, I think I understand how you feel," she said. "We've read through the reports of the court case following your accusation against Mr Harris and, in my opinion, the investigation wasn't handled very well, nor was the court case itself. Perhaps you'd like to tell us your side of the story."

He looked across at her under his brows, then he got up, thrust his hands deep in his pockets and began to pace up and down in the small space there was behind his desk. "I thought I'd put all that behind me," he said, then added, his tone accusing, "and now you've raked it all up again."

"We're sorry about that," Dilys said, and she meant it, "but we need to know as much as possible about—"

"I know, I know," he sighed. "Look, Caleb was never a close friend of mine, but I knew him and he was a good lad, never made me feel like some of the others did, you know, he didn't look down on me because of where I came from. Things weren't too good at home and that's why I started going to the youth club. That bloody pastor came to our school and talked about it, and I decided to give it a try. It got me out of the house, see, away from my mam and da rowing and... and other stuff. How was I to know that he was – well – fucking recruiting is what it amounts to."

"How old were you when you first went to the club?" Matt asked.

"Ten, eleven." He sat back down. His expression was brooding and tinged with an emotion that was hard to decipher, a mixture of pain, anger and shame.

"I know this is difficult," Dilys said gently, "but can you tell us what happened. We've read the reports, as we told you, but we'd like to hear it from your point of view."

He let out his breath in a gusty sigh then rubbed a hand across his mouth. After a moment he began to speak.

It was a sadly familiar tale. A disturbed and lonely child from a dysfunctional family finding friendship in an environment completely unlike his home. A strong and charismatic man, making him feel that he mattered, giving him attention and what passed, in the child's mind, for love of a kind. This wasn't exactly how Tom Beddoes described it, but this was what came across to Matt and Dilys.

"I thought – well – I felt important, as if I'd been singled out. Oh, I knew it was, sort of wrong, but he kept telling me he cared about me, that I was the only person that mattered to him, and, of course" – his voice became bitter and full of self-mockery – "he said it was a secret between the two of us, that other people wouldn't understand so I must always keep it a secret, what we— what he did to me." He took a shuddering breath and Dilys felt her stomach churn with a mixture of pity and anger as he went on. "When my da buggered off with some totty he picked up at the pub, my mam told me I couldn't go to the club anymore, I had to stay home and help her with my sisters and brother. I let her think, like, that it was a pain, that I wanted to keep going, but deep down I was dead relieved."

"Do you remember exactly when you stopped going?" Matt asked.

"About two years after, I must have been nearly thirteen by then."

Dilys found his story believable, she was sure he was telling the truth, and glancing at Matt she felt that he thought the same. She leant forward, trying to get across to Beddoes that they were on his side. "Do you mind telling us why you decided to accuse him of abuse, what was it? Nearly five or six years later?"

"It was around when I got done on a drugs charge. I was an idiot, I know that now." He gave them a straight look as if trying to convince them. Matt nodded but neither of them said anything.

"Anyway," Beddoes went on, "I got sent to the Parc in Bridgend for a few months and he was a prison visitor there. Sod's fucking law, that. He behaved as if we'd never met, just blanked me. It made me real angry and I told myself, once I got out, I'd get him, but it wasn't till I got the job here, through one of the warders at the Parc, real tidy sort he was, that I finally had the courage to report him. Shouldn't have bothered," he said bitterly. "A posh bastard like him was always going to wriggle out of it with the help of his fancy friends. But I tell you what, in a way he did me a favour, made me determined to make something of myself, show him he couldn't... couldn't bring me down, and he hasn't." He thumped the table with a fist. "No way," he said and stared defiantly across the desk at them for a moment, then gave a sneering smile. "But then you probably don't believe a word of this, do you? Just like that fucking Fairweather that comes in here, winding me up and–"

Dilys gave Matt a startled glance. Matt looked grim. "That's Sergeant Gerry Fairweather you're talking about?"

"Yea. One of yours, he is. Always coming snooping around, hinting that I'm using steroids, says because of my 'history'." He loaded the word with scorn. "He says he has to check, keep an eye, then asks if he can have a discount for a few sessions. Pain in the arse, he is."

"I'll see what I can do about that," Matt said, and Beddoes looked across at him in disbelief, but behind it there was a touch of hope in his eyes.

"So, you think that shit Harris might have something to do with what happened to Caleb, do you?"

"We're investigating all angles at the moment," Matt told him carefully. "We'd be grateful if you'd keep this conversation to yourself for now, but we might want you to come into the station and sign a statement if we make any progress."

"I'm not gonna lie to you, I don't want all that crap raked up again, but if it means that bastard gets taken down, I wouldn't stand in your way."

Matt smiled and held out his hand. "Thank you very much for your co-operation, Mr Beddoes."

Beddoes got up and took Matt's hand in a firm grip then turned to shake hands with Dilys, gave them a rueful grin, a very different man to the one they'd first encountered. "You're not so bad, for coppers, and tell your girlfriend, the artist, she can come and do those drawings if she wants to, might get a tidy bit of publicity for the club, that."

"Thank you," Matt said.

As they walked towards their car Dilys glanced at Matt. "Somehow I think he's telling the truth. I don't quite know why, but he does come across as, sort of, authentic, don't you think?"

"Yes, I agree. I'm not sure I can pin my finger on it either, but it does seem that he got a raw deal when he reported Harris, and he's being straight with us. We're going to have to interview the pastor again, but I don't want to put him on his guard, we'll just let him think we want background information on Caleb Morgan, stuff like that, and see what comes to the surface."

"And what about Gerry Fairweather?" Dilys asked as they got to the car.

They both got in and buckled up. Matt didn't answer her question until he'd manoeuvred out of their parking space. "Yea. Bloody Foulweather. I'm not sure what he's after with Beddoes. I might have a word if the opportunity arises, but I'm definitely going to keep an eye on him."

Chapter 26

Matt had arrived at Fabia's late on Sunday evening and, after just one look at him, she hadn't asked any questions, just put a bowl of soup into the microwave and cut him some thick slices of granary bread.

"Get that down you," she'd told him.

Now they were in the sitting room, lights low and a log fire blazing in the grate. Matt's long body was stretched out on the settee as Fabia handed him a glass of malt whisky, poured one for herself, then sat down and swung her slippered feet up on to his lap.

"Now," she said as Matt slid off her slippers and started massaging her feet, "tell me all."

He began by telling her about their visit to the Shaftesbury Boxing Club. It took him a while to tell her everything as she kept interrupting with questions, as she always did, but he finally came to the end of his account.

"I'm really glad he says I can do the sketches. I think that could be a really interesting project, perhaps he'd like to have them framed and put them round the gym."

"Maybe, but make sure you ask a good price."

"We'll see. And what else has happened today?"

"What indeed," Matt said wearily, leaning his head against the back of the sofa. "This afternoon Dilys and I went and had a word with Selwyn Harris. That did not go so well."

"How so?"

He didn't give her a direct answer, but smiled and said, "Dilys has nick-named him Slippery Selwyn, and she's not wrong."

"Somehow that doesn't surprise me. I have to say I didn't take to him at the funeral. I felt that the eulogy definitely had shades of criticism of Caleb's way of life, and all that business about how God will forgive all sins, with its implication that there was plenty Caleb had done that merited forgiveness, made my toes curl."

"What? These?" Matt said, running a finger down the sole of Fabia's foot.

"Stop it!" she said, pulling her feet away from his lap and tucking them under her. "Come on, tell me more."

Matt grinned at her, but then was serious again. "You're right. When we asked him about the court case, he came over all sort of… how to describe it? As if he entirely understood why Beddoes made the accusation. He insisted he held no grudge and kept going on about what a terrible childhood Tom Beddoes had had and how he needed attention at any price, and his theory is that that was the reason he accused Harris of abusing him. We couldn't shift him on that. We went on to ask him about Caleb and he said how much Caleb's 'way of life' had hurt his mother. That she'd asked him for help in turning the boy from his sinful path, was the way he put it, and that he'd talked to Caleb but didn't feel he got anywhere with him. He repeated what he'd said to Chloe—"

"What did he say to her?"

"He implied that Caleb's university friends were into drugs and that they'd pulled Caleb into that way of life; one person in particular was mentioned."

"Iolo Beynam?" Fabia asked.

"Got it in one. How did he put it? That Caleb had an unnatural relationship with one of his housemates, but he didn't want to name names. Of course, since the other two housemates were female and presumably, to Harris, that wouldn't be unnatural, Iolo Beynam had to be the person he had in mind. We pushed him on it, and he finally admitted that it was Beynam. Then we got to the interesting bit."

Matt took a slow sip of his whisky and Fabia waited impatiently. After a moment she said, "Come on, Matt, what interesting bit?"

He gave her a lazy smile. "His theory is that Caleb and Iolo Beynam had a quarrel because Caleb wanted out of the relationship."

"But how did he work that out? Did Caleb speak to him? Surely not."

"No, but Caleb's mother did. As I told you, she went to him for help when she found out about the relationship and then, a few months later, according to the pastor, she told him she was sure Caleb realised that the relationship was sinful, as she put it, and that he was trying to extricate himself, but that Beynam was obsessed with him. She actually suggested to Harris, a few days ago, that Beynam was the one responsible for Caleb's death as a result of this supposed quarrel."

"And do you think that's possible?"

Matt rubbed wearily at his face. "Of course, it's possible, but I'm not sure, nor is Dilys. We'll have to have another word with Iolo Beynam, obviously. Dilys is fixing that up. But this afternoon, once we left Harris, we decided the best thing was to have a word with Caleb's sister. Luckily we were able to catch up with her at her office, she'd gone in to catch up on paperwork in spite of it being a Sunday."

"Poor girl," Fabia said, with ready sympathy. "She's still going in to work while all this is going on?"

"Yes. I think she might be one of those people that finds concentrating on work helps."

"I can go with that, and she struck me as a pretty strong person when I met her the other day. What did she have to say?"

"Can I help myself to some more of that whisky?" Matt asked.

"Stay where you are, I'll get it."

Once she was settled back on the sofa, Matt answered her question. "It was interesting. She didn't say it in so many words, but I got the impression she's not a great fan of the pastor. She said she remembered her mother going on about some kind of conversion therapy that he said he could provide. Apparently, she persuaded her mother that it would be wrong, and she told the pastor that to his face."

"Wow, that must have taken some guts at that age," Fabia said, impressed. "What would she have been? Twenty? Twenty-one?"

"About that, yes, but then I don't think she lacks courage. And anyway, she says that Caleb wouldn't have anything to do with it. She says by then he'd accepted his sexuality and no longer felt it was wrong to be the way he was, and she insisted he was happy with Iolo Beynam. Happier than he'd ever been, was the way she put it. Dilys asked her how long all this was before Caleb disappeared and she said it was in his second year of uni, he and Iolo had been together for about six months then. She remembers it as the last time he'd been to the family home, there was an enormous row and when he left, he swore he'd never come back. Her mother was devastated."

"But I thought that he kept regular contact, that's the impression I got at the time he disappeared."

"I think he did, but only by phone. He refused to go home, wouldn't go near the place."

Fabia grimaced. "That is so sad. Why do people have to put their religion before their children? It just doesn't make sense." Then she saw the expression on Matt's face and put out her hand. "Oh, darling, I didn't mean your parents. I realise they were pretty preoccupied with their faith and all that, but not like this."

Matt's memories of being brought up in a vicarage were not always happy ones, what with an unworldly theologian for a father and a mother who took her vicar's wife role to extremes at times. He glanced at Fabia and his eyes were bleak for a moment, but then he smiled. "I know you didn't mean them, and anyway, that's long gone now, and Pierre isn't like that."

"Of course, he isn't," Fabia said. "Did Nerys tell you anything else?"

"There was one more thing. She asked if we'd considered a random homophobic attack on her brother. We said we had, but if that was the case, we warned her we may never find the person who killed him."

"I suppose not, but I wouldn't give up on the idea quite yet."

"For goodness sake, Fabia, as I said to you the other day, if that's the case we're screwed."

"Did she tell you anything about the others? Filly Jenner, have you lined up an interview with her?"

"Dilys is doing that, we're hoping to see her on Tuesday morning."

"And what about Gaenor Baptiste? And there's also the Clare woman, the one they had the confrontation with after the funeral."

"She did mention her. She said she and Caleb were really close when they were younger, and she got the impression Clare was rather put out when he came out as gay. She thinks that's one of the reasons she went off to Australia, which is plausible enough."

"Yes, that follows."

There was silence in the room for a while. A burnt through log settled in the grate, hissing as it did so. Matt leant back and yawned cavernously, and Fabia glanced at her watch. "Twenty to one," she said, "time for you to get some shut-eye."

She bent to dampen down the fire then gathered up their now empty glasses. "Come on, love," she said.

Matt dragged himself upright and gave her a quick hug. "Thanks for listening, it always clarifies everything in my mind when I go through things with you."

"Good, now bed."

* * *

In Fabia's dream there was a persistent ringing, but slowly she came to as she heard Matt's voice mutter, "Bloody hell, Aidan, it's half six in the morning, this better be good." There was a pause while he lay back on the pillow and listened.

Fabia pushed herself up on one elbow, trying to get some idea of what Aidan was saying. "What? You're already at the station?" Matt glanced across at her, smiled sleepily, but the next moment the smile was wiped off his face as he listened intently. "They're sure about this, are they?" Another pause and then Matt said, "Okay, I'll be in" – he glanced at his watch – "in about half an hour, traffic shouldn't be too bad this time of the morning. And, Aidan, well done."

As he cut off the call, Fabia asked urgently, "What did he say? What did he say?"

"It seems the telecoms specialist team who've been analysing Caleb's sim card have actually retrieved some of the information on it, and Aidan says he's also got some other information which could change the whole emphasis of the case."

Matt rolled towards her, put an arm over her body, buried his face in her neck and groaned. "But I'd much rather stay here with you."

She stroked his back. "I know, love, but come on, you've got time for a quick shower."

"You, my Fabia, are a slave driver."

"Yup, that's me." She pushed him away. "Come on, Matt, I'm longing to know what Aidan's found out. I'll go and make you a cup of coffee while you shower."

Matt forced himself out of bed and Fabia rummaged for her slippers, flung on her dressing gown and went downstairs. Within fifteen minutes he had gulped down the scalding coffee, given Fabia a rib-cracking hug, strode out to his car and, as the sun was coming up, he made the familiar journey from Pontygwyn to the station.

But when he arrived there was no sign of Aidan and, when Matt got to his office he found a note in Superintendent Rees-Jones's black scrawl demanding that he go up to the Super's office immediately when he arrived. What the hell's he doing in the office at this time of the morning? Matt thought. And why can't he text me? Or phone? But Charlie Rees-Jones had his own little ways and leaving scrawled notes on people's desks was one of them.

The fact that the boss was in so early gave Matt a sinking feeling. This didn't look good. Ah well, better get it over with, so he took the stairs two at a time to the next floor up and knocked on a door at the end of the corridor.

"Come," growled a voice from inside.

Matt went in and, keeping his expression blandly neutral he said, "You wanted me, sir?"

The man sitting behind the desk was hawk-faced and thin-lipped, his receding grey hair brushed in a sparse comb-over which did little to hide the encroaching baldness. He sat back as Matt came in and the expression on his face didn't bode well. Glaring at Matt, he nodded towards a chair in front of his desk. Matt sat down, cross legged with his hands folded in his lap, then he waited.

For a moment Rees-Jones fiddled with a pen, swinging it back and forth between finger and thumb. Finally, he spoke.

"I've had a complaint, not official as yet, but I'm taking it seriously. It's about your conduct on the Caleb Morgan case."

Matt wondered what on earth he was talking about. Maybe Harris had complained about his questioning. It was always possible. But then another possibility presented itself. Ah yes. He thought he knew where this was going now. There was definitely someone else who might have made a complaint.

"I'm sorry to hear that, sir," he said, keeping his voice as calm as he could. "Is it about the original case, Caleb Morgan's disappearance, or the present murder investigation?"

Rees-Jones frowned across at him and Matt didn't think he'd been expecting that question.

"Largely about this present one," he said. "You came to me a few days ago with some screwball idea of making ex-Superintendent," – there was an emphasis on the 'ex' – "Havard some kind of special constable to help with the present investigation, because she was involved in the search for the boy years ago?"

"Yes, sir, but I accepted your rejection of the idea."

"I should think so too," Rees-Jones snapped. "Fabia Havard failed to find him then–"

"And so did I, so did we all."

"Yes, yes," – he waved a dismissive hand – "but she was in charge, and I told you there was no way I was going to co-opt her now."

"You did, sir, and she hasn't been." Matt felt he ought to cross his fingers when he said that, as it wasn't exactly true, so he added, "Sworn in as a special constable, that is."

"But I've been told she's been poking her nose in. We just cannot have retired police officers behaving as if they're still on the force, Chief Inspector, you should know that."

"I'm sure you're right, sir," Matt said, doing his best to dampen down the anger that was starting to rise up inside him, "but I thought it would be very useful to get Fabia Havard's slant on the present situation as she was deeply involved when the boy disappeared. She has an excellent memory and her input, so far, has been extremely useful."

"And does that include her resurrecting other closed cases?"

Now we're getting to it, Matt thought. "What others, sir?"

Rees-Jones leant forward and crossed his arms on his desk, his attitude more conciliatory. "Look, Matt, I'm aware of the fact that you have... er... a personal relationship with Fabia Havard, but I'm afraid that may blind you to the inappropriateness of involving her in your work."

As Matt opened his mouth to speak, his boss held up a hand to stop him.

"Do you remember a case, some years ago, where a young tearaway accused a respectable Baptist pastor, Selwyn Harris, of abuse. Pure mischief, it was, and the case was thrown out."

"I remember it well, sir."

"This pastor lives in Pontygwyn, same as Fabia Havard – she may know him. The lad that accused him now runs a boxing club over by Shaftesbury Park–"

"Tom Beddoes. I know him, he was a friend of Caleb Morgan's way back."

"Ah, I see you're up to speed." He gave a humourless smile, which just made Matt angrier.

"I sincerely hope so, sir," said Matt, doing his best to keep the irony out of his voice. "We've already interviewed him as part of this present investigation."

"That's all very well," he said, and he was no longer smiling, "but so has Fabia Havard, and she should not have done so." He thumped his desk in time to the last few words.

"How do you mean, she's interviewed him?"

"She was interrupted in doing so a few days ago."

Although Matt was fully aware who did the interrupting, he said, "May I ask by whom?" And this time he knew he wasn't entirely successful in keeping the anger out of his voice.

"I really don't think it's necessary—"

"I think I have a right to know, sir. After all, if others are becoming involved in one of my cases, I would like them to be answerable directly to me and, with all due respect, any information they have should be passed on to me and my team, don't you think?"

There was a tense silence in the room for a few moments. Matt sat still, his hands still clasped tight in his lap as he looked steadily across at his boss, waiting for an answer.

Rees-Jones leant back again, frowning back at Matt. The silent battle of wills dragged on, then the Chief Superintendent said, "Apparently Sergeant Fairweather is a regular at the Shaftesbury Boxing Club and Gym, where Beddoes works, and he walked in on Fabia Havard interrogating Beddoes a few days ago. He was of the opinion that she should not be doing so, that her interference could jeopardise the investigation, so, quite rightly, he brought his concerns to me."

"Rather than straight to me?"

"He felt your… er… relationship with Fabia may make it difficult for you to see that her behaviour is inappropriate; after all, you did run that special constable business past me."

"I did, sir, and as I said, I took it no further, as you instructed."

"That's as may be, but that message doesn't seem to have got through to your girlfriend." The scornful tone he used fanned the flames of Matt's anger, but he gritted his teeth and forced himself not to react.

"There is a simple explanation for Fabia's presence at the club," he said, his voice quiet and steady. "You do know she's been making a living as an artist since she was forced to retire, don't you? The reason she was there was that she's arranged to do some sketches of boxers in the ring which Tom Beddoes will probably be putting up on the walls around the gym, and he'll possibly be using them for advertising purposes. That is the sum of her involvement with Beddoes. I'm sorry Sergeant Fairweather didn't bother to come to me with his concerns, I could have put his mind at rest."

Matt could see that his boss didn't really believe his explanation. Tough. That was all he was going to get. He pushed himself forward in his chair. "Will that be all, sir? I've some information just come in that I really must go and check."

Rees-Jones gave a curt nod and Matt got up and went to the door, then turned with his hand on the doorknob. "You ought to know, sir, that one of the people we are investigating in relation to the death of Caleb Morgan is actually Pastor Selwyn Harris. Caleb attended his youth club for some years and, obviously, we're taking into account any contacts he had in his past, including Tom Beddoes of course."

Matt didn't wait for a response to this but opened the door, snapped it shut behind him, and strode off along the corridor and down the stairs. As he marched through the main office, several people looked up, ready to speak to him but, seeing his expression, every one of them changed their minds, except Aidan, now sitting at his desk.

"Okay, what have you got for me, Aidan?" Matt demanded. "Come into my office."

Chapter 27

Gaenor was worried about Filly. She'd phoned on Saturday as promised but Filly had said she had to go and see her mother. They'd decided, instead, to meet for a drink at their favourite wine bar on Sunday evening, but Filly hadn't turned up. Gaenor had texted her, and tried to phone, but she'd got no response. Although she hadn't thought much of it – Filly could be notoriously absent-minded – she did begin to worry the following morning when, on texting her again, she still got no response. Instead of worrying away about it, she decided, before going into work, that she'd drop in at Filly's flat to check up on her.

Gaenor managed to park a few yards down the road from the terraced house where Filly had a flat on the first floor; the one on the ground floor was empty, but Filly had told her a new tenant was due to arrive soon. Glancing at her watch as she went up the short path, she saw that it was only just half past eight – surely Filly would be in at this time of the morning. She rang the bell and waited, but there was no answering voice from the intercom grille. She rang it again; still no answer. Leaning back, she looked up at the first-floor window which she knew gave on to Filly's sitting room, but the curtains were firmly closed. What to do? She could just leave it and go to work, try the shop later on, or she could let herself in. She stood on the doorstep, hesitating, then rummaged in her shoulder bag and brought out her keys and was about to unlock the door when it was flung open.

"Oh my God, thank goodness!" exclaimed a woman, her greying hair wild, her bright red dressing gown clutched around her. She was a complete stranger to Gaenor. "But–" she said, "I thought you were the ambulance."

"I'm sorry, what ambulance?" asked Gaenor anxiously.

The woman stepped back to let her in. "I'm from the downstairs flat. It's Filly, look." As she stepped aside, Gaenor saw that someone was sprawled at the bottom of the stairs, slippered feet on the bottom step, brown curly hair stained with blood. For a moment she couldn't work out who it was, then realised it was Filly.

Gaenor rushed over and bent down beside the unconscious form. "What happened?" she asked, looking up at the woman.

"I'd just got up and I was in my kitchen, over by there" – she indicated a front door to the side of the hall which stood open – "and I heard this awful noise – banging and crashing. I grabbed my dressing gown and came out to see Filly like this and someone rushing out of the front door. I think it was a man, he was tall enough, but I just saw the back. He was wearing jeans and a hoodie. I couldn't believe it. I shouted after him, but he took no notice, just kept running as if the devil was on his heels." She put a hand to her chest. "Oh dear, oh dear," she said, her eyes wide with distress.

Gaenor looked up from where she was crouching beside Filly. "How long ago was this?"

"About ten, fifteen minutes. I couldn't rouse Filly, and I didn't think I should try to move her, so I phoned for an ambulance. That's who I thought you were."

"No, I'm a friend of Filly's. Gaenor Baptiste."

"I'm Mary Thomas. I only moved into the flat last week, but I've met Filly several times already. She's such a sweetie."

"One of the best," Gaenor said, her voice shaking a little. She bent closer to listen for a moment. "I think you did right not to move her. At least she seems to be breathing okay. We'll just have to wait until the paramedics get here. Can you describe the person again?"

"Tall, sort of powerful-looking, must have been quite young at the speed he was going. I did go to the door and saw him jump into a bright yellow car, don't know what sort, and then he did a U-turn and drove off."

"Was the car a sort of egg yolk colour?" Gaenor asked sharply.

"Yes, it was. Do you know who it could be?"

"No, not really, at least—"

Before she could say anything more, they heard an ambulance siren approaching.

Mary pulled open the front door and a moment later two paramedics arrived on the scene.

* * *

After Matt had left, Fabia had tried to go back to sleep, but she soon gave up. There was far too much going round and round in her mind for her to settle. It was so frustrating not to be able to go with him and hear first-hand what Aidan had turned up. But, as she sat at the kitchen table having her breakfast, she thought of one thing she could do. As she'd promised, she could phone and check on Filly.

Fabia scrolled down to the number and stood gazing out of the kitchen window as it rang and rang. She was just about to give up when it was answered.

"Hallo?" a voice said.

"Is that Filly?" Fabia asked, not sure she recognised the voice.

214

"No, it's Gaenor Baptiste, and you're Fabia Havard – I saw the name before I picked up."

"Hallo, Gaenor. Is Filly there?"

"No. She… she–"

Fabia could hear the distress in her voice. "What's wrong? Please tell me."

"Oh God! It's so awful."

"Gaenor," Fabia said, firm but gentle, "take a deep breath then tell me what's happened."

After that it all came out in a rush, her decision to call on Filly because she hadn't been able to make contact, Filly lying unconscious, the helpful next-door neighbour, her description of a man rushing out the front door and driving off, and the arrival of the paramedics.

"They said she had a nasty injury to her head and one of her arms might be broken. They wouldn't say whether she'll be alright, just told me to contact the hospital later to find out, but I'm not the next of kin so I really don't know if they'll tell me anything. And I know I should go and tell Filly's mother, but I just can't face it yet. She's so frail and she won't be able to go to the hospital either, I don't think she'd be up to it. What should I do?"

Fabia's mind was racing. But first she must try to reassure Gaenor. "She's in the best hands, so leave the hospital to do its work. And until you know more, I shouldn't bother her mother. Wait until there's more news." She paused briefly, then said, "You say the next-door neighbour – what was her name?"

"Mary something, I can't remember her surname."

"Mary described the person who rushed out. Did you recognise the description?"

"No, not really," said Gaenor, but there was something in her voice that made Fabia ask.

"Are you sure?"

"I don't know," Gaenor said, sounding anguished.

"How about you tell me exactly what Mary said?"

"She said he was tall, and she described him as powerful-looking, but I don't know if she meant he was big or just had an air about him. She said he was wearing jeans and a hoodie, which doesn't help at all. And there was something else, she said he drove off in a bright yellow car, but she doesn't know what make it was."

"Have you called the police?"

"Do you think I should?"

"Absolutely, Gaenor," Fabia said firmly, feeling a little exasperated at the time that was being wasted. "And they'll need to talk to Mary as well."

"When you say the police," Gaenor said slowly, "do you mean that Chief Inspector Lambert?"

"Well, yes, that would be the ideal. There might be a connection to the case."

"I don't see how. I mean, I know what you're saying, but I don't feel I can just phone and pour all this out," Gaenor protested. "They've no idea who I am, and they're hardly going to put me through to anyone important, are they?"

"I think they might well do so," Fabia said. "Particularly with the on-going murder enquiry in the background. They've interviewed all of you who knew him, but there may be people connected to the case that you don't know anything about."

"How did you know they'd interviewed us?" asked Gaenor.

There was no way Fabia could get out of giving her a direct answer. "Chief Inspector Lambert asked for my help since I was involved in the original search for Caleb when I was in the police force."

"I did see you together, but I didn't realise that. Then could you speak to him?" Gaenor asked eagerly. "Since you know him. Please? Could you?"

Fabia thought for a moment. If the truth were known, she wasn't at all reluctant to get involved, and she knew she'd be able to get through to Matt much more quickly than Gaenor would. "Okay, leave it with me. Give me your own mobile number."

Gaenor dictated it and Fabia grabbed a pen and jotted it down on the edge of a newspaper lying on the kitchen table. "I'm pretty sure the Chief Inspector will send someone round to talk to you, and to the next-door neighbour."

"You can tell him I'll be at work. I have to go in, I've got tutorials, but I'll be home by four."

"I'm sure Filly is in good hands. I have a friend who works in A&E at the Heath. If I give him a ring later on, he may be willing to tell me what's going on."

"Thank you so much," Gaenor said, sounding much calmer now.

"And try not to worry," Fabia said, but as she cut off the call, she couldn't help thinking what a stupid platitude that was. Try not to worry! I wish, thought Fabia.

Sitting down at the kitchen table, she dialled Matt's number, leant her elbows on the table and waited for him to respond. He didn't. What to do? She decided to try the main station number and hope that she'd get through to him that way. After negotiating the switchboard and waiting, impatiently, for quite some time listening to tiny music repeating itself over and over, with the occasional interruption from a mechanical voice telling her she would be connected soon, she finally got through to Dilys rather than Matt. Quickly she explained why she was calling.

"Hold on, Fabia," Dilys said once she'd heard the details, "I'll hand you over to the boss, he's right here."

There was a muttering in the background, then Matt came on the line.

"Fabia, you've got something for us." His voice sounded curt, but she took no notice, this wasn't the time to worry about inessentials. She repeated her story to Matt.

"Do you know how bad she is?"

"No, I don't. Gaenor says she was still unconscious when they put her in the ambulance."

"We'll get someone round to speak to the neighbour. You say Gaenor has left the flat?"

"Yes, but you could send someone to speak to her at the university, and she said she'd be home by four."

"There's something else, isn't there?" Matt said.

"Well, yes. That yellow car, it rang bells."

"Oh? How come?"

Fabia told him and he said, "I missed that. Thank goodness for your powers of observation, love, that's really useful."

"Glad to be of service."

"Right." There was a pause and Fabia waited for him to go on. "Look, those developments that Aidan turned up, they're pointing in the same direction. I'll get someone round to A&E in case she comes to. Hopefully Hari Patel is on duty, which should make things easier. I'll give him a ring now, and thanks, love, your so-called interfering turned up trumps this time."

"You're too kind, make sure you get back to me as soon as you can. This hanging around is doing me no good at all."

"I'll do my best," he said.

Chapter 28

When Matt had marched through the main office and ordered Aidan Rogers into his own, Aidan had calmly pushed his bulk out of the chair, picked up his laptop, and followed him in. Nothing ever persuaded Aidan to move fast and getting flustered just wasn't in his nature. He'd taken a seat beside Matt, calmly opened up his laptop and, his fingers deft on the pad in spite of their size, he'd searched for what he needed. He brought up an Excel spreadsheet and both he and Matt leant forward to study it as Aidan pointed to what was being displayed.

"I've made a comprehensive chart of all the information I got from the embassy, from UK Visas and Immigration and from the airlines' records. You see there, sir, that's the date of application for an ETA, that's an electronic travel authorisation which she'd need before leaving. You can see here when it was granted, and then here we have the actual airline used, the date of the flight and the departure time. The name is clear there on the manifest." He'd turned to Matt, his eyes appearing enormous behind his rimless glasses. "It's all pretty conclusive, sir."

Leaning back in his chair, Matt had clasped his hands behind his head. "It is, isn't it? This opens up the whole case." He'd jumped up, gone to his office door and searched around for Dilys. She was just hanging her coat on the back of her chair. "Dilys," he'd called, "come in and see what Aidan's got for us."

Quickly she'd made her way across the main office. "Look at this," Matt said, pointing to Aidan's laptop.

There was silence as she stood behind Aidan and studied the screen. "Well, well, that's a turn up," she'd said, with a wide-eyed glance at Matt.

"But that's not all." There'd been a note of triumph in Aidan's voice. "That sim card, from the victim's phone, my London pals actually managed to get some bits and pieces off it." He clicked away at the laptop and then leant back to give them room, grinning as he did so. "This is a transcript of what they managed to retrieve."

Once again silence had reigned while Matt and Dilys took in what Aidan was showing them. There were several fragments of texts that had been sent and received, an arrangement to meet, a place and time, and a longer piece which appeared to be a plea for understanding.

"We're going to have to set up another interview as soon as possible. Dilys, can you look after that? And Aidan, keep working on this. Knowing you, there's probably more you can pull out of all this information. I owe you. Well done."

* * *

An hour later, as they sat in his office, Matt cut off the call from Fabia and turned to Dilys and gave her a rundown of what had been said.

"Do you think she disturbed an intruder?" asked Dilys.

"Looks like it. But there is that distinctive car."

"Yes, that puts a slightly different slant on it, although I didn't notice any car like that when we did the interviews. But why would we?"

"True," Matt conceded. "Anyway, I'll see if I can get hold of Hari Patel, warn him we'll be sending someone along to sit with Filly Jenner until she's able to tell us what happened. I hope to God she can, we really need her side of the story."

Dr Hari Patel was a close friend of Matt's and had been an important witness in a case that Matt and Fabia had been involved in the year before. Matt scrolled down to the number on his mobile and was delighted when Hari responded almost immediately.

"That was quick," he said. "How are you doing, Hari?"

"Fine, fine. I've just this minute come on duty. But I'm sure you haven't phoned to ask me about my health, what's up?"

"You should have a young woman in A&E by the name of Felicity Jenner, fell down some stairs. I think she's got a head injury."

"Give me a moment, I'll just go and check."

Matt sat waiting as patiently as he could, grateful that Hari hadn't wasted time asking why he wanted to know. It wasn't long before Hari came back to him.

"Yes. She's here."

"How serious is it?"

"She's showing signs of coming round."

"That's really good news."

"But we can't tell yet how badly she's injured. There's some severe bruising to her arm but I don't think there are any bones broken, we'll know more once it's X-rayed. The head injury is more difficult to assess. We'll be doing tests, a scan, etc., and we'll know more after that. Anyway, what's up?"

"We think she might have been pushed down the stairs rather than simply fallen."

"Ah, I see, part of a current case, I presume?"

"It could be," Matt said. "How long do you think it'll be before we can interview her?"

"Matt! I'm not a clairvoyant. I'll come back to you once we've done all the tests. How did you find out she was here?"

"Fabia. The friend who found her spoke to Fabia and she got through to me."

"Ah the gorgeous Fabia!" Matt could tell Hari was grinning. "There's far more to this than you're telling me. I shan't let you keep me in the dark for long, but now I must get back to work. There'd be no chance of anyone speaking to the patient for a couple of hours, I'll let you know if and when she's up to it."

"If?" asked Matt anxiously.

"I'm just hedging my bets, Matt."

"But can I send one of my constables round just to keep an eye on things?"

"Yes, so long as he or she doesn't get in the way," Hari told him.

"Understood, and thanks, Hari. You're a star."

Matt got up and went into the main office. Dilys looked up as he came in. "I've had a word with Inspector Richards from Traffic about that car, sir," she told him.

"Good. And I spoke to Hari Patel, he says there'll be no chance of interviewing Filly Jenner for a couple of hours at least. We can send someone, best be in uniform, just to keep an eye at A&E."

"I'll organise that, and I've sent Watkins and the new girl, Becca Pugh, round to her flat. I thought you'd want us to have a word with the neighbour, and they could go on to speak to Gaenor Baptiste. They haven't reported back yet."

"Good work, Dilys, let me know when they do, and fix up someone to go to the hospital."

* * *

It wasn't until later in the morning that they had any more news. When the call came through, Matt was going over Aidan's evidence for what felt like the tenth time, standing beside Dilys while she brought it all up on her computer. She picked up, listened for a moment, then held the phone out to Matt.

"Inspector Richards, sir."

People nearby looked up and stopped what they were doing to listen while he took the call. "Hallo, Alun, what have you got for me?"

"I think we may have sight of your yellow Fiat."

"Great. Where?"

"A PC spotted a car of that description at the Magor services, filling up with petrol. The registration of the car is CG68 BYV, driven by a tall chap wearing jeans and a hoodie. Does that sound right?"

"Could be. Any more than that?"

"Not at the moment, but we've got one of our unmarked cars tailing it, and they're heading towards the Severn Bridge."

"Okay, can you intercept them at the bridge?"

"We'll do our best," Alun said.

"Of course, it could come to nothing."

"Granted, but it's worth a try. I'll get back to you."

"Thanks, Alun, I owe you a pint."

"Or one of Fabia's Sunday roasts?"

Matt grinned. "That's not up to me, but I'll ask."

"You do that, butt."

Matt turned to give Dilys the good news. "It could always be a completely innocent driver. We'll just have to wait and see."

"I have a hunch it'll turn up trumps."

"Hunch indeed! You're getting as bad as Fabia."

But all Dilys did was grin at him and tap her nose.

* * *

"Dilys is getting as bad as you with her hunches," he told Fabia when she called a little later.

"What do you mean, as bad? They're bloody useful," Fabia protested, "but never mind mocking our undoubted talents, what I was phoning about was, well, I've had this idea."

"You have?" said Matt, sounding wary.

"Have you heard from Hari yet?"

"I spoke to him earlier. We've sent Dave Parry along to keep an eye, and Hari's going to phone me when Filly is in a fit state to be interviewed, which I hope will be before the day is out."

"Good, so what I thought was why don't I go along and be there when you, or whoever's going to do it, speaks to her." She rushed on before Matt could protest. "She's so timid, Matt, so it might help if someone she knows is there, don't you think?"

It didn't take her long to convince him and, as a consequence, Fabia was driving into Newport later that afternoon ready to sit in on Matt's interview with Filly.

Hari Patel came out to greet her at reception, a smile on his dark face. Although he was half a head shorter than Fabia, he reached up to kiss her on both cheeks.

"How very good it is to see you, Fabia."

"And you, Hari. Is Matt here yet?"

"Yes, he's in my office, come through."

Fabia followed him past various cubicles – some empty, some occupied, some with their curtains drawn. There was a general air of bustle and activity, the murmur of voices, a soft laugh in one direction, quiet sobbing in another. They arrived at a tiny room at the end of the ward to find Matt waiting for them.

"Hallo, love," Fabia said, smiling at him.

Hari pulled a chair forward. "Sit, sit," he urged her.

"Hari has had her wheeled into a side room so that we can speak to her in private," Matt told her. "She's come to and is waiting to go up to the ward. He says he wants to keep her in until they're sure about the injury to her head, but her arm is just badly bruised. She's very lucky, it could have been much worse."

"All the same. Poor girl."

"Would you like me to tell you what she has told us so far?" Hari asked. "Not that she's said much. Your chap has been sitting on the side lines taking notes of course."

"If you could give us the gist," Matt said.

Hari nodded. "Well, so far the nurse has reported that she seems to be very worried about her diary, she keeps muttering about needing to find it. From what they gathered she'd written something in it that made someone angry. They said they don't think she's talking about an appointment diary, but do people keep the old-fashioned kind anymore?"

"Oh yes," Fabia said, thinking back to a diary which had helped her and Matt solve a case a year ago.

"She's mentioned her mother several times, so we thought maybe that was who would be angry about her diary entries, and she's also mentioned someone called Gaenor. Is that a friend of hers?"

"Yes," said Fabia. "Along with Filly's next-door neighbour, Gaenor arrived on the scene soon after she'd fallen down the stairs."

"I see. And she keeps saying 'Poor Caleb, poor Caleb' over and over."

Matt explained, briefly, about the case they were working on and Filly's connection to it.

"I think I saw something about that on the news a couple of days ago," Hari said. "What a waste of a young life. So, she was one of his university friends?"

"Yes," Matt said. "Along with several others, most of whom are in the frame at the moment. Some more than others."

A nurse poked her head round the door and said, "Can I have a word, Doctor Patel?"

At the same time Matt's phone rang. He rummaged in his pocket and looked at the screen. "It's Dilys," he said to Fabia.

While Matt took the call, Hari smiled at the nurse and said, "I'll be with you in a moment." And then he turned to Fabia. "Why don't I take you along to see her?"

Fabia followed Hari, and Matt took up the rear, still talking away on the phone. As they went, Fabia tried her best to work out what Dilys was telling Matt, but he was doing more listening than speaking. In the end she gave up but, as they arrived at the door of a side room down a corridor, he turned to her and said, "I have to get going, Dilys needs me back at the station."

"What's up?"

"I'll tell you later. Can you see what you can get out of Filly?"

"I'll do my best," said Fabia, secretly delighted that he was asking her to get even more involved.

"Thanks, Hari," Matt said, clasping his friend's arm, "this has been very helpful." And with that, he dashed off.

Chapter 29

Dave Parry got up from a chair in the corner of the room as they came in, a look of surprise mixed with pleasure on his face. "Afternoon, ma'am," he said, "are you deputising for the chief?"

"You could say that, Dave," Fabia said, smiling at him, "unofficially, of course."

"Of course," Dave repeated, grinning.

Hari had been having a quiet word with a nurse who was standing by the bed, but now he turned to Fabia. "I must get back to work now, but I'll see you before you go." And with a wave of the hand, he too was gone.

"If you'd like to sit here," the nurse suggested, indicating a chair to the left of the bed where Filly lay.

Filly's head was bandaged, the curly hair almost invisible, and there was a cannula in her right hand attached to a bag of fluid rigged up beside the bed. Her eyes were half closed, as if to open them completely would be far too much effort.

Fabia did as the nurse suggested, then asked almost in a whisper, "Which arm is the one that's bruised?"

"This one."

"Can I take her hand, just to let her know I'm here, or will it hurt her?" asked Fabia.

"Just be careful," she said.

Fabia leant forward and gently slipped her hand beneath Filly's. At first there was no reaction then slowly she opened her eyes and turned her head a little, groaned then said, "Oh, hallo" – her voice sounded as if her throat was sore – "it's… it's Fabia, isn't it?"

"Yes, it is. How're you feeling?"

"A bit sore, and my head aches. What are you doing here?"

"I came to see you," Fabia told her, without elaborating.

"So kind," said Filly, and closed her eyes again.

Fabia waited, the minutes ticked by, then Filly suddenly opened her eyes wider. "When we had lunch, I shouldn't have said anything, I shouldn't…" Her voice trailed away.

"Who did you have lunch with, Filly?" Fabia asked urgently. "What did you say?"

"I said I put it in my diary," she whispered; then more firmly she asked, "have you found it? Have you found my diary?"

"No, Filly, is it lost?"

"No, no, it was taken away, it was in the shoulder bag."

"Whose shoulder bag, Filly?"

But her eyes fluttered and closed again. Fabia resigned herself to a long wait.

* * *

Matt got back to the station and took the stairs two at a time up to the main office. "Okay, Dilys, what have you got for me?"

"A bit of luck, sir," Dilys said, grinning. "Our friend in the yellow car decided to make a bolt for it, crept up to over eighty-five, at which point Alun's lads intervened."

"And who is it?"

"Exactly who we thought."

"Great," Matt said, clasping his hands and rubbing them together. "Are they coming back in?"

"Yes, sir, delivering straight to us. Should be here in about an hour, depending on traffic," Dilys said. "They're going to do a proper search of the car when they get it back in."

"Good. Let's hope that turns up something useful."

"What happened at the hospital?" Dilys asked.

"She's coming round, talking a bit. I left Fabia and Dave sitting with her and I'm hoping they'll be able to get something useful for us by the end of the day. Okay, come into my office, let's go through all the info we have so far and decide how we're going to approach this interview."

Dilys followed him into his office and they sat down to plan their strategy.

Half an hour later Matt's phone rang.

"Hallo, love, anything useful for me?" He listened for a moment, concentrating on what Fabia was saying while Dilys sat on the side lines full of curiosity.

"Okay, that's useful. All night? … Time enough to do a search while Filly slept… and she's sure it was taken… good… in her bag? … Is that the point she was pushed? Okay, great. Can you get Dave to come back in and type up the info, then we'll have it with us when we do the interview. Thanks, Fabia, that's really useful. You got that much sooner than I thought you would. I hope to see you later, but I've no idea what time. This could be a long haul."

He cut off the call and, turning to Dilys, related what Fabia had told him. "It looks like we've got a case. I just hope we can make it stick."

* * *

The woman sitting in the bleak interview room was very different from the one Matt and Dilys had interviewed the Wednesday before. Then it had been her strength and charm that had dominated the room, now it

229

was her anger. She swung round as they came in and pushed herself up from the chair.

"Oh, it's you. Why on earth have I been brought here?" she demanded, pushing the hoodie back from her head. The long, blond hair was scraped back into a ponytail and the velvet hairband was gone. And gone was the sad smile. It had been replaced by a hard, angry frown. She watched them go around the table and take their seats opposite her.

"You haven't answered my question," she snapped.

"Please sit down," Matt said, and after a moment she complied.

Dilys switched on the recording equipment as Matt said, "This interview will be recorded and may be given in evidence if you are brought to trial—"

"Trial? What d'you mean trial?" she demanded.

"—if you are brought to trial," Matt repeated calmly. "We are in an interview room at Newport Police Station, the date is Monday 3rd April and the time" – he glanced at his watch – "is 3:00 p.m. I am Chief Inspector Lambert, also present is Sergeant Dilys Bevan. Please state your full name and date of birth."

While Matt had continued speaking, she had sat as if mesmerised, her eyes wide behind her glasses, then she exclaimed, "Bloody hell! I was only speeding. You don't usually arrest people for that, do you? What is going on here?"

"The speeding offence will be dealt with by the traffic department. Please do as I ask."

For a moment he thought she'd refuse, but then she drew herself up and spat out, "Clare Edwina Jeffreys, 25th May 1989. Okay? So why have I been dragged in here?"

"Before we start this interview, I must remind you that you are entitled to free legal advice, either in person or by telephone at any stage," Matt told her calmly. "Do you wish to speak to a legal advisor now or have one present during the interview? If you don't have a solicitor of your own, we can contact the duty solicitor on your behalf."

"Why would I want a solicitor? Until I know what bee it is you've got in your bonnet, I think I can manage on my own, thank you very much."

Matt glanced at Dilys then said, "Clare… may I call you that?"

She gave a curt nod.

"We would like to ask you about an incident earlier today."

"What incident? I don't know what you're talking about."

"A friend of yours, Felicity Jenner," Matt said, watching carefully for a reaction, but the scowling face gave very little away, "was badly injured when she fell down the stairs at her home early this morning. She is in hospital and the doctors don't yet know the extent of her injuries. The prognosis is not good."

"Oh poor, poor Filly. Is she conscious?" Now the expression on her face showed nothing but concern. "How did it happen?"

"That is what we're trying to establish."

"You said it doesn't look good, she…" Her voice trailed off, then she added, almost in a whisper, "Is there a chance she won't recover?"

"There is always a chance with a head injury," Dilys told her.

"But why have you brought me in here to tell me about it?"

"Because we believe you were with her at the time it happened."

"What!" The word was gasped out, then she started to laugh. They sat and waited for her to get control of herself and, after a moment, she said, "You have got to be joking."

"We have two witnesses – Miss Jenner's downstairs neighbour, and Miss Jenner herself."

"But you said she was in hospital, the doctors – you lied to me," she spat out.

"No," Matt said calmly. "I told you she was seriously injured. I did not say she couldn't communicate with us."

There was silence in the room. The expression on Clare's face went from anger to fear, then to cunning. She leant forward, her folded arms on the table, and gave them an apologetic smile. "Look," she said, "I don't want you to think I had anything to do with Filly falling down the stairs. I was, well, scared and—"

"So, you admit you were there when it happened?" asked Matt.

She didn't give a direct answer, so Matt asked again, "Do you admit you were with Felicity Jenner when she fell down the stairs?"

"I didn't know what to do," she wailed in protest and tears filled her eyes. "I was so scared. I just... just panicked and ran when that woman came out from the bottom flat. I thought it was empty, but it wasn't, and I thought, she's there, she'll be able to look after poor Filly. I'm so sorry, I know I should have stayed."

"You say you thought the bottom flat was empty," Dilys said, her voice sharp. "Is that why you thought it would be okay to push Filly down the stairs? There'd be no-one to see you do it?"

She sprung up from her chair and leant her hands on the table, shouting, "No, no, no," across at them.

"Sit down, Clare," Matt said firmly, and then added more sharply, "Sit down."

After a moment she subsided back into her chair and crossed her arms over her body, dropped her chin on to her chest and stared at the floor.

At that moment they were interrupted by a knock on the door. Matt frowned in irritation but when Tom Watkins came quietly into the room and said, "Sir? Could I have a word?" he got up to go over to him while Dilys recorded Tom's presence.

Clare had shown no interest in Tom's arrival, neither did she show any interest in their muttered conversation.

She sat motionless and continued to stare at the floor as Tom handed an evidence bag to Matt then left the room. Coming back to the table, Matt handed the bag to Dilys and glanced down. She took the hint and placed the bag on her lap, out of sight.

"Let's go back to what happened last night," Matt suggested. "When did you arrive at Felicity's flat?"

After a moment she looked up, her expression sullen. "Sunday evening."

"Was this by arrangement?"

"Yes."

"Felicity had invited you?"

"Yes."

"We understand that Felicity had arranged to meet Gaenor Baptiste that evening," Matt said. "Did she say anything about this? It seems strange that she should invite you round when she already had another arrangement."

"Bloody Gaenor," she spat out. "Why should she–? Filly said something about that when I got there, but I persuaded her to stay in with me."

"Am I to understand that you hadn't been invited, you just turned up?"

"What does it matter? Invited? Turned up? Filly was… is my friend, I can go around to hers, can't I? I don't need bloody permission."

"No, but I'm just trying to establish exactly what happened," Matt said patiently.

Dilys sat forward and asked, "What time did you arrive at the flat?"

"Around half six or seven, I suppose."

"And you persuaded her to stay in with you rather than go out as she'd planned?"

"Yes, haven't I just said so?"

"Did she let Gaenor know about the change in plans?"

"No. She said her phone was dead but, in the end, she said the sainted Gaenor would understand."

Matt sat looking at her in silence for a moment, thinking about what she'd told them so far and wondering what direction to take next; after a quick look at Dilys, he allowed her to take over.

"You can be very persuasive, can't you, Clare?" Dilys said.

A ghost of a satisfied smile flitted across her face but quickly disappeared. "I suppose, but Filly was quite happy to stay at home, she said she didn't really feel like going out, what with the funeral and everything. And anyway, I'd brought a couple of bottles of Prosecco with me just to cheer her up, it's the only alcohol she'll drink."

"And you stayed the night."

"Of course, after all that fizz, I could hardly drive home." She gave a little triumphant smile. "I would have had one of your lot on my tail if I had, wouldn't I?"

"And did you talk about Caleb Morgan at all?"

She looked up, then her face crumpled, and her eyes filled with tears. She rummaged in her sleeve and brought out a tissue, pressed it to her eyes and said, in a choked-up voice, "Yes, we did. We were his two best friends back then, the only ones who really knew him. I think Filly was a bit in love with him too, so when he disappeared, she took it very hard. I remember her e-mailing me in Australia to tell me all about it, saying how much she missed him; it was awful. But there was nothing much I could do to comfort her, being so far away."

"And do you remember exactly when it was that she e-mailed you?" asked Matt.

"Like I said, just after I arrived at my cousin's in Australia."

"And when exactly was that?" he asked.

She frowned across at him, then gave a twisted smile. "You've got a short memory for a policeman. I seem to remember telling you that when I came in last Wednesday – off my own bat because I knew it was my duty, I have to remind you."

"Humour me," said Matt. "Tell me again."

She spoke very slowly, as to an idiot. "It was in May 2010, a week before my 21st birthday. I left on the 16th and arrived in Sydney on the 17th."

"Are you sure?"

"Of course I'm sure." She was getting angry now, but Matt was sure there was fear lurking behind the anger.

"It wasn't, perhaps, a week *after* your 21st birthday?"

"No!"

He held out his hand to Dilys and she put the evidence bag into it. Matt placed it on the table and opened the seal, took out an A5-sized, red leather-bound notebook, a little battered and scratched. Clare watched him, her eyes darting from the notebook to his face and back again as the blood drained slowly from her face.

Chapter 30

Early on Tuesday evening Fabia crept into her sitting room and looked at Matt who, once again, was sprawled on her sofa, this time fast asleep. In her hands she had two glasses of wine. She bent and put them on the coffee table, then leant down to kiss his lips.

"Umm, nice, do that again," he murmured, reaching for her.

But she side-stepped him. "No, no. Time for wine and an up-date. When you got here earlier on, I was willing to let you rest while I got dinner ready, but the casserole's in the oven now and it's time for you to tell me what happened. A few brief texts are no good, I want the details – all of them. What happened all those years ago? How did you get your confession? Come on, Matt, I'm dying of curiosity."

He pushed himself upright and stretched, then reached out for his wine. Fabia sat down next to him and he put his arm round her shoulders.

"Where to start?" he said, taking a gulp from the glass. "Of course, you know all about what Filly Jenner said, after all, you were asking the questions. After that knock on the head, I was surprised at her recall of the evening before."

"So was I, but she seemed pretty sure of herself," Fabia told him. "Not long after you had to get going, she seemed to perk up pretty quickly. Hari was really pleased, but he says she'll have to take it easy for a while. She phoned me this morning to say she was going to stay with Gaenor for a few days when she gets out of hospital, so she should be fine."

"Good. She'll be called as a witness and, without her, we might not have nearly as strong a case. It's clear from Dave Parry's notes that she told you she remembered Clare was just behind her when they left the flat, and the last thing she remembers is feeling this hard push in the small of her back.

"That's right."

"What she didn't know is that, once she'd gone to bed the night before, after Clare had been asking her all about her diaries, as she told you, Clare searched for and found the one that covered 2010 and put it in her bag. That's the one we showed her during the interview; we'd retrieved it from under the seat of her car. I think she must have pushed it under there when Alun's chaps stopped her on the bridge. It clearly states that Clare left for Australia just over a week later than she told us. Filly remarked in the diary that she was surprised that Clare actually went ahead with it as, by then, they were all busy helping Nerys put posters around the place asking if anyone had seen Caleb.

In the diary she remarks that she's surprised how little Clare seemed to want to get involved. She wrote, in a sort of apology for Clare, that maybe she was just too grieved about his disappearance, though she does speculate on whether or not Gaenor or Nerys warned Clare off. Anyway, it's there in an entry dated 25th May, 'Clare went off to Australia today, she must be halfway there by now, I just can't understand how she could go.' All this, of course, is borne out by the information Aidan turned up: her ETA application, the immigration records, and her name on the airline manifest. Why she didn't think of all that is a mystery to me; but then I think we're dealing with a supremely arrogant woman, and maybe you could call her sociopathic – she certainly seems to have an overblown idea of her own importance."

"A narcissist?" suggested Fabia.

"Yes, I think so, and in a way that was her downfall."

He paused and Fabia, used to these occasional silences while Matt's thoughts wandered, waited for him to go on, but she couldn't bear to wait long.

"Come on, Matt. Tell me more."

"Not until I get a refill."

"Stay here, I'll get the bottle."

Fabia dashed out to the kitchen and was soon back. She bent to refill their glasses, then sat back down and turned eagerly to face him. "What I want to know is why she did it. From all we've heard, she adored him. Why kill him? And how?"

"It took us a while to draw it all out of her, but in the end we had a pretty clear picture." Matt sighed, his face bleak for a moment. "Such a waste of a life, of two lives really. As you say, she adored him, to the point of obsession, I think. The bits and pieces of texts that were retrieved from his sim card give us a pretty clear idea that she was begging him to meet up with her and, in the end, he must have given in. We pointed that out to her, and she finally admitted that they'd met up for a walk down by the river in Caerleon. Remember, he was a student at the campus there. She said she knew – that's the word she used – she knew she could persuade him to leave Iolo and be with her, and she followed that up by saying, 'but then the accident happened'."

"The accident?" Fabia said, incredulous. "What did she mean, accident?"

"How did she put it?" Matt said, frowning a little. "She said she was very angry with him because he kept telling her that he and Iolo Beynam were in love. She was very scornful about that, kept insisting that Iolo had some kind of malign influence over Caleb. A bit like what his mother said, in fact."

"And?"

"They met up for this walk." Matt took another long sip from his drink as Fabia waited for him to go on. "From what she said, and it was all a bit garbled by this time, he said that he never wanted to see her again, he got really angry and told her he was glad she was going to Australia because then he'd be free of her stalking. That seems to have tipped her over the edge. Apparently, they'd stopped walking by this time. She told us they were sitting down, and she put her arms round him, tried to hold him close, but he pushed her away. Then, she said, 'the next moment he was lying dead'."

"But how? Did she explain?"

"After an awful lot of questions, going back and forth over the events, she finally admitted that she'd grabbed a rock and hit him. It must have been a pretty frenzied attack – it usually takes more than one blow to do the sort of damage that was done to Caleb's skull – but I think she'd completely lost it by then. Of course, then we asked her how he came to be buried." Matt looked at Fabia, his expression bleak. "She was talking like an automaton by now and just described what she did. She said she dragged his body into the scrub, I suppose she was just going to leave it there, but she kept insisting she needed to bury him. It was rather creepy. How did she put it? 'It was my way of saying a proper goodbye to my darling'."

"What on earth? Like some kind of ritual?"

"I suppose. She found what she called a deep hole beside a fallen tree, probably where the root ball had been torn out. She smiled at us and said it was just the right place for 'my Caleb'. She told us he loved walking in the woods beside the Usk and so to bury him in the woods was 'fitting'."

"Oh dear. It sounds as if she'd gone completely over the edge."

"That's the impression we got," Matt told her.

"So, what did she do?"

"She tipped his body into the hole, pushed a pile of earth over him, added some rocks, then pulled some fallen branches over and that was it. She finished off by saying that 'her' Caleb had always loved nature and she made sure he went back to nature, that she left him where he should be: in the heart of the woods."

"Apart from anything else, all that must have taken her ages. The chance of someone seeing them, her, must have been pretty high."

"I know. She got lucky, if you can put it that way."

"And you've charged her?"

"Oh yes. Tomorrow Chloe and I will go and inform the family, and Dilys is looking after talking to the other friends."

Matt stretched his arms above his head and yawned, then straightened up suddenly and grinned at her. "I knew there was something else to tell you. You're going to love this."

"What?"

"Your least favourite copper, Gerry Foulweather, is in deep shit."

"How come?" Fabia asked, a look of delight on her face.

"Dilys told me just before I left the office," he said. "Had I mentioned we've got a new PC, Becca Pugh, who's joined us from the Hampshire force? Winchester, I think."

"No, go on."

"She came to us about a month ago. She's really bright and doesn't take any crap from any of the men."

Fabia gave a gurgle of laughter. "And Gerry tried it on with her?"

"Exactly. She's reported him for sexual harassment, and Dilys has added her little store of notes to back it up.

What's more, she's persuaded her friend, Lois Le Feuvre, to make an official complaint about his behaviour before she moved. So, it looks as if early retirement, or maybe worse, is staring our Gerry in the face. He'll be lucky to keep his pension at this rate."

"When it comes to early retirement, I feel for him."

"Do you?" Matt asked, surprised.

"Nah, not really," Fabia said and laughed. "And I've got a little story to tell you."

"Go on, I like stories," Matt said, turning to face her.

"When was it? Sunday, that's it, I was coming back home via the bridge and I saw this black 4x4 slowing down to negotiate the narrow bit and I recognised the driver. It was Tom Beddoes."

"What on earth was he doing round here?"

"That's what I wondered, but today I think I found out."

"How come?" Matt asked, sounding sleepy.

"Listen, listen, I was on my way down the high street this afternoon. Well, I had to do something to keep from chewing my nails to the quick, wondering what the hell you were up to. Shopping's as good a distraction as any, and I bumped, literally, into Pastor Harris. We did one of those this side, that side pavement dances, and I realised he wasn't his usual immaculate self."

"In what way?" Matt turned to look at her, interested now.

"He had a split lip, a spectacular black eye, and when I bumped into him, I'm sure he winced. I said something about his having been in the wars and he brushed it off, said he'd fallen in the garden, tripped over a hoe left lying around. The thing is, he hasn't got any garden to speak of, it's all paved over – Cath told me. So, what on earth would he be doing with a hoe?"

"What indeed?" Matt said, grinning.

"Don't laugh at me, you horrible man. Look, I put two and two together–"

"And made five?"

Fabia punched his arm. "Will you listen? I said something about having a horrible feeling he'd been beaten up, and he went beetroot red, glared at me, snapped that that was a ridiculous idea, then stepped round me and strode – well, sort of limped off at speed. You know what, I think Tom Beddoes might well have got his revenge."

At this, Matt sat up, frowning. "What? Beaten him up?"

"Absolutely."

"Harris hasn't reported anything, at least, not as far as I know. Well, well, but there's nothing we can do unless he makes a complaint."

"And I don't think he will, Matt."

Fabia snuggled down next to Matt, her head on his shoulder and for a while all was quiet, except for the crackle of the fire.

It was Matt who broke the silence. "I haven't thanked you for all your help. As usual, it seems, I couldn't have done without you."

"I don't know, I wasn't that involved this time."

"But just having you there helps so much," Matt said, not so sleepy now. "And it'd be even better if we lived in the same place, I'd have you on hand all the time." He turned to face her. "What about it, my lovely Fabia? Can I move in?"

She put up a finger and touched it to his lips. "Ssh. Come to bed. I'll tell you in the morning."

Acknowledgements

A few thank yous, to my writing gurus, Jeannie and Dallas, and to Ros and Caroline for their double-checking abilities, to all in the Guernsey Writers' Group, for their support and encouragement, particularly Linda Roberts for her sim card idea. To the fantastic team at The Book Folks. And most of all, thank you to Niall for listening and contributing, for his unfailing encouragement, and for never grumbling when he has to do all the cooking.

If you enjoyed this book, please let others know by leaving a quick review on Amazon. Also, if you spot anything untoward in the paperback, get in touch. We strive for the best quality and appreciate reader feedback.

editor@thebookfolks.com

www.thebookfolks.com

Also by Pippa McCathie:

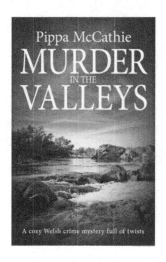

MURDER IN THE VALLEYS

The first book to feature Fabia Havard and Matt Lambert

Having left the police following a corruption investigation, ex-superintendent Fabia Havard is struggling with civilian life. When a girl is murdered in her town, she can't help trying to find the killer. Will her former colleague Matt Lambert stop her, or realize the value of his former boss to the floundering inquiry?

Available in paperback, audio and FREE with Kindle Unlimited.

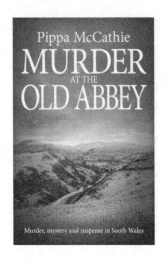

MURDER AT THE OLD ABBEY

The second book to feature Fabia Havard and Matt Lambert

When an overbearing patriarch and much begrudged ex-
army officer is found dead in his home, there is no
shortage of suspects. DCI Matt Lambert investigates, but
struggles with a lack of evidence. He'll have to rely on his
former boss, ex-detective Fabia Havard, to help him. But
will their fractious relationship get in the way of solving
the case?

Available in paperback, audio and FREE with Kindle Unlimited.

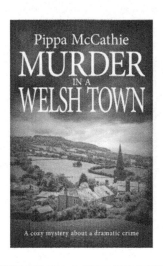

MURDER IN A WELSH TOWN

The fourth book to feature Fabia Havard and Matt Lambert

Hopes for a town pantomime are dashed when a participant is found murdered. The victim was the town gossip and there is no shortage of people who had a grudge to bear against him. Detective Matt Lambert leads the investigation but draws on the help of his girlfriend, ex-police officer Fabia Havard. Can they solve the crime together?

Available in paperback and FREE with Kindle Unlimited.

LIBERATION DAY

A standalone romantic thriller

Having become stranded in the English Channel after commandeering her cheating boyfriend's boat, Caro is rescued by a handsome stranger. But when the boat is impounded on suspicion of smuggling, she once again finds herself in deep water.

Available in paperback and FREE with Kindle Unlimited.

Made in the USA
Coppell, TX
25 April 2021

54501368R00152